The Play's the Thing…

The Play's the Thing...

Acting in a world of great untruths

Dermod Judge

The Book Guild Ltd

First published in Great Britain in 2023 by
The Book Guild Ltd
Unit E2 Airfield Business Park,
Harrison Road, Market Harborough,
Leicestershire. LE16 7UL
Tel: 0116 2792299
www.bookguild.co.uk
Email: info@bookguild.co.uk
Twitter: @bookguild

Copyright © 2023 Dermod Judge
Photo courtesy of Theatre on The Bay, Camps Bay, Cape Town, South Africa.

The right of Dermod Judge to be identified as the author of this
work has been asserted by them in accordance with the
Copyright, Design and Patents Act 1988.

All rights reserved. No part of this publication may be
reproduced, transmitted, or stored in a retrieval system, in any form or by any means,
without permission in writing from the publisher, nor be otherwise circulated in
any form of binding or cover other than that in which it is published and without
a similar condition being imposed on the subsequent purchaser.

This work is mostly fictitious and bears no resemblance to any persons living or dead.

Typeset in 12pt Adobe Jenson Pro

Printed and bound by CPI Group (UK) Ltd, Croydon, CR0 4YY

ISBN 978 1915352 637

British Library Cataloguing in Publication Data.
A catalogue record for this book is available from the British Library.

Dedicated to all brave playwrights and all honest actors.

Introduction

You can't substitute a play for real life even when it seems more authentic than the world outside the theatre. The play caters for our need to believe in two contradictory worlds – the one on the stage and the one on the streets. But, all too often, the play's illusion doesn't last even though the transient world created by the writer and actors is about what's worthwhile within us; all we yearn for, all we love, all we laugh at – and all we fear.

And all we know but are afraid to say.

That's why great theatre is the bane of an unjust society.

It is at the time when the world outside is at its most dishonest that we need the truth of theatre the most. Such a time was during apartheid in South Africa when a few theatre folk screwed their courage to the sticking place. Thanks to them, many theatregoers experienced the world outside the theatre from inside the playwright's mind and suffered the blows on the streets from inside the actor's personal experience. And eventually a whole society strove for a peace outside that had been longed for inside the playwright's soul.

The South African circumstances were not unique. The same insidious sedition happened in Ireland in the early twentieth century during the dying days of English overlordship. Dublin theatre crackled with indignant pride on the stage of the Abbey Theatre and played a significant role in the emergence of the Irish Republic.

Great theatre tells you what you know but are afraid to say.

Chapter One

The play's a scalpel that exposes our darkest depths and lets in the light. It lays out all the faults, all the glories, the victories that illuminate our histories and the defeats that set us aback. The play's a mirror of mankind, the prism through which the good intentions of rulers are wryly viewed and the suffering of populations bleakly exposed.

"But she's black!" exclaimed Bernard.
"So?" said Michael.
"Listen, China. Where you come from, that doesn't matter but, in this country, what you have in mind is against the law."
"And the law is against common sense."
"That's as maybe but in this country the law beats common sense to a pulp. Which is what you'll be if you fall into their hands."
"A pulp?"
"Listen to me. You're here on a permanent resident's permit, right?"
"Yes."
"Well they'll deport you so fast that you'll think your arse was greased. But her? They'll be tougher with her."
"But she's not really black, more of an ivory colour."

"There are no shades of blackness in this land of the eagle-eyed racially prejudiced. They can spot a black person, even in total darkness. They'll lock her up for a while and then throw her back into her home town, probably under house arrest."

"That's a bit extreme."

"Yes. It's extreme. Very extreme punishment for ignoring their favourite law – keeping us apart."

"But what you're doing here is against the law too. How have you manged to get away with it for so long?"

"I think the powers that be consider this place a bit of a safety valve. A few liberals gather together of an evening to see a play that's banned. They bask in their feelings of righteousness and a whiff of fear for a while and think themselves very brave. 'Useful idiots' Lenin would have called them."

"You old cynic."

"That's me. Come on. We'll be late for rehearsals."

He was right, of course. Blacks acting in front of white audiences was illegal, as more whites acting in front of black audiences. But the Arena got away with it. Even with mixed casts on occasions. Every so often a particularly goading play would be closed down after a few performances but by and large, the authorities left them alone. The legal nicety used to carve out this admittedly precarious manoeuvring room was the entrance fee charged; part would be for the production itself; the rest would be for a twenty-four-hour membership of the Arena Club and, in doing so, making the performance private and supposedly immune to censorship. That was the game and the government played it. That was why he had come here, to act at the Arena and get his teeth into some very juicy parts. The theatre was known around the world for its battle against the authorities and a stint at it would look good on his CV. It had been formed by an established playwright, a leading actor and a crazy theatre lover who knew how to tread delicately around the rules and push the boundaries just so far. If the subject matter was explosive, there would be no mixed casts; if it was a safe subject, the cast would be mixed, increasingly so, as time went on. The reputations of some of the playwrights and the leading actors were such that to confront them was a delicate matter, not to mention the pesky publicity that the Arena garnered in intellectual journals and popular newspapers throughout the Western world. So, the game went on. Snoots were cocked at the sanctimonious; foibles were flaunted; and shibboleths were confronted.

The current production for which he was rehearsing was *Richard the Third* and he was the lead with the lovely Thandi Kubeka as the Lady Anne. They were about to work on the great scene where Richard, having killed Anne's husband – and her father-in-law – on his gallop towards the throne, stops her as she follows her father in his coffin and woos her as never a lady had been wooed before. The play itself presented no challenge to the government, so it was decided that it would be totally integrated, black and white actors in gaudy costumes having a brave stab at the demanding dialogue, with variable success. The play had been performed several years ago at the State Theatre which stood deep in the bowels of the corporate section of town. The wide steps to the intricate and confusing entrance occupied more real estate than the entire footprint of the Arena and several Arenas would have fitted into the foyer with its plush carpeting, soaring staircases and intimidating balconies. But being funded by the government, the theatre management was above such mundane matters as budget constraints or profit and loss. Their *Richard the Third* had been, from all accounts, a dry, superficial but beautifully pronounced reading of what is considered by some as Shakespeare's most frightening play. Michael, and Bernard – who was directing the Arena version – were inspired by the superb level of the Bard's work staged in some of the Western world's finest theatres and Michael intended to extract the maximum fear and loathing out of his Richard. For both of them the high point – low point would perhaps be a better indicator – of Gloucester's (the soon-to-be King Richard's) evil cynicism, was his wooing of the Lady Anne as she is following the corpse of King Henry, her father-in-law, whom Gloucester had recently killed shortly after he had killed her husband, Edward. They had studied the scene very carefully and worked out the rhythm required to communicate the swooping determination and guile with which Gloucester had bludgeoned the poor woman until she caved in to his oh, so implacable will. And Thandi Kubeka was playing Anne. She had a very mobile face which Bernard was trying to subdue somewhat so as to make sudden, passionate outbursts all the more powerful. Her diction was perfect, the result of careful teaching by the Irish nuns, and her voice had a surprising range. Michael was becoming more and more enthralled by her as rehearsals proceeded.

Bernard was setting the scene for them both.

"This scene will unlock Richard's character and it's all to do with rhythm, of the words and of both your emotions. Get it right here and you'll get it right through the play. The first seventy-odd lines are all about her loathing for him who killed her husband and his father. It starts to sizzle when he orders the bearers to set the corpse down and threatens to kill them if they don't. Thandi, let's have it."

Anne: *What? Do you tremble? Are you all afraid? Alas I blame you not; for you are mortal, and mortal eyes cannot endure the devil.*

Thandi continued to pour rage and scorn on his head as Michael ducked and weaved, totally unabashed by his own behaviour.

"OK," said Bernard. "Carry on until he suddenly admits he's the killer. This stops you in your tracks, Thandi."

She carried on and had the complete measure of the piece.

Anne: *Didst thou not kill this king?*

Glo: *I grant ye.*

"I just love the throwaway manner of that. You could almost polish your nails on your chest as you say it. Now carry on until you admit your lust for her."

Soon it came.

Anne: *He is in heaven where thou shalt never come.*

Glo: *Let him thank me, that holp to send him thither; for he was fitter for that place than earth.*

Anne: *And thou unfit for any place but hell.*

Glo: *Yes, one place else, if you will hear me name it.*

Anne: *Some dungeon.*

Glo: *Your bedchamber.*

"Whoa! You're shocked, Thandi," said Bernard. "Astounded. For an important split second, you're taken aback. And the audience must see that and feel that. But you summon up your rage again immediately. So, it's a split-second dip in your rage but when you pull yourself together, you're in a higher state of anger. Go on until you spit on him.

"A real spit?"

"Of course. What do you think this is, a pantomime?"

They carried on until she spat on him.

Glo: *Why dost thou spit at me?*

Anne: *Would it were mortal poison, for thy sake!*

Glo: *Never came poison from so sweet a place.*

Anne: *Never hung poison on a fouler toad.*

"Aren't you going to wipe it off?" she asked.

"No. You will," said Michael.

"When?"

"Don't know yet. We'll find a place."

"Good idea," said Bernard. "It will be a part of her submission."

The place suggested itself when Richard offers her his sword and tears open his shirt. She starts to stab him but pauses.

Glo: *Nay, do not pause; for I did kill King Henry, but 'twas thy beauty that provoked me. Nay, now dispatch; 'twas I that stabb'd young Edward.*

She starts to stab again.

Glo: *But 'twas thy heavenly face that set me on.*

She drops the sword.

Glo: *Take up the sword again, or take up me.*

"There! That's when you wipe my face with your sleeve. Right, Bernard?"

"Yes. Right there. OK. Now on to the finish."

They carried on until the now submissive Anne leaves and Gloucester gloats.

Glo: *Was ever woman in this humour woo'd? Was ever woman in this humour won? I'll have her* (maniacal laugh); *but I will not keep her long.*

"Good. Good. I love the laugh," said Bernard. "Let's take a break."

"How's the coffee?"

"It's fine, thank you."

Michael and Thandi sipped in companionable silence in the small coffee shop in the foyer of the Arena. It was the only place in the neighbourhood where they could do so together. It was noisy, cramped and fun and Michael, studying the creased brow of the girl, knew that a problem was bothering her. It wasn't long in coming.

"I'm having difficulty with this scene. My reactions to your… outrageousness is so hard. I have to stand there and not react too obviously."

"Listening. The secret is in the listening – active listening. Very few actors really listen. They're waiting for their cue word. Gloucester is such a bastard that the audience – the important part of it – are outraged and watch you like a hawk so see how you're coping with him."

"I'm so afraid of overacting."

"Then let your eyes do the work, not your face. They'll see it, believe me. They are so sympathetic to Anne that there's almost an invisible bond between her and the audience."

She pondered this for a long time, and he watched her closely as she processed the thought.

"You're right. Why did nobody tell me that before?"

"Not many people know it. That's why it's the secret of the universe."

She laughed and her entire upper body joined in. Hell, she was lovely.

"We'd better get back," she said.

"Can we meet afterwards?"

She looked shocked.

"Where?"

"Anywhere."

"Anywhere! No. We can't."

"Why not?"

"Because it's against the law. Or hadn't you noticed."

"Oh yes. Of course I've noticed. But—"

"But what?"

"Michael, the Arena is probably the only place we can ever meet. In the coffee shop or in the theatre. If we were together anywhere else, we would be denounced by the general populace or arrested by the police. You'd get a severe warning, but I would be punished and that would be the end of my acting career. And I don't intend to put that at risk. Just when I'm starting. So thanks but no thanks. Now let's get back."

She stood up and strode away and he was reluctant to let her go. He caught up with her and detained her in the corridor back to the rehearsal room.

"I'm sorry, Thandi. I didn't mean. I didn't think—"

"No. You didn't."

"I'm sorry."

"So am I. I would like to have been friendly with you but it's not possible in this country. Why did you come here anyway?"

"To act at the Arena. It will look good on my CV."

"You worry about your CV, and I worry about my papers that allow me to visit this city during daylight. I must go back to where I live before it gets dark or I'll go to prison, for God knows how long. Days. Even weeks, and any time spent in their jails is very dangerous. So, let's forget you ever asked me what you asked me and let's just act together. That's more than enough for me."

She strode away and a much-chastened Michael followed her.

Chapter Two

Every play has a taste of blood and more than a whiff of gunpowder. Each requires a suspension of disbelief, of safety and of imminent retribution. The ages ring of players and writers chastised, reviled, exiled, condemned, apostatised and incarcerated by those in command at the time of playing and who are generally deposed before the applause has died down.

"Jesus, Michael! What were you thinking?"
"I like her."
"So do I. Very much. That's why I wouldn't dream of playing fast and loose with her career."
"It's all so…"
"Yes. It is, but here it's an awful reality and not some subject for a mild flirtation."
"I wasn't flirting! I like her."
"Then think of her safety and don't put her at risk."
"She said she has to be out of town before it gets dark. How does she manage that if she's in a play?"
"We play the game according to the rules. After each performance, we pack the black actors or stagehands into a dark-windowed van and drop them back in their areas. Except for Fridays and Saturdays. In the attic here there's accommodation

for about ten people. We let them stay there because it's too dangerous to go into their areas, especially with some wages in their pockets."

"Well, in that—"

"Don't even think about it. No visiting. We make sure of that. We're not going to risk this whole house of cards for a randy white man."

"That's not fair!"

"No. It's not. I'm sorry. But we are not going to damage this arrangement. OK?"

"OK."

"Now let's nail this play. Redirect all you anger at Richard's rivals for the throne."

The play was well received, and Michael got rave reviews for his role. He was interviewed on radio and on TV where excerpts from the production were flighted but, of course, Thandi didn't appear in them. Michael was furious but it was so treated as normal that he could get nothing more than shrugs from his colleagues. He spoke to Thandi as she was waiting for the van to take her to her neighbourhood.

"It's not fair," he said.

"It's normal. But I did get a good notice in the evening paper. My first rave. Even though it's a single sentence. I've sent copies to my family. They'll be so excited. I read all your notices and I saw your interview on TV. You were great."

"So were you."

"Well, my chance will come."

"When?"

"I don't know. This is my first professional role after all. I'm happy with the coverage I got."

"Do you intend to stay in theatre?"

"Of course. I'm hooked."

"Where?"

"There's a small theatre in my city. It's amateur and I should be able to land a few good parts."

"Can you make a living out of that?"

"No. But I'll go back to my day job."

"Which is?"

"I get regular work for typing. Business reports. Stuff like that."

"Oh, hello you two," said Bernard. "I need to speak to you both. Got a minute?"

"Yes," said Thandi. "The van doesn't leave for another half hour."

"I'm at your disposal, Bernard."

"Good. Let's go in here."

The Arena coffee shop was deserted, and they sat at a table in a dark corner.

"I've got a new play. By Rupert."

"Hey! That's good. He hasn't written for a while."

"No. He hasn't. He's been saving up his rage."

"Is it going to stir things up?"

"I hope so."

"What's it about?"

"It's about the arrest of a white man and a black woman because they are lovers."

"Wow! That'll set the cat amongst the pigeons."

"That's what Rupert wants."

"Will it get banned?" Thandi asked.

"Yes. Undoubtedly. That's what Rupert's banking on."

"Then what's the point?" she asked again.

A tall, bearded figure strode through the door and loomed over them.

"Because it's been accepted by the Edinburgh Festival," it said.

"Jesus, Rupert," said Michael. "Smooth move."

"Yes. Those bastards won't know what hit them. We will announce the staging of the play here and its acceptance by

Edinburgh in the same press release. The slippery bastards will have no room to manoeuvre."

Thandi spoke up. "Why are you telling us this?"

"As if you didn't know, my African flower. I want you and Michael here, to play the lovers. And I'll play the cop."

The table was silent for a long moment. Then Rupert lit a stinking pipe and strode up and down as if he was addressing an audience. Which, in fact, he was – the state.

"Loved your Anne, Thandi. Loved the way you played against this evil bastard. With quiet strength. That's what I want for my heroine. A quiet attentive dignity. A listener. Michael, I admire your stage presence. Rupert Blenkinsop."

He held out his hand and Michael shook it, surprised at the hardness and firmness of Rupert's hand.

"Michael Driscoll. Very pleased to meet you."

Thandi and Michael exchanged glances.

"What's the game plan?" he asked.

Bernard took up the narrative. "Next week we go into rehearsal. You know how Rupert operates. Well, if you don't, it's a work in progress right up until closing night."

"I didn't know that," said Thandi.

"No. I don't suppose you did," said Bernard. "You'll both be paid all through rehearsals and an additional amount when it's banned. And you'll earn well at Edinburgh. We have generous if discreet sponsors."

"It's a three hander," Rupert butted in. "I'm not concerned – yet – about the arrest scene when you're both caught kissing or in bed. I haven't decided on which. Probably just light and noise as the world crashes in on you and you're taken away to be destroyed by the system. Well? Are you in?"

The question was directed at both of them but, shielded somewhat by the vile smoke, Rupert was watching Thandi.

"Of course I'm in," said Michael, but they were all looking at Thandi.

"It's more than…" They all waited. "It's more than I ever dreamed of."

"And I will play the policeman," said Rupert who then spoke with the directness that his plays had made famous.

"We live in a time of plague and are privileged by our white skins but you, my dear, are much more vulnerable. I am hoping that the authority of the Edinburgh Festival will provide some protection for us all, but I am not, none of us are, at all sure of the repercussions *you* will face at the hands of the state. Be sure. Be very sure that you are ready to take on this risk."

Thandi collected her thoughts and, seemingly unconscious, she reached out and grabbed Michael's hand in a fierce grip.

"When I decided to go into theatre, I accepted that I would struggle to find work that paid enough to justify the hard work. I had hoped for a career, a few decent parts and some exposure in places like the Arena. But I had never dreamed of an opportunity like this. A part written—"

"For you," Rupert intervened.

"For me and developed with me," she said and Michael winced as she twisted his fingers as if they were her thoughts. "I know the risks. We could be closed down on the second night and I could be sent back home to rot. I know that the state would probably like to make an example of me to deter others and to teach me a lesson. But the chance of Edinburgh! How can I refuse? I can't! It's too… theatrical."

Rupert roared with laughter and, leaning across the table, planted a hairy, malodourous kiss on her forehead.

"Too theatrical! I'll have to write that into the script. However, I have made the state my life's study and while most levels of it are vindictive, there is a layer of pragmatism at the top and those on that layer would see the potential of the international kudus to be gained from a magnanimous gesture. I can't guarantee it of course but I'm pretty certain."

He stood up and relit his pipe.

"Well, *Richard* closes next Saturday. You'll have a day off on the Sunday and we start at 9am on Monday."

"What's the title?" Bernard asked.

"*Black and White*. Working title. It's cudgel time."

He strode out and silence fell on the table.

"Well. That's something to look forward to," Michael finally said.

"It certainly is. Mind you, it's going to be hard work," replied Bernard.

"Good."

"No. I mean *hard* work. Rupert likes to keep his options open as long as possible. There will be more changes than you can imagine."

"You've worked with him before?"

"You don't work with Rupert. You work for him. You try everything four, five, six times before he's happy and then he changes it. He likes to keep his options open and let other people make decisions so he can be totally objective. He sits in the mind of the audience. And it's a privilege to work on his plays."

Thandi suddenly became aware that she was holding Michael's hand very tightly.

"I'm sorry."

"That's OK. It's sort of nice to be a part of your thought process. You're sure about this?"

"As sure as I have ever been about anything."

A horn sounded.

"Oh. The van."

She was gone in a flurry of waves and bag handling.

"What are the chances of her being in trouble?"

"High. And she knows it. But if I were her, I would take the risk too."

"You're a funny lot. All of you. Why don't you all kick this lot out?"

"Oh, we will. Someday."

Chapter Three

The playwright is the conduit, the irrepressible outlet for mockery and mimicry, through whose pen flows the abnegation of the authoritarian and the wicked; in rage, in warning and, most deadly of all, in laughter.

On Monday morning they arrived in the rehearsal room early to find that Rupert was waiting and ready for them.

"Good. Let's get started. Your characters have just met and liked each other immediately. However, you live in a land where love across the colour line is strictly forbidden. If you are caught, you will both be punished. It's totally unfair and neither of you can really understand the people who made this law. You must have to understand the logic – or lack of logic – of this law before you dare to break it."

He produced a slim, tattered paperback book from his pocket, folded it open and bent it back brutally. Glancing at the text, he continued.

"This is a book by JD Laing, a strange and brilliant man and the favourite of the counterculture mainly because he was an anti-psychiatrist. I want us to discuss one of his gems. He tells of how people tie themselves in knots with contra-indicatory thinking. It may help you to get the psychology of the state into perspective. For example, he posits that parents can, on the one hand, think that they are blessed because they have brought their children up properly to love honour and obey them. If they don't love honour and obey them, there must be something the matter with them and they must be punished. Or, conversely, there must be something the matter with the parents for not bringing them up properly. What does this suggest to you in terms of the society we are operating in?"

"Paternalism."

"And stupidity," Thandi suggested. "If you punish a child, that child will fear you but will most certainly not love or honour you. Even if that child obeys you."

"Arrogance too," Michael said. "They're thinking it's their children's duty to honour and obey them. Once anybody talks about 'duty', head for the hills."

"Duty to them," said Thandi. "And in the state's case not to a society but to a small group, usually men, who have the power."

"For now."

"Yes. For now."

"And 'obedience', how many times have I heard that at my home and in the church?" Thandi ventured. "As if God's law was all about obedience."

"Or being 'proper'. How I hated that word."

"Me too."

Rupert carried on.

"But if they don't love honour and obey them, there must be something the matter with the parents because they did not bring the children up properly."

"But hold on," Michael said. "They admit that they may be in error. But it's a grudging admission to say the least. They lay the blame in the end on the children."

"Their logic is crazy and you could go crazy trying to follow it," said Thandi. "What is this fellow…?"

"JD Laing."

"What's he trying to demonstrate?"

Rupert held up the book so they could read the title.

"*Knots*," Michael said with a dawning of the concept."

"I don't get it," said Thandi. "Oh. Yes. I do. People tie themselves in knots, trying to justify their beliefs."

"And their beliefs are themselves illogical. Like their thinking."

"Correct," said Rupert. "This state is illogical and ultimately self-defeating. Their logic may have made some brutal sense in the days of slavery, but a truly modern state cannot exist based on such knotted thinking."

Rupert closed the book.

"I suggest that you dip into this book. There are many self-contradictory statements in it that invariably lead to the breakdown of logical thinking that will lead ultimately to self-defeating processes. My play will challenge those mindsets and, hopefully, indicate some anomalies in the state. In one of my classes, I divided the students into two groups and gave each one the end of a rope, which a student in the other group held by the other end. Then, when I read out some of Laing's crazy examples, with inherent contradictions in the thinking, each would change places with the person next to them. This would entangle the rope."

"What happened?"

"It ended up like some demented piece of macramé with the students in a frightful tangle on the floor. The purpose of this play is to entangle the policeman character in his own faulty logic as he tries to justify his treatment of an act that is illegal in his mind until he doesn't know his arse from his elbow."

"How are you going to do that?"

"I have no idea. We will work it out in rehearsal."

"Can we use ropes?" Michael asked.

"Yes. Can we? It would be such fun."

"We'll see. But first let's deal with how you meet."

And so, the rehearsal unfolded at its own pace and with its own logic. The couple set up a normalcy of a meeting, a liking and a falling in love. The official disapproval of their relationship was iterated by each character, she more than him because she would have to bear the brunt of any repercussions. A tension was created through their dialogue and actions which grew throughout the first act and exploded when they are caught by the policeman in *flagrante delicto* and arrested. Rupert discussed and rehearsed various acts of intimacy they could be caught at, ranging from deep embracing and kissing to simulated coitus. The latter, when attempted, affected the hormones of Michael and Thandi to such a degree that the rehearsal became somewhat distracting to say the least and Rupert pulled back.

"Apart from the fact that such intimacy is… blunting your focus, it is too much for any local performance. It would be so outrageous that the state would have no hesitation in banning the work – and, sadly, the audiences would agree. We must soften it a trifle. At least for local performances. We'll see about Edinburgh later. Let's take a break."

He left them alone to calm down. Michael's excitement had manifested itself so obviously that they were both stimulated and disturbed and they were silent for a while. Michael was the first to speak.

"I'm sorry that I got so excited, Thandi. It is so unprofessional."

"I was just as affected."

"You were?"

"Yes, Michael. My reaction was not as obvious as yours. But just as intense."

"Are you blushing?"

"I suppose I am."

"I didn't know black people could blush."

"Well, you know now."

At the lunch break, they both felt like some fresh air, and they took a stroll down the street outside and towards a busier street at the end. Michael strode along, trying to ignore the looks they got, which varied from surprise to resentment and even anger, but Thandi got more and more nervous and soon made it plain that she would rather walk ahead of Michael than by his side. As they tried to cross the street at an intersection, a police car slowed down next to them and the driver and his companion looked hard at them both before exchanging glances with each other. This made Thandi so distraught that she almost ran away from Michael. He started to run after her but thought better of it and walked back to the theatre, where Thandi joined him.

"Welcome back to this little cocoon," said Rupert.

"That's what it is," said Michael. "A cocoon of sanity."

"I'm sure the play will get banned," Thandi ventured.

"And if it is, what will happen to you?"

"I'm not sure. Some form of punishment, I suppose."

"Doesn't that worry you?"

"Yes. A little." She looked at Rupert who thought a bit before replying.

"It's not likely to happen. The chairman of the Edinburgh Fringe Festival is coming to watch the rehearsals just before the opening. He is already committed to taking this work to the festival and will say so – very publicly. Since he is a lord and a high court judge he carries some weight with our lot. They will not want to cross swords with him, believe me."

He turned to Michael.

"How did you feel on the street?"

"Nervous. Worried about Thandi. Angry."

"Nice soft, middle-class emotions. Easy to control. Safe. And you, Thandi?"

"Afraid. Really afraid. When the cops looked at us from their car, I was really scared. I know that there was no hope of any form of assistance. I… I could see it ruining my career even before it's starting."

"Real emotions. Real fear. Michael, unless you can feel what Thandi is feeling, unless you can really walk in her shoes, her black skin, this play will not work."

They went on with the rehearsals, with Rupert pushing them – hard. He probed the sore spots with Thandi until he brought tears to her eyes, to such an extent that Michael started to get very angry with him but any inclination to interfere was immediately quashed by her reactions. To her, it was as if she was biting on a sore tooth to bring a swift, cleansing pain that eliminated the resentment and instilled a burning anger, even rage. This Rupert sensed and exploited, pushing her deeper and deeper into her innermost self until she was at times literally screaming at the injustice of the world and her inability to cope with it. Sometimes he would have to give her time and space to process all the fury and at those times Michael would sit very still and look at her in amazement, envying her depth of feeling and her ability to harness it and bring it into the process. This had demonstrated to him the shallowness of his style of conventional acting which relied on movement, facial expression and standard emissions of the 'actor's art'. These, he was discovering, weren't enough to do justice to the situations that the rehearsal evoked and probed. The script, such as it was, slowly emerged, typed up each night by Rupert and almost totally changed the next day. At the beginning, this frustrated Michael until, to his surprise, he realised that he was going deeper and deeper into his character which was being developed and transformed each day. Rupert took them through the stages of romance: flirting, increasing intimacy, intimacy and fulfilment. By the time they reached that stage, they were both truly in love, but this emerging relationship was disrupted brutally when Rupert adopted the role of a bullying, racist and ultimately unfulfilled policeman carrying out his duties. His character expressed his conviction in such a powerful manner that he destroyed the comfort Michael and Thandi had derived from devising *their* characters and so were immediately cowed and lost. Rupert let them stew in their indecision over lunch and when the afternoon session started, he appeared with Bernard who appeared with two ropes in his hands.

"Let's get knotted. Thandi, hold one end of this rope. Michael, take this one. I will stand in the centre holding the other ends. I will utter a line and each of you will circle me in opposite directions as Bernard speaks an obviously counter line."

They got into position, and each held the ropes as instructed. Bernard stood to one side holding a piece of paper. Rupert adopted his loud, bullying tone. "What you are doing is against the law."

Bernard countered, "What we are doing is compliant with the natural law."

Thandi and Michael circled Rupert in opposite directions so that his arms were twisted around his body.

"The natural law doesn't apply here," Rupert said.

They pulled on the ropes but did not circle until Bernard said, "That's unnatural."

Another circle. This time the ropes got tangled.

"Unnatural or not, it is the law of the land."

"Then the law of the land is unnatural." Another circle, another twisting of Rupert's arms and another entanglement of the ropes.

"I am here to uphold the law of the land," he gasped.

"Then you are unnatural." Another twist.

"So are you to go against the law?" he asked grimly.

"It is lawful to go against an unnatural law so we are lawful."

They pulled hard on the rope-enwrapped Rupert until he protested.

"OK! OK. That's enough. Don't kill me."

"I enjoyed that," said Thandi.

"So did I," said Michael as he gave the rope a last tug.

"Thanks Bernard. No. Don't go. Sit a while and watch."

He turned to the other two.

"Now that is the underlying structure of the entire play. We must confront the policeman with the Adamite injustice of the state and its way of thinking until… well, until we'll see where his character takes us."

"You mean you don't know what will happen to him?"

"Haven't a clue."

"Is that OK with you?" Michael asked Bernard.

"It's the way he works. He hasn't slipped up yet."

"It's an onion we are exploring here," said Rupert. "Layer after layer we pick at the leaves until we come to the innermost part which, in an onion, just contains the possibility of more leaves. There is no real core, just as there is no real truth buried in the reasoning of the state."

"Will the policeman buy it?" Michael asked.

"Probably not. But let's not get ahead of ourselves. Let each character find his or her final shape."

"So, we keep challenging his state of mind?"

"You won't. The play will. Perhaps he firmly believes in the law to start with and perhaps he doubts more and more as he is exposed to the couple's anguish and fear. We'll see."

Chapter Four

The making of a play demands the construction of drama from detritus, it's a dithyramb of dissonance, a knowledge of the raw material of societies in various stages of demolition. Story calls for desperate characters in search of the exciting forbidden while being confronted by insuperable forces in search of the comfortably mundane.

And see they did.

The rehearsals proceed with a surgical intentness. Rupert made changes all the way, but they grew less and less as the play began to take shape. The characters were stripped down and the work lost all semblance to a written piece and became a searing reality to them all. The relationship between the two lovers became tempestuous as the situation got more and more ominous and, because Rupert forbade any contact between the two of them outside the rehearsal, they felt the separation on a visceral level. It deepened as they confronted the harshness of the policeman and the ruthlessness of the state he represented. At one stage, Rupert contemplated giving the policeman some semblance of remorse but instinctively they all felt that it weakened the drama, so Rupert decided – as definitively as his process allowed – to play him in a torment of indecision as they are both given heavy sentence and he delivers a tormented soliloquy, pinned to the stage by the harsh light of a slowly dimming spot. As usual, Rupert left the final judgement of the character to the audience.

The work was approaching completion when they arrived at the rehearsal room to find Rupert sitting with the tallest and thinnest man either of them had ever seen. He had an enormous moustache and a twinkling pair of startlingly blue eyes. Rupert rose and advanced on them.

"Your Lordship, this is the remainder of my cast. Two brilliant actors with a great future ahead of them in theatre. May I present Thandi Kubeka and Michael Driscoll. His Lordship is the Chairman of the Board of The Edinburgh Fringe Festival who has kindly come over here to see the rehearsal."

The Lord stretched out a languid hand which Thandi shook firmly. Michael was tempted for a moment to bow over it, but the twinkling eyes seemed to read his mind and his hand was shook firmly and swiftly.

"Delighted to meet you both. Rupert has sent me glowing reports of your talents and how much you have brought to this play. Knowing Rupert's ability and having been a fan of his for years, I have committed the festival to accept this play for performance at its opening in one month's time. I am aware of how close to the wind Rupert has always sailed. That is why we have accepted his latest work. I don't doubt that I will be as impressed with this as I have been with his other works and that opinion will be expressed forcibly at a press conference in the next few days, which Rupert is arranging. Now, please try to ignore my presence during the proceedings. I shall be as quiet as a mouse."

"Thank you, Harry. By the way, I've decided to call the play *The Kingfisher Couple*."

"Halcyone and Ceyx?"

"That's right."

"You give your audiences a hard time, don't you?"

"Yes. Because the state makes everything all too simple. Anyway, the audience – some of them – deserve a hard time. There is nothing like a conundrum or a difficult question to take them away from the dreadful simplicity of their government, which has taken the old adage of 'divide and rule' to its ultimate and, hopefully, self-destructing conclusion."

"And where will the halcyon days come into it? Or will they?"

"Of course. The blissful days of their love affair."

"What are you two talking about?" Michael asked.

"Forgive me," said Rupert. "In the Greek myth, Halcyone was the daughter of Aeolus who ruled the winds from his cave and only let them out when the gods instructed him. Halcyone was married to Ceyx the king of Tachis and their love was so famous that the gods peeped into their bedroom and were angry when they heard them calling each other by the names of the gods Zeus and Hera so they told Aeolus to send the wind to find Ceyx on a ship and sink it. The drowning Ceyx asked the sea god Poseidon to bring his body to his wife. Morpheus, the god of dreams, sent a dream to Halcyone, telling her that Ceyx was dead and where to find his body. At the body of her love, the distraught Halcyone threw herself into the waves in a tormented and vain effort to find Ceyx. The gods were so upset and ashamed by the two deaths that they transformed them both into kingfishers so that they could be together forever."

Thandi looked perplexed.

"So, I'm Halcyone and Michael is Ceyx. The wind is the policeman."

"And the law. Yes. Go on."

"Michael gets killed and I find him and kill myself. It's all so hopeless. I was thinking that this play should be a message of hope."

"It can be."

"How?"

"I suspect that you shall become kingfishers and herald the halcyon days again."

"Without dying?" asked Michael.

"Perhaps."

"How will you do that?"

"I have no idea. It will emerge."

"Really, Rupert," said the Lord, "aren't you making it very difficult for the two of them."

"No more difficult than it is for me."

"Will we both die?" Thandi asked.

"Not sure. I don't think so. There are seven days on either side of the winter solstice when storms do not occur, they are the halcyon days. As I say, they could be the days of your ill-fated love affair or perhaps you have a brief moment of acceptance and peace before the end. We shall see. When it feels right, we will incorporate it."

"It's a helluva journey," said Michael.

"Did I promise you a rose garden?"

"You certainly did not."

"OK. Let's get started. By the way, Thandi, you had better get started on obtaining the travel documentation you'll need to get to Edinburgh; Bernard will help you as he has helped other actors, and he has obtained the necessary letters from Edinburgh, the British Arts Council and from me, whatever good *that* will do. You had better take some time off to do that."

Doing that was exhausting. Thandi had identity documents from her part of the country but to travel to another country she had to go through an exhaustive administrative process that took very little regard to her actual living conditions. On paper, she actually had to relinquish her right to be in the city and use the fiction that she was an inhabitant of the area of her birth, for which she was 'granted' citizenship. This tortuous legal legerdemain would facilitate her passing through the national border to Scotland on one visit only in the prescribed period. It took all of Bernard's negotiation skill to get this arrangement through the channels in the time allowed and it was the

Edinburgh commitment that did that trick. When she arrived back in the country, she would be subjected to another procedure to re-establish the status quo. She felt demeaned by all this, and Bernard spent much of the time assuring her that it would be alright and would not have any serious repercussions when she came back. Meantime the next days of rehearsal were exhausting. Rupert pushed and pulled the action and the dialogue in various directions, some of which he would change the very next day, but slowly and steadily, the story emerged, the motivations clarified and the play took on a tangible and inexorable shape. The perpetual changes drove Bernard, who was stage managing, close to despair. His pleas for some sort of finality which he could base his stage business fell on deaf ears. Rupert demanded total freedom to shape the play as he went along. This forced Bernard to keep stage business to a minimum, so he decided to use pools of light on a totally black stage. The spots would all be on tracks directly over the actors, containing each of them in a tight circle of light. He supplemented them with soft lighting on each side of the stage to soften the shadows. Wherever the actors moved on the stage the spots would follow them and he could manipulate the columns of light at will, using fractured mirrors that could send shards of light in any direction. He also devised a shivering mechanism which could make the columns tremble and sway as if in a high wind, which he was sure would be a feature in the story. This lighting plan gave Rupert all the freedom he required. The intimacy in which the lovers are caught by the policeman had been expressed forcefully but not graphically. They were well into the final scene and the possible moment of peace and serenity that Rupert had been groping towards when the Lord held his press conference. It was attended by a good cross section of the serious newspapers, the magazines and radio. There was also a TV crew there with the presenter of a well-thought-of arts programme. At the back sat three granite-faced men in dark suits who Rupert immediately identified as security police and next to them sat a man he recognised as a government minister. Good. They would hear something of importance from His Lordship who was well into his announcement.

"I have committed the Edinburgh Fringe Festival to staging Rupert's latest play which is even now finishing rehearsals," the Lord said. "It will open the festival and, I am sure, astound the theatre world and the world's press when it is staged. It is called *The Kingfisher Couple,* and the two principal actors are black and white. It is worthy of note that it is the first racially mixed cast that this country has seen in the modern era. For this forward-looking production, I think the current government is to be congratulated on its far-sightedness."

At this point he caught the eye of the government minister who gritted his teeth and smiled nervously at the camera that turned on him.

Well finessed, thought Rupert as the proceedings came to a close.

Chapter Five

Love thrives in a sympathetic climate, blossoms from a thorny bush and blooms in a soft breeze. Love feeds the aspirations, the needs and the appetites of the young and blesses the angst of the old. With love, full living is mandatory but fleeting, without it, living is empty and endless.

The government kept its peace as the play was discussed in the local and international press and on TV and the required travel documents for Thandi were produced on time and without undue hassle. The company made its way to Edinburgh for some more rehearsals before the very well-attended opening night. Bernard got to work on his lighting well into each night with the assistance of four locally recruited freelance stagehands. Central Edinburgh and the Fringe Festival were culture shocks for Thandi. To contain costs, many performance venues shared several shows each day, sometimes up to six or seven. Consequently, the High Street was buzzing, and one venue provided nightly showcases of Fringe fare to allow audiences sample shows. There were also significant places for after-hours socialising, even though Edinburgh's licencing hours closed the pubs at 10pm. This free mixing of races and nationalities was a joy to Thandi and Michael, and they made the most of it. Rupert was at first nervous as to the impact all this giddiness would have on their performances, but they were both so keyed up with the freedom and excitement that they excelled themselves at rehearsals, and the opening performances were a tour de force.

They had all agreed, when working on the sexually incriminating scene, that it would be sufficiently explicit if they were shown moving towards each other in their own light until they blended to occupy one single spot where they embraced, with Thandi's back to the audience. Michael lowered her dress to the waist as the spot faded. But before it disappeared, the policeman emerged suddenly and dramatically in his own bright spot and screamed abuse at them. They cowered in the column of light as it swayed and shattered as if in a gale before disappearing into the surrounding darkness. Rupert had decided that, since the play would be monitored by security operatives, they should not show an unsubtle demonstration of interracial love which would inflame things back home. The scene was sufficiently erotic and dramatic to make a forceful point. The play itself had reached a stage of completion unusual for Rupert, although, he assured them, he was keeping his options open so that he could fine tune it to the reactions of the various audiences, but his changes were so incremental and made so much sense that Thandi and Michael accepted them confidently and the work had improved throughout the run. Rupert had finally come to the fundamental conundrum of the halcyon days and had located them in the first days of their love, when they focused their entire beings on the moment and thrust off the inevitable day of reckoning. Indeed, the joy the characters experienced in the brief period sustained them through the torment of their arrest, and, in Thandi's case, brutal interrogation. The policeman was the embodiment of the very forceful wind sent out of Aeolus's cave to wreck their lives, but he too was subjected to the vagaries of the tempest he had unleashed and, in spite of his background and thought processes, he was drawn into the tragedy and changed beyond all recognition.

Inevitably, the lovers had to be separated, but the impact their mutual fidelity to each other affected the policeman immensely and the last scene had him imprisoned in a brutal shivering spotlight as he contemplated the horror that he had imposed on the two of them. The image of them both as being free, in their mutual love, of the world that he was forced to rule with a fist of iron, prompted him to imagine them both as birds, as kingfishers, which Aristotle had said made their nests on the sea in a period of winter calm, the halcyon days, which are now synonymous with summer. On this bittersweet note of a tentative redemption, the spotlight went out and the play ended. The sizable audience was ecstatic in their response, and they demanded seven curtain calls. Both Thandi's dressing room and Rupert's and Michael's shared room were mobbed by reporters, some famous theatrical personalities, the festival administrator and other event officials introduced by the Lord, as well as local bigwigs. They all crowded in to lavish praise and congratulations on them both, and when Michael finally escaped his admirers and fought his way into Thandi's dressing room, she was both aglow and weeping and looked more beautiful than he had ever seen her. He stood at the back and watched as she accepted her well-earned approbation. Bernard, who had accompanied them as stage manager, finally cleared the dressing rooms so that they could gather themselves and prepare for the noisy reception they would get at the nearest socialising venue.

"How do you feel, Thandi?" Rupert asked when the crowd abated.

"I feel on top of the world."

"Where you belong."

"I wish I could stay here forever."

"So do we, but you and I have to return at the end of the run or face stiff consequences. Michael here is not under the same pressure to return but—"

"I have to go back with you and face whatever consequences arise. We're all in this together."

"I've managed to have brief words with some of the more important journalists and they assure me that this will be the main highlight of the festival," said Rupert. "However, I strongly suggest that you both be circumspect about conditions back home. You should restrict your remarks to the play and how grateful you both are for its reception and being allowed to perform here. Our government is torn between a grudging pride and being peeved that we, in a way, tricked them. The three of us, particularly you, Thandi, are on a tightrope. So be careful. Now, let's mingle with the human race."

The next two hours were hectic. Everybody in the hall wanted to speak to them and all were glowing in their praise. A few tried to draw them on conditions at home, but they all managed to steer their questions back to the play itself and how much its acceptance at the festival meant to them. When Thandi and Michael finally made their escape, they strolled along the Royal Way, marvelling at the good-natured tumult and the occasional flattering remarks thrown their way. Hand in hand they got lost, found their way again and slowly arrived back at the hall where they were staying in makeshift dormitories. In the darkness of the foyer, they embraced, kissed and clung to each other.

By the time the run ended, they were both feeling the frustration of being celibate in the midst of such love, so, after a late-night stroll beneath the romantic loom of Edinburgh Castle, they stopped under a tree in the shade of the ponderous walls which had shielded Scottish royals on Castle Rock since the twelfth century. After a passionate embrace they looked at each other with complete understanding. Michael was the first to break the emotionally laden silence.

"On Monday, I will book a room in a small hotel I found in a courtyard off the end of the high street. For Monday night. For the two of us. Is that OK?"

Her silence was acquiescent, but he wanted more.

"Is that OK with you? I have to know."
"Yes," she said. "But…"
"But what?"
"We have to be careful."
"Of course. I'll make sure of that."

The show closed on the Saturday night in front of an enthusiastic audience, and they spent the Sunday mixing and snacking with the departing participants, many of whom had been supportive to the two of them and were curious about what would happen when they got back home. Both of them – and Rupert – were very discreet about that. So, the day passed, and they both retired to their dormitories agreeing to meet the next morning. Kissing her gently on the lips, Michael said he would be a little late meeting her, as he had some business to attend to. The next morning, Michael hurried down the high street, scanning the shops on either side. He was halfway down before he saw what he wanted: a barber's shop. He opened the door to see the usual row of chairs, only one of which was occupied by an old man being shaved by the thickset, swarthy barber. There was a bench along the wall on which sat four other men, waiting patiently. They all looked at Michael, and the barber nodded towards the bench. Michael stood there and made a beckoning movement with his head. The barber exchanged glances with his customers and approached. Michael leaned towards him and spoke in a low tone.

"I'd like… a packet of French letters."

"*Si,*" said the barber as he moved towards a wall cupboard. He slid the door open and looked inside then looked back towards Michael.

"*Lubricato?*" he called out.

Michael blushed to the roots of his hair and nodded. Every eye in the place was on him. The barber took out a packet and moved to the reception desk. He rang up the price and Michael handed him a banknote. It seemed forever before he received the packet and his change and, when he did, he practically ran out into the street. He and Thandi spent the next day on their own, wandering around the city, admiring the buzz, sipping coffee and enjoying a light lunch in a very old-fashioned tea shop which Thandi loved. It was full of gentle old women talking in various soft and varied Edinburgh accents. They all smiled at the two of them and nodded complacently at them as they ate their delicate sandwiches and sipped the surprisingly strong tea. Later they checked into the hotel and after a quiet meal in the dining room, they decided to walk some more under the full moon that had suddenly broken through the clouds. They decided to return to the castle and stand under the same tree to view it. In the pale moonlight, the massive fortress looked incredibly romantic.

"Hard to imagine the torment that thousands of prisoners went through in there," Michael said.

"I'd rather imagine the great, lavish banquets they held there, with kilts, pipe bands and gowned ladies swooping around the dance floor."

They started to dance on the cobbles beneath them, but it was hard to dance gracefully on the uneven surface, so they clung to each other, laughing in amusement and delicious anticipation. Suddenly their mood was rudely shattered.

"What's this? One of those fucking actors."

"Yeah. With a black woman."

"Jesus! They have no shame."

There were three large young men standing around them, exuding anger and alcohol fumes.

"Here! Whoever the fuck you are. We don't approve of this."

"Black and white! It's not natural."

"Let's show them Edinburgh doesn't fucking approve."

Michael was grabbed roughly by two of them while the third punched him savagely in the stomach and then in the face. Thandi stood there trembling and stunned with horror. As the man stepped back ready to kick Michael between the legs, another voice came out of the gloom.

"What's going on here?"

It was one of the two policemen who suddenly stood there.

Thandi spoke hurriedly.

"Thank God. We're part of the festival, and we were just strolling around when these men attacked us for no reason."

"All right, you lot, scarper. We don't want no trouble during the festival. You should know that. Get out of here."

The policemen watched as the men slinked away. Michael was aghast.

"Aren't you going to do something?"

"It seems we have. We've stopped you getting the hell beaten out of you. Or worse."

"Yeah," said the other. "What business do you have roaming around at night? With her?"

"We have every right—" Thandi started to say.

"You're not from round here, are you?"

"No, but—"

"Well, keep your black mouth shut. OK?"

The two policemen walked off, laughing quietly to each other, and Thandi rushed to Michael's side.

"Are you alright?"

"I think so. Only my dignity is hurt."

"That was awful."

"And I thought we had taken you away from the violence."

"Hah! It's everywhere. Let me see your face."

"It's OK. The Scots don't punch very hard, it appears."

He rubbed his stomach and winced.

"Well, not always."

"Seriously. Are you hurt?"

"No. I'm OK. Let's go back to the hotel."

"Are you up to it?"

He grinned.

"Yes. Nothing seriously damaged."

They were at the hotel in ten minutes and in the room at 11pm. They stood facing each other silently until Thandi started to unbutton her dress. He watched for a while and then took over the unbuttoning. It soon slid off her shoulders and he wondered again at the polished darkness of her skin. He kissed each of her shoulders lightly, inhaling her scent and then divested her of her underwear. Soon he joined her in nakedness, and they stood there, holding hands and looking at each other in delight. She kissed his bruised face and when she stepped back to look at a naked man for the first time, she saw the bruise on his stomach and pressed up against him, her stomach warming and soothing his.

"That feels so good," he said through a very dry mouth.

He kissed her passionately and then hurried her to the bed and tossed back the covers. She slid between them, pulling him after her, kissing him all the while. His unfamiliarity with the condoms, which had made him apprehensive, prompted gentle laughter and loving assistance as he fumbled. Soon they were locked in the ultimate embrace which was all the more powerful and moving because of their growing closeness and intimacy of the previous weeks. The only worrisome event at the hotel was the fact that the three French letters they had used would disappear down the toilet the next morning only after six noisy flushes.

Chapter Six

The devil's blandishments, citing of scripture and good tunes have a crepuscular air, no matter the time of day. Buried impulses respond to recognition, from whence it comes. The deep-rooted ache and the secret fear are easily awakened, and the unmistakable but unspoken innuendoes sink like a trident into the oh, so fickle flesh which resonates to enticements.

Going home was depressing for both Thandi and Michael but not so for Rupert. He was ready to don the armour and do battle with the windy windmills, as he termed them. For the two lovers, the hard part was ostensibly severing the relationship as soon as they got on board the national carrier. They could sit beside each other but that was as far as it went until the lights were switched off and they could caress each other under the flimsy blankets. This was exciting but depressing because they both knew that a grimmel blanket would be thrown over them as soon as they landed and were confronted by the stony-faced minions of the system at the passport counter. One of whom, indeed, glared suspiciously at Thandi as she tendered her passport, looking off into the middle distance as it was stamped resentfully. The play opened locally at the Arena to full houses and no sign of security people, much to everyone's relief. The reception was excellent, even though the subtleties which the Edinburgh audiences had loved, were missed by the local audiences, or so it seemed. The reviews were good for the most part and excellent in a few of the more serious newspapers, and the work settled down for a comfortable three-week run. Rupert of course had made some adjustments to tune in better to local sensibilities and these kept the actors on their toes and consequently there was no slacking off of energy or intensity in their performances.

The social restrictions were a trial for the lovers which was mitigated somewhat by the fact that in the attic were two small dormitories for those black actors to stay in on Friday and Saturday nights, when going back to the black areas, especially with a week's wages in their possession, made their journeys home very dangerous, especially approaching midnight. As there was only Thandi to accommodate, she and Michael managed to spend those nights together, in spite of Bernard's reservations, and so their relationship deepened and, at the same time kept society at bay. At one performance during the second week, Bernard, who was examining the audience from a peephole in the wings, spotted two dour men enter and take a seat in the middle of the second row. Immediately it flashed through the cast and the staff that they looked suspiciously like security men and, since nobody recognised them, the thought was that they were from out of town, sent in to keep a low profile. The play started and from his vantage point, Bernard kept a close eye on the two men but not one expression crept across their stony faces. At interval they left their seats and headed towards the entry, with Bernard in hot pursuit. As they were about to leave the building, he confronted them and innocently asked them if they were enjoying the show or not. There was a moment of confusion and they started to speak to each other – in Portuguese. It turned out that they were leaving because they hadn't understood one word of the play. There was relief among the cast and the staff, and the play proceeded. Halfway through the final week, two genuine security cops arrived just before the opening bell was sounded. They showed their identification at the box office and asked for the person in charge. Rupert and Bernard were there in seconds and were handed an official note banning any future performances of the work. When the theatre was emptied and closed the cast and crew assembled on stage and Rupert addressed them.

"That's how they operate. They let the play run long enough to demonstrate to the world how tolerant they are, and they close it just before the end of the run to demonstrate to us that they are still in charge. Well, I have another idea I want to develop so I'll go back to my little cottage and start on it. What will you two do?"

Thandi was the first to speak.

"Bernard says there's another role coming up for me," said Thandi. "But he doesn't know when. I'll look for a job of some sort to keep me going."

"You won't go back home?"

"There's not much there for me. Very little work, no accommodation except in my parents' shack, and they can't afford another mouth to feed."

"It is terrible what we are doing to our best and brightest youngsters."

"You're not doing it. They are."

"They are an extension of us, much as they try to forget that. So, we must keep the pressure up any way we can. When enough of us come to realise that the system is wrong, we will change it, perhaps with a little help from overseas. But the rejection must be initiated by us. What will you do, Michael?"

"Bernard also told me there's another role coming up. I can hang on until then, I suppose."

"Well, I wish you both success. You've chosen a hard way to make a living, anywhere in the world but particularly here. I'll stay in touch."

He embraced them both closely and went off, his brow furrowed, whether from anger at the system or the challenge of his next work. Probably both.

"Let's have a coffee."

They sat silently in the coffee bar looking at each other sadly.

"Where will you look for a job?" Michael finally asked.

"Oh, I'll make enquiries amongst my friends. They usually know about the few opportunities."

"But what sort of work would it be?"

"Anything that pays. Typing, waitressing, cleaning, maybe domestic work. I'll find something."

"You should be basking in glory after your success in Edinburgh."

"It's no help, you saying that!"

"But they loved you there!"

"That's no help either."

Michael shook his shoulders in frustration.

"There must be some way…"

"Why? *Why* must there be some way? There's no way. There's the law and that's that. You may be able to shrug it off or ignore it, but I can't."

There was a long pause as they both pondered on the unfairness of their situation. Finally, Thandi spoke.

"Maybe it's better if you go back home. Out of this country."

"And leave you?"

"And leave me. You'll have to anyway, as soon as we walk out that door. Michael, we had such a good time together. A taste of a real life. But it's over."

"We could be in another play soon."

"Yes. If one comes along, but I don't think the authorities will allow me to act with another white person. They'll have their eyes on me. And you to a lesser extent. But they certainly won't let us act together. This is a brave little theatre, but I don't think they'll risk using me again, at least not for a while."

"Let's leave. Go overseas."

"They won't let me go."

"They let you last time."

"And they'll be regretting it now."

"I'll do something."

"What? To make it better?"

"Yes. Even if it's just a little." Michael sighed. "I feel… so fucking hopeless."

"Welcome to the majority."

There was another pause as they looked at each other. Thandi finally spoke.

"Do Rupert's plays. They'll change things."

"That's so slow."

"It's the only way. They'll change people's minds. The way they think. And he's working on something right now. Be a part of it."

"It's *so* slow."

"But sure. Promise me you'll work on everything he does. You're his perfect mouthpiece."

After a long pause, "I promise."

They parted in sadness. She went to look for work and he went to see what was on offer at the Arena. They were not to meet again until things had changed beyond recognition, and each carried the other in their minds, but the image lost touch with the reality slowly but inexorably because the heart can stand only so much pain, and the heart's only defence against pain is to dull the source of it. Wear it away, bit by bit until the pain dulls into an ache and gradually dissipates. That way, one can get on with the life dealt by situations and pressures and thrust the guilt into a deep core where it dulls but never fades. Not entirely.

"What's coming up?" he asked Bernard.

"Some good stuff. We've got the rights for a Woody Allen comedy and there's a great part for you in it. As a ridiculously suave special agent."

"But Allen doesn't allow his plays to be performed here."

"He does at the Arena but no other theatre."

"But me? In comedy?"

"Why not? It's time you developed a light touch. You've been wallowing around in misery and evil too long. Even seeing your picture on a poster plunges the city into gloom."

And Bernard was right. Michael's ability to portray utter conviction became a valuable comic tool when it came to Allen's insane logic and ponderous self-inspection. This talent took some time to emerge but, with Bernard's sensitive direction and encouragement, it was soon keeping the rest of the cast in an uproar and Michael began to experience the certainty that comes from being deep inside a character. The sense of timing he had developed in all his previous heavy roles empowered him to drop a ridiculous line with gay insouciance that they all knew would light up the audience; they needed an evening of laughter to cushion them against the sense of injustice that threatened their staunch audience's peace of mind. The play opened and thundered into a four-week run to full houses and Michael found he was greeted cheerily in the streets as he went about his business. Slowly the image of Thandi faded from his mind and the easy comfort with which he was surrounded cushioned him from the manifest injustice of the system. When the show ended its run, he went to see the latest, big-budget production at the State Theatre which was also playing to packed houses. At the break he was suddenly pounded on the back with a vigour that slopped some of his gin and tonic.

"Michael Driscoll. You're a sight for sore eyes. Let me have a quiet word in your ear before the next act."

He was dragged to a quiet corner of the cavernous foyer by a nattily dressed man, wielding a glass of champagne who imperiously waved away the approaching intending conversationalists. His captor was Dominick Stygfeldt, the manager of the State Theatre and the shrewd chooser of its fare.

"Listen to me. I admire your work. You were utterly convincing in *Kingfisher*, and I just loved your Woody Allen.

What a range! I would like to push that range to its limit."

"That's a pretty ambitious aim."

"And I intend to achieve it. Listen to me. I'm planning a season of the best of American theatre. Four of the most important plays written this century. And…"

There was a pause for theatrical effect.

"*And* I want you to play the lead in all of them."

Michael came close to choking on his gin and tonic and Dominick snapped his fingers and pointed at Michael's glass. With almost supersonic speed, Michael's glass was replaced, and Dominick's champagne glass was not at all behind.

"Now listen to me. Lost soul Willy Loman in *Death of a Salesman*. Miller's finest and probably the most poignant character to ever be portrayed on stage. That got your balls on fire? Then there's James Tyrone, character-imprisoned actor in O'Neill's *Long Day's Journey into Night*. That's going to be followed by the abusive George in *Who's Afraid of Virginia Woolf?*. We finish with Miller's *The Crucible*, written in response to Senator Eugene McCarthy's communist witch-hunt that ruined so many careers in America. You will play John Proctor, the doomed lead. How's that for a sizzling quartet? You ready for that?"

The theatre bell chimed but Dominick ignored his aide's agitation.

"We'll use the private entrance," he said and turned back to Michael. "Listen to me. We'll spread the plays out over the period of a year because we can't feed the be-fucked denizens of this benighted country too much culture too quickly. Otherwise they'll choke. Let's go in."

Michael wasn't fooled by Dominick's outwardly subversive language. He was a died-in-the-wool racist and the government gave him lots of elbow room. In allowing such a prominent person to shoot off his mouth at them and the system they had created, they appeared as tolerant and broad-minded. In fact, had anybody else uttered Dominick's sentiments they would have been buried under a ton of bricks. Michael could barely concentrate on the play. His mind was spinning at the implications of the offer. It would keep him away from the Arena and probably Rupert's next play, but that was seemed a small price to pay for such a theatrical opportunity. The overpowering despair of the lead in *Death of a Salesman* is a litmus paper test of the depth of an actor's talent. The lead's nostalgia in *Long Day's Journey into Night* allows the character to belie his shabby lifestyle but limits his further career, while the despairing self-flagellation of the lead in *Virginia Woolf* affords some force-ten acting bravura seldom given to an actor. Finally, the doomed seventeenth-century John Proctor, the lead in *The Crucible* calls for a down-to-earth, sincere style of acting seldom tackled in twentieth-century plays. Any one of the roles would be a godsend. Four such would be a life-changing opportunity and would catapult him onto the world's stage. During Michael's musing over the subject, the play ended and he and Dominick parted company in the foyer.

"OK," said Dominick. "I'll stay in touch. We'll be preparing the contracts in a few weeks and embark on the schedule. There will be a gap of about two months between each play which will give you time to live out your other life, if you have one. Meantime, listen to me, stay well and keep your nose clean."

He was gone in a cloud of cologne and acolytes, and Michael walked home in bemusement. Where had this thunderbolt come from? And why him? His appearance on *Kingfisher* and its subsequent banning should, he would have thought, alienated the authorities, the string-pullers, and made him anathema to them. After all, their strings would indubitably have the State Theatre enmeshed in them. Dominick had appeared all too casual in his invitation, but Michael felt sure that the implications and publicity of such a noteworthy event would have been carefully evaluated at the highest level and undoubtedly, they would have weighed up the advantage – or disadvantage – of having him star in all four plays. Was it another cynical manipulation, as the late banning of *Kingfisher* had been? Or was it a sincere appreciation of his acting ability? They were clever. Devious and clever, and he mustn't forget for one moment that he was totally in their power. He arrived back at his modest flat, his brain seething and, after a steadying cup of tea, he went to bed and tossed and turned all night.

Chapter Seven

The suppurating tie that binds man to the powers that be is not opened like the Gordian knot – with a swift and surgical swipe of a blade – it has to be prized open, bight by bight, with nail- and nerve-less fingers. But it is a prerequisite that the knot itself desires to be undone.

"It will be a two-hander. A highly conservative father and a rebellious son, arguing over the father's will. I will play the father and you, Michael, will play the son."

Rupert was striding up and down the rehearsal room, hands clasped behind his back as Michael and Bernard watched.

"There will be conditions attached to the father's considerable will, each intended to perpetuate the family's way of life and the vast possessions that the family had preserved over the generations. There will be conflict of course. Lots of it. I am thinking that it will take place in real time. The conversation, the argument, the clash of wills, lasting as long as the performance. I am toying with a very simple structure. The first act will end with the father having a heart attack. The second act will be in the bedroom where the father is recovering – or not – from the heart attack. And the play will end in his death caused by his discovery that the son rejects all he stands for."

He stopped talking but kept pacing and Michael and Bernard kept silent while Rupert's brain was still running at high speed.

"I need a week of improvisation on this subject. You and I, Michael. To explore the polemic and devise the dialogue flow. Then I will require a month to write the first draft before going into full rehearsals. How would that suit you?"

Michael walked to the window to collect his thoughts and to think about the schedule. The week's improvisation wasn't any problem, but rehearsals in about six weeks would complicate the State Theatre's schedule, presuming that they would mount the four-play project in the current year. He toyed with dissembling, but he respected Rupert and Bernard too much.

"I have to tell you that…" He paused for thought and they waited patiently.

"I can't play the son. It's just that… I may have an opportunity – a once in a lifetime opportunity – that could get under way, properly, in about two months."

"How long would it last?" Bernard asked.

"A year. Maybe longer."

Rupert butted in, "At the State?"

"Yes."

"So it's true. The American programme?"

"Yes."

"And you have been invited to participate."

"Yes. I mean the contract hasn't been decided yet but it's… pretty likely."

"Which role?"

"The lead. In all of them."

"And they are?"

"Two Millers, an O'Neill and an Albee."

Bernard was taken aback.

"Four leads in four plays?"

"Yes. Well, Dominick says—"

"That prick. Surely you don't believe him?"

Rupert butted in, "He's telling the truth. Stygfeldt wouldn't rashly commit himself, even to a promise only. He's too sure-footed for that. Will you accept? Of course you will. It is, as they say, the opportunity of a lifetime."

"They're not as important as your next work."

"It's kind of you to say so. But they are much more important in your life plan. You'd be foolish to turn it down."

"Maybe I could still help you with your improv?"

Bernard butted in, "No. That wouldn't work. You know Rupert's way."

"Perhaps you could," Rupert said. "You have the sort of theatrical instinct that I value. Bernard, I don't suppose there would be any chance of a modest payment for his input?"

"Certainly not. All or nothing."

"I'll do it," said Michael. "I've got some money."

"Good. Let's start tomorrow."

"Who will you get to play the son's role?" Bernard asked.

"Not sure yet. I have a couple of people in mind."

They started to break up, but as Michael was getting ready to leave, Rupert asked him to wait. Bernard left and Rupert took Michael over to a side table and gestured to him to take a seat. There was a moment's silence before Rupert spoke.

"Michael, it looks as if you will start to earn some big money. What are you going to do about it?"

"Well, I'm not sure. I haven't really thought about it."

"You had better think about it and soon. And you had better invest it wisely."

"Isn't it a little early to talk about investing money I haven't earned yet?"

"No. It's never too early. People like Dominick and his like are very fickle. They are using you."

"Listen—"

"No. You listen. They have a plan for you. It will prove to be complicated and you would be better off if you started preparing for it as soon as possible."

"OK. I trust your judgement. What should my plan be?"

"You will earn a considerable amount of money through this American project, and you should put it in a safe place where you can access it, should you and Dominick fall out."

"Well, I'll try to invest it wisely, so I would welcome any advice you could give me."

Rupert tore a page out of his notebook and wrote on it.

"Here is the name and number of somebody who could assist you if anything went awry."

"Awry? I'm sure they'll pay me what I earn."

"Oh, they will. I'm not concerned about that. I'm concerned about the future, if and when you want to… shall we say… place it where they can't reach it."

Michael felt a chill in his spine.

"You don't think—"

"Listen to me. Apart from the money you make from the shows here, there will probably be earnings overseas which will be paid here, so I suggest you place it in the hands of this man. He handles all my investments, and he is very resourceful – and discreet. Contact him and make arrangements. He will understand your needs, especially when he knows I suggested him to you."

The improvisation was exciting. Michael felt privileged to be in at the very start of the project which was so timely and apt, the handing over of a stagnant state to a younger generation. It mirrored the inevitable handing over of the nation, a society in stasis, to younger politicians, the older generation fearful of change and the younger scared of the challenge. A world which has to change, irrespective of the repercussions. The work hadn't the same degree of dramatic action as *Kingfisher*, but it probed deeper, seeking to expose the very souls of the father and son. The angry denial that strips down the father's ego culminates in a heart attack and, ostensibly, the end of their relationship. Consequently, the second act is one of reconciliation which raises hope of a conversion. The near-death experience of the father makes him realise that their relationship is of fundamental importance, so he tentatively reaches out. But his change of heart confuses the son and, to hide his long-suppressed pain and confusion, he lashes out in anger which re-establishes the conflict and escalates it to such an extent that it engenders a fatal heart attack. Bereft, the son faces a lonely, guilty and empty life, knowing that his father had been a guiding, if a misguided, star to him. Michael assisted in getting the structure of the play into shape and he started to regret that he would not be a part of its completion and staging. But a phone call from Dominick soon jerked him back to reality.

The cutlery was very thick and very heavy. The napkins were as stiff as a mainsail in a gale and the waiters were as obsequious as convicted French traitors on a tumbril. But the oysters were divine; the white burgundy was superb; and Dominick's cajoling was increasingly irresistible. There is a certain ambience in a high-ceilinged, high-priced and highly exclusive restaurant that raises the temperature if the goal is intimacy and lowers the guard if the goal is seduction. Resonance has no room in such a temple of gourmandising; the ponderous drapes, the plush carpeting and the damask tablecloths soak up the sound; the space around each table dulls it; and the cavernous emptiness above the diners dissipates it. Each table is enveloped in a cocoon of silence, enabling a rare depth of confidentiality, and Dominick took full advantage of it. His blend of boisterous bonhomie and shameless flattery was working on Michael. Details of the contracts had been spelled out, and all were favourable to Michael. All that remained was to sign them.

"You'll work your arse off, but it will be worth it. Four great roles that will catapult you into the stratosphere and open up opportunities anywhere in the world. Great directors and a first-rate supporting cast. You'll think you've died and gone to thespian heaven and all your understudies will wish you had. I hear you helped Rupert with his next piece. Is it as subversive as the last one?"

"On a deeper level it is. It's going to make a lot of people nervous."

"Good. They're a ragbag lot, and they need shaking up every so often. Besides it takes their minds off the real troublemakers out there and gives them a bit of a rest. How's that black girlfriend of yours, Thandi Kubeka? Heard from her lately?"

"No. Not a word." A stab of guilt shot through Michael. "I don't know where she is now."

"She's up to no good. Mixing with the *real* troublemakers."

"How do you know that?"

"You can't break wind in this fucking country without somebody knowing. She's on some very inconvenient lists. Ah! The main course."

All conversation stopped as the food was served dexterously, and a bottle of red wine was opened. Michael watched the ritual and thought of somehow getting word to Thandi about this dangerous tracking of her, but where was she? He had heard nothing for several months. Perhaps Rupert would know how to warn her. The meal proceeded in the comforting atmosphere of rare roast lamb, strong wine and Dominick's exciting recital of how and when the events would unfold: a launch press conference which Michael was to attend, several interviews with the media, in-depth articles to be prepared and circulated to the relevant media and, of course, a demanding schedule of rehearsals. But before all that, the directors of each play would have to be met and consulted on all aspects of each work. It had been decided that a single actor for all the leading roles would be very newsworthy and fascinating but a different director for each would be equally advantageous.

"I must tell you that the powers that be are very interested in this project. You should be flattered."

"Flattered? I'm a little nervous."

"Nervous! No need to be. The Minister for Culture himself sees this as a very pivotal exercise in terms of internationally repositioning the country as a force to be reckoned with in the theatre world. He has ordered multi camera recordings of each play to be distributed initially through the PBS – the Public Broadcasting Service – which is fast becoming America's most prominent provider of serious television. He has great plans, starting with initial visits to the PBS and the American government – not many of *those* have taken place, I can assure you. You will be a key component in his presentations, an internationally acclaimed actor, lauded at the Edinburgh Festival and on English television, tackling the most challenging roles back-to-back in America's most revered dramas. You will accompany him on his tour. Have some more wine."

Michael was almost overwhelmed, by the wine fumes, the succulent lamb, the combination of both and Dominick's smooth blandishments, the thought of such international exposure and, of course, the glamour of the roles. It was seldom, in any country, that an actor at the beginnings of his career, was granted such a launching pad. The minister… he was drawn up short by the image of that blustering, imperious bully… but that was immediately supplanted by an image of himself in the American mainstream media. Dominick, who was reading him like a book, decided to draw him back towards reality. They both finished the magnificent meal and Michael sipped the remainder of the wine while Dominick ordered a crème souffle to be supported by a Grand Marnier liqueur. When that course had delivered its magic and they were savouring the coffee, Dominick slipped in the stiletto-pointed coup de grâce.

"You will, of course, be squeaky clean in all of this. You acting with a black woman in a love story is considered beneficial to the country's image but consorting with her would be to your disadvantage."

"Consorting? No. We were close during the run of the play but—"

"I'm glad to hear it. As a talented actor your presence at all the required public occasions would be invaluable but as a consort of a black woman, which is manifestly and unequivocally illegal, would…let us say… hamper your involvement. It would be more than the powers that be could stomach. Do I make myself clear?"

"Of course."

"Good. One more thing, before the required stages of the operation are completed. If you could reach Thandi, please inform her that she is being watched and that she should desist from any further associations with…" Dominick made imaginary double quotes next to his head, "…enemies of the state. If she does so, she will be left undisturbed."

He suddenly leaned across the table and grasped Michael's arm.

"Listen. We're both men of the world. I know only too well, how attractive women of a different race can appear, especially if they are accomplished actresses. But, be sure of this, if you…"

He leaned back and nodded in the direction of the heavy drapes as if he and Michael had exchanged some meaningful confidence. Then, catching the eye of the hovering waiter, he indicated that he required the bill.

"Just warn her to stay under the radar and all will be OK. OK?"

Chapter Eight

Imminence of the moment should be followed by experience of the moment and then experience of the experience. Man is a tourist, like Faust and not a participant like don Juan. Or a Dante with no donna gentile Beatrice to guide him and no Virgil to stiffen him in a strange, dangerous and seductive land.

The walk back to the Arena seemed to take forever. He made his way to Bernard's pokey office and found him bent over a small portable typewriter. He looked up as Michael came in and nodded.

"I hear you've been slumming."

"Yeah. You could say that. How have you been, Bernard?"

"As well as can be expected. No salary again this month. The sooner Rupert finishes his next play the better. You?"

"Good. I'm good. I need to get hold of Thandi."

"Thandi? Why?"

"I have something to tell her. It's important."

"She's up country somewhere. Not sure where. She's keeping her head down."

"She should too."

"Why do you say that?"

"I heard something today that I think she should know. Are you in contact with her?"

Bernard looked hard at him.

"Is she in trouble?"

"Not that I know. But she could be soon if she's not careful."

Bernard looked hard at him in silence.

"Come on, Bernard. I'm very fond of Thandi. I just want to help her stay out of trouble."

"You sure?"

"Yes."

Bernard tore a corner off a sheet of paper and wrote something on it. He folded it and handed it to Michael.

"Memorise this number and then tear this up. You can leave a message for her there."

"Thanks. Can I use this phone?"

"Are you mad? Use your own phone. No. Better still, a public phone."

"Thanks. Well, I'll be seeing you. How is Rupert's play looking?"

"Good. It'll do well."

"OK. Well… thanks again."

Bernard just nodded and went back to his typewriter. Michael left the theatre and headed towards the end of the street where he knew there was a public phone. He reached into his pocket and found only two small coins. Damn! Well, he'd use the phone at his flat.

As he walked there, he took the number out and tried to memorise it, but the alcohol fumes had not yet cleared so he put it away and got to his flat in a matter of minutes. There was a phone in the corner of his small and untidy lounge. He lifted it up, took out the paper and dialled the number. After a few rings, a deep male voice spoke.

"Yes?"

"Is Thandi there?"

"There's no Thandi here."

"I have a message for her."

"What is it?"

"Tell her Michael says to keep your head down."

The other phone hung up and as Michael sat pondering the situation, he became aware of a hollow echo on the line which he had never heard before. He listened for several seconds and then there was a click and the normal dialling tone came back. Jesus! Was his phone tapped? No! It couldn't be! Then he thought of Dominick's smug 'enemies of the state' warning, and he felt cold. From his shelf he took down a well-thumbed copy of *Kingfisher* and tucked into it, was the name of the financial advisor that Rupert had suggested. Next to it he positioned Thandi's number. He replaced the document and sat and pondered on the significance, if any, of Rupert's warning and Thandi's number being in juxtaposition until he fell into a deep sleep.

The American public relations trip was exhausting. The team checked into a downtown New York hotel and made preparations for the first press conference. Dominick briefed Michael carefully as to the limits of what he could say. No matter what questions he was asked, he must stay focused on the plays and not be diverted into political topics by some 'smart-arsed reporter with a chip on his shoulder'. He was backed in this by the Minister for Culture who commanded Michael to leave all questions on national affairs to him and concentrate on the plays and the wonderful opportunities they afforded him.

"I know how to handle the press," he intoned. "I've had lots of experience. Reporters are always looking for interior motives—"

"Ulterior motives?" Michael interjected and immediately wished he hadn't.

"That's what I said, young man! They are always trying to paint us in a bad light. So, no politics."

In spite of the minister addressing the invited press, radio and TV reporters like an unruly class of adolescents, as indeed his teaching background prompted him, and in spite of his pounding the table with his fist after he had delivered a particularly cutting remark, the conference was a success. There was, after all, a significant amount of news value in the project. It was the first time such an ambitious program had been mounted anywhere and the reporters were keen to probe advantages afforded to the image of American theatre. Dominick was much more adroit and handled them with flattering attention and genuine newsworthy quotes, which Michael could see many of them wrote such gems down, unlike the total absence of notetaking during and after the minister's address. There was only one awkward question about the lack of any black actors in the program. Before the minister could summon up his ire, Dominick stepped in with the fair observation that none featured in the scripts and that doing so would raise issues that none of the playwrights had intended.

"However…" he paused for emphasis, "we intend to include black actors and actresses in *The Crucible*, to give it extra resonance for seventeenth-century Salem. Mr. Miller was quite pleased with the thought and agreed."

One reporter then asked if the inclusion of black people in the cast was a condition for Miller's granting permission to perform the play in Dominick's country. Dominick became eminently reasonable and pointed out that Miller's plays had been performed there before with all-white casts, but that the playwright had been pleased nonetheless. When another reporter asked Michael if he was happy with that, he responded that he was and that, anyway, it was not up to him as an actor to distort the purity of the great plays he was honoured to act in. Back in the hotel they watched that evening's cultural TV program in the minister's room and it screened part of the press conference. It gave a flattering view of the project and mention was made of the inclusion of the black actors. However, when the broadcast ended it was evident that the TV producers had no interest in anything the minister had said. He appeared in one wide shot at the start of the ten-minute insert and that was all.

"What... what happened? Where am I? They cut me out! I'll have words with the authorities about this! Just who do they think they are? Hey?"

Only the producers of some of the world's most authoritative TV programming, Michael thought, but he kept his thoughts to himself and watched Dominick try to sooth the minister's anger and resentment. The minister stood up abruptly and strode out, muttering about going to bed.

"I don't suppose he'll feature in any other media," Michael said.

"Probably not."

"How did he get to his position?"

"That, my friend, is a question asked by many. Anyway, it's all gone well and if that insert is representative of the media's reaction, we have done a good job."

At breakfast they perused the morning papers and those that featured the project were all favourable and indeed complimented the government's significant support of the arts and its attitude towards race.

"They'll be pleased at home, but I fear the minister will have noticed his absence in the press reports too. Duck. Here he comes."

The rest of the meal was uncomfortable as the minister pounded the table, making the cups rattle and their eardrums ring. Dominick and Michael tried to look sympathetic as the minister swore to take it up with International Affairs before stomping off in high dudgeon.

"Come on," Dominick said as he left. "Let me show you some of New York's attractions."

So, for the next four hours, Michael soaked in the vivid and enthralling sights of the most vibrant city in the Western world. Then it was off to the airport and a flight home that was relaxing mainly because the minister travelled first class, leaving them to the tender mercies of business class.

"Thandi's missing," said Bernard. She disappeared two days after I gave you her phone number. You did destroy it?"
"Yes. As soon as I made the call."
"What did you say to her?"
"I didn't speak to her. I just left a message that she should keep her head down. It must have arrived too late."
Bernard looked at him long and hard.
"Where did you make the call?"
Michael blinked.
"At the phone on the corner."
"You sure?"
"Of course, I'm sure. You don't think—"
"I don't know what to think. She was in deep cover. She should have been OK."

Chapter Nine

The actor remains the focus of all, the tip of the spear, the edge of the sword, the barrel of the gun, the power of the trebuchet. The actor assails the audience with words, postures, emotions and pretences until its disbelief and detachment metamorphose into involvement, acceptance and conviction.

"Michael. You're too young to play Willy Loman."

Len Hayward, the director of the first play, *Death of a Salesman*, was speaking. He was nervous, balding, a perpetual smoker and a ferocious nail-biter. He was also a notorious bully, and Dominick had advised Michael to stand up to him from the very first as this was the only way to get treated by him as an equal. It was common knowledge in the theatre world that Len believed that theatre was a jungle, and it was 'eat or be eaten' there. According to Dominick, he was a typical case of breast deprivation, bad toilet training and an Oedipus complex but this walking bundle of neuroses was a brilliant director who would make *Salesman* a revelation and find depths in it that a mere mortal could not even imagine. Armed with this inside information, Michael knew that this was a challenge, an all-balls-out declaration of impending war and a sticking place at which things stopped or went on, a place wherein to plunge the killing knife. Right! It was war or peace.

"Give me half an hour and access to the wardrobe department and I'll prove you wrong."

Len shrugged and nodded at the assistant director who stood up hurriedly and beckoned Michael out of the cavernous rehearsal room. In the wardrobe, Michael headed for the men's section and started to root through the suits. He soon found a dark, rather baggy suit a little too large for him, a striped shirt with a white celluloid collar pinned to it, a gaudy tie and a pale grey trilby with a feather, which he bent, and then a pair of boots a size too big for him.

"Good. Now I need access to some make-up."

"There should be some in the other dressing room. The play they were doing ended last night."

"Lead on."

Sure enough, this dressing room was littered with discarded costumes, smeared cotton wipes and several make-up boxes. Sitting in front of an illuminated mirror, Michael got to work. The eyebrows were easy, just a backwards wipe with white greasepaint made them appear grey; some oil on his hair made it appear like a cap which he parted crisply and brushed back behind the ears. Stuffing a roll of a wipe into each cheek, he created jowls, which he accentuated with some dark, flesh-toned greasepaint underneath until they stood out. Then he made the slight furrows in his forehead deep and ageing. Some shading under the eyes to make them look slightly droopy and some vertical stripes up his neck to make sinews pop out on either side. He gazed for a while at the results before grunting in satisfaction.

"Get me an old, battered suitcase while I dress."

Dressed he soon was in the ever-so-slightly baggy suit, with a towel stuffed in over his stomach to give him a paunch, with a stiff collar too big for the scrawny neck and shoes shined but so big that they forced him back on his heels and made him flat-footed. He then applied a dark grease spot in the indentations on either side of the front break in the hat and placed it on his head, tilted ever so slightly back. He slumped his shoulders and was regarding himself critically in the mirror when the assistant director entered with the suitcase and stopped in surprise.

"That's… that's amazing."

Michael took the suitcase and made his tired, flat-footed way back towards the rehearsal room. The rest of the cast applauded as he came but Len looked long and hard at him and, curmudgeon as he was, merely gave a movement of his head that could have been interpreted as an approving nod.

"To put *Salesman* into perspective…" Len said, "…when it played in America, it was roundly condemned a piece of communistic propaganda by the Catholic War Veterans and the American Legion, but Miller is on record as saying that he was invited by two of the largest corporations in the States to address their sales organisations. Go figure, as they would say over there. Throughout all his plays, there are many moments of suspense, when the audience does not know what the hell is going to happen next. But they are often followed by revelations. You probably won't notice them in the read-through, but I'll point them out. Miller wanted to change the audience reaction from 'what happens next?' to 'oh, God! Of course!'. Only a truly great playwright can do that. Now, let's read it."

Michael stayed firmly in character as they commenced the read-through. At the very start the salesman replies to his wife's call of 'Willy!' when he comes through the door just after he had left on his usual sales trip. He answers that he is all right. No, nothing had happened. No, he hadn't smashed the car. He was just tired to death. That's why he had come back. He just couldn't make it.

And so, they began to tell the story of an exploited victim of a system to which he remains a devoted adherent until the end. The journey to destruction of a man who carries himself in his bags as he goes out there, 'riding on a smile and a shoeshine'. A lost soul who can't forget his past or explain his own guilt to himself. A small man who outlives his huge dreams and foolish imaginings until it all becomes too much for him to bear.

At the final speech from Linda after Willy's suicide, all were in a sombre mood as she delivered the closing loving condemnation and requiem. She can't cry. Why did he do it? She can't understand why, just as she had made the last payment on the house too. They were free dear… free… free.

The opening of *Salesman* at The State was an astounding success and received seven curtain calls, three of which Michael took alone before beckoning the rest of the cast forward again. After the show Michael was feted in a very crowded dressing room and was honoured by a personal visit by the minister whose nose was slightly out of joint because Len Hayward had forbidden anyone other than the cast to appear on stage at the curtain calls.

"I should have been there on the stage," he complained to Michael. "After all, I made the entire project possible."

Michael was saved from responding by the push of people, all of whom wanted to congratulate him and the minister, who, confused and dismayed by the lack of recognition of his position, soon drifted away, stout wife in tow, muttering something about bringing it up with the prime minister. Rupert was among the crowd.

"Well done, Michael. We're all proud of you. I missed your input into my play, though, and you would have been magnificent as the son. Let's catch up when this project is finished. Local theatre needs you in local roles. That's where the true power lies."

"Thank you for that, Rupert. I really look forward to working with you again."

Rupert looked at him closely for a while before moving away to make way for the next admirer. The noisy, congratulatory crowd soon dissipated, leaving only Bernard who stepped forward to shake his hand.

"I'm proud of you, lad. Stay in touch with us lesser mortals."

"Aah. Come on, Bernard. Don't be like that. I'm sorry I missed Rupert's latest. No. Honestly. Is it as good as it deserves?"

"Better. And when you see it… you will come and see it?"

"I… I hope so."

"You'll regret having passed it up."

"I'm sure I will."

Bernard looked around the spacious, well-appointed dressing room.

"Well, I'll leave you to your just rewards."

He headed towards the door and paused, his hand on the door handle.

"By the way, be at the Arena coffee shop at noon tomorrow. I have a surprise for you."

He turned to the door, paused and looked back.

"You haven't forgotten where we are, have you?"

"Of course not."

"Good. Tomorrow at noon."

He was gone and Michael sat at the table and looked at his image in the mirror. Suddenly his face, with the remains of his make-up smeared over it, seemed like the face of a stranger.

"This play is about a man destroying himself," he said and, grabbing a cotton wipe, he doused it in face cream and started to clean his face.

Chapter Ten

The perfect moment that we want to stay in, the universal applause that we bask in and the heady whiff of gratification is all the devil needs. He is within us, so a long spoon is redundant, but an emetic is perhaps a prerequisite.

Thandi was sitting there as if the past months had not elapsed. He stood in the doorway, looking at her as she read a local newspaper. She was as lovely as he remembered. Thoughts of their past intimacy came into his head, and he started guiltily as she looked up, as if his thoughts had been communicated to her. Then she smiled that lush, bright smile and stood to welcome him. He crossed to her, and they embraced and held each other for the longest time, each looking over the other's shoulder as if trying to see their past times together. They both sat down and held each other's hand as they looked silently at one another. Finally, she spoke.

"Congratulations are in order," she said.

"Thanks."

"A great review. And three more plays to follow."

"Yes. It's all a bit overpowering."

"Oh, you'll manage. What's the big time like?"

"Great. I've got to admit. I'm trying not to let it all go to my head."

"You've got a level head. You'll get used to it."

"I hope not. I'd hate to become blasé about a once-in-a-lifetime opportunity."

"It's a pity I can't see it."

"I could probably arrange something."

"Don't. I couldn't go into that place. It represents all I hate about this country."

"Yes. Of course."

There was a pause that threatened to become awkward.

"Coffee?"

"Please."

He rose and walked to the counter where he ordered and turned to look at her. She was calmly regarding him and smiling gently. He took the coffees and brought them back. They sugared them and sipped.

"How have you been?"

"Not bad, considering the special branch are on my case."

"I don't believe it!"

"Believe it. I was followed here. I'm followed almost everywhere I go."

"That must be…"

"Terrible? Yes. It is. But you get used to it. Don't look so shocked. It's par for the course."

"What course?"

"Of being black. It's not so noticeable when you have a low profile, but when you stick your head above the parapet, as I did, it becomes bothersome."

"Is there nothing—"

"No. There's nothing I can do but ride it out and hope they don't arrest me."

"But—"

"Michael. I can't believe you are as naïve and as deliberately blind as the rest. You've been here long enough. Don't disappoint me."

"I'm sorry. It's just that, seeing you again has rammed it home again."

"Well, you have had some privileged time here in the meantime, haven't you?"

He froze with guilty embarrassment and looked into his coffee. She reached out and took his hand.

"I'm sorry. I didn't mean to make you feel bad. I just wanted to see you again. Honest."

He smiled and returned the pressure of her fingers.

"It's so good to see you again, Michael. Let's just enjoy this little time together. I'm so proud of you. But I can't tell anybody. That's the sad part."

"What do you do?"

"Oh, little enough. I try to keep low and do some little things for the cause."

"Isn't that dangerous?"

"Yes. But so is being black."

"Where are you—"

"Don't ask. And don't send me any more messages."

He caught his breath.

"After you rang that number and left a message, the place was raided and the man who was passing on messages disappeared."

"And you?"

"I got away. And moved. A lot. It's sad that I have to do that in my own country, isn't it?"

"It makes me so angry."

"Oh, Michael. Don't go all liberal on me. Not while you are basking in the privileged world that the system has created at the expense of the majority. There. I've upset you again. I didn't mean to. Honest."

She squeezed his hand again.

"I… I don't know what to say."

"Then don't say anything. At least not about the situation. It doesn't help. Tell me about the plays."

Swallowing his guilt, he began slowly to describe his enjoyment – his joy of the project and especially the role of Willy Loman, and she listened with genuine interest and pleasure for him, tinged, perhaps, with a little resentment which she covered up successfully. They spoke for a long time before she took a glance at her watch and sat up straight, relinquishing his hand.

"Must go."

"When can we meet again?"

"We can't."

"Can't I call you?"

"Again?"

"Sorry."

"No. You can't call me. But I have several ways of getting a message to you, if it's required. *You're* easy to find... now."

She stood up and kissed him gently on the cheek.

"Goodbye, Michael. We'll speak again. Keep up the good work."

Then she was gone, and Michael felt bereft.

The Saturday night performance was among the best the cast had ever delivered, and Michael was heaped with praise from all sides. They were approaching the final performance and the audiences were as enthusiastic as they had been at the first. The theatre bar was buzzing after the show and one handsome woman collared him and explained that she was the arts correspondent for the glossiest women's magazine in the country, a local edition of an international publication. She wanted to do a deep interview with him which would occupy the prime position in the early pages and include a cover portrait by a leading local photographer. In the bustle, they hurriedly arranged a meeting on the upcoming Wednesday and a photo shoot the following week. Then she was gone, and Michael was surrounded by admiring fans and plied with another celebratory drink or two – or three or... by the time the bar emptied, Michael was as drunk as he had ever been and mightily glad that tomorrow was Sunday. Dominick came in as the bar was emptying and descended on Michael like a hawk diving on a lure.

"Hail the conquering thespian! Let's grab a seat. I have something of import to communicate. A bottle of champagne, barman and close the door when you can prize the last imbiber out into the real world."

"No thanks. I can't drink champagne now. I've had more scotch than I deserve."

"More than you deserve? Nonsense," said Dominick sliding into the comfortable bench between the table and the photo-studded wall. "Why isn't your photograph up there?"

"They plan to take one this week. That's two sittings I've lined up."

"What's the other? That female rag?"

"Why do you call it a rag?"

"Because it is. But it will be good for you. A cover pic too I believe?"

The champagne arrived and was opened and poured with panache. Dominick sipped and nodded his satisfaction.

"Sure you won't have some of this?"

"No thanks. I've had enough."

There was something unsettling about Dominick's bonhomie. Michael tried to gather his befuddled wits about him, but he knew he couldn't manage so he vowed to keep silent. One never met Dominick by accident. Each contact had some important information – or message – at its core. This time was no different. Dominick sipped the champagne, discreetly sloshed it through his teeth and swallowed it. Then he placed the glass to one side and leaned forward.

"It's time to sort out some procedural factors. You have been chosen to take the lead in a series of plays of international – and local – significance. This has raised eyebrows in certain quarters and temperatures in others. Considerable pressure has been brought to bear on the project. Why you? Some are saying. Why not a local actor and not a foreigner with a resident's permit? Why should you not fully commit to the project by changing your stature, by becoming a citizen of this country? These questions have been asked in certain places and have made some influential people slightly... shall we say... nervous. Rest assured, there are key people who have full faith in you and consider you the logical choice for the roles, certainly on a professional level. But the question of naturalisation remains a thorny one. After all, there is nothing to stop you garnering all the glory of the project and reaping the benefits of it in some country other than this. There are, certainly, some restrictions on citizens of this country in certain places around the world but, on the other hand, a commitment on your part would allay some of the nervousness in certain places in government. Think about this, Michael, carefully. Before rehearsals for the next play commence. Now, if you are not going to share this champagne with me, let's consider this little confidential chat as completed."

Dominick took another mouthful of champagne and stood up to examine the photographs on the wall. The interview was over. Michael muttered a farewell to his neatly tailored back and escaped to think about this as rationally as he could, but he was convinced that no clear decision was possible until his head cleared.

Chapter Eleven

He that says 'stay' to the moment presages his own demise. If a soul is the price, is the gaining of a whole world a profit or a loss? The devil, however, will laugh as he laughed of old: "For art? Is that clever?"

Bernard looked savage and Rupert looked sad. Michael sat, subdued, between them and waited for their reactions.

"I never thought you would cross over!" Bernard burst out.

"Cross over? This is not a war."

"Oh no? Ask Thandi. If you can find her."

"That's not fair."

"Not a war? Not fair? Jesus, Michael, get your head out of the sand."

"Rupert, what do you think?"

Rupert sighed and spoke softly.

"Let's look at the situation and weigh up the advantages – and the price – of each possible course of action. I don't blame the authorities. They don't want a foreigner... yes, I said a foreigner... to derive the major advantages from the project. So, they want you to share the glory with the nation. It's how they think. Always have. It is clear that if you don't comply, they will drop you. Now what are the benefits of you complying? On the one hand, you achieve a once-in-a-lifetime success and will be lauded here for it. And offered more and better roles. But, and it's a but worth thinking about, it will constrict your acting career in several countries. And limit it, because you will not be offered the really important roles as a citizen of a pariah country. Not in the serious theatres around the world where you want to act. Having experienced the pinnacle of an actor's career, you would most probably spend the rest of your career at the lower end of the spectrum and it's no fun down there. If you decide not to become a citizen, you will end your acting career here and the rest of the world will not care, beyond a passing moment of regret at the loss of a great actor. That moment will be brief and will confer very little kudos on you because most people don't know or don't care how cruel this society is or how vindictive. Now don't ask me for advice. I rarely give it because those who need it most don't listen and usually resent what I suggest. I will say that if you take out citizenship, they will have a stronger grip on you that you will probably find very restricting. There. I've said enough."

They all sat in silence before Michael sighed and stood up.

"Well. I have a decision to make. See you."

As he reached the door, Rupert called out, "About that advisor—"

"Yes. I've called him. Well… I've arranged to call him."

Rupert was silent as Michael walked out.

The procedure went much quicker than Michael had thought possible. The few occasions he had visited the home affairs offices, he had been treated with lofty distain in a grim room with a glass pane between him and the official. This time, when he had filled in the completed forms and had brought prints of the required photographs, he was directed to the director's office and invited to take a seat facing an enormous desk on which stood a telephone, a family photograph and a national flag. He was not kept waiting long. The director breezed in and strode over to Michael to shake his hand.

"Mr. Driscoll. I am delighted to meet you. My wife and I enjoyed your performance so much and I believe that there are more great roles on the way. We both look forward to them. I have been advised that your application for citizenship should be given top priority. And so it shall. So it shall."

He reached into a drawer and took out a programme for *Salesman*.

"My wife has asked me to ask if you would kindly autograph this programme, right next to your picture."

"Certainly. I'd be glad to."

He took the proffered pen and started to write.

"What is your wife's name?"

"That's very kind of you. Andrea. She keeps a scrapbook of all-important photos and articles and… suchlike."

He took the signed programme and inspected it before placing it carefully on the desk in exact alignment with the square base of the flag.

"Very kind. Now that your application has been accorded the highest priority your new passport and all relevant documentation will be delivered to you by the end of the week."

He pressed a bell on the side of his desk and the door opened immediately.

"My colleague will escort you down the hall. First to a justice of the peace who will hear you swear to uphold the laws of the land and then to have your photograph taken. Now, is there anything else I can do for you?"

Michael found himself back out on the street in less than half an hour. Not a long time at all to change his nationality, swear fealty and alter his standing in the country – and the world – forever. The thought of Thandi flashed through his mind but he thrust it away guiltily and strode off.

The rehearsals for *Who's Afraid of Virginia Woolf?* started and Michael's life was again hectic. It was a superb cast; the tall, handsome woman playing Martha was the perfect foil for Michael's George, a failed, disillusioned history professor who had married the daughter of the head of the university and disappointed both father-in-law and wife. The other couple, newcomers to the university, were also well cast, he a rather lightweight intellectual and she an immature and spoiled wife. The play consists of a perpetual sparring match, rather like a game of ping-pong with a hand grenade as the ball. In the real-world game, the ball must rest on an open palm thrown into the air to be struck with strength by a hard paddle, but in the play, it is held in four tightly clenched and frustrated fists and delivered as if by a rubber paddle which lowers the speed of the balls but increases the wounding power and the hurt each hit causes. At carefully placed moments in the play an emotional grenade explodes with devastating effect and four lives are brought very close to disintegration. The fact that each character gets progressively drunker means that guards are lower, and they become more vulnerable to the slings and arrows of frustration and disillusionment. Hovering over them all are the ghosts of two lost children, both figments of tortured imaginations. The name for the play is from the jingle:

Who's Afraid of Virginia Woolf
Virginia Woolf
Virginia Woolf
Virginia Woolf

At the first rehearsal, Sylvia, who was playing Martha, sang it as in *The Big Bad Wolf* but the director, Adrian Major, pulled her up sharply.

"Not to that tune please."

"But that's the tune I always associated—"

"Yes. Yes. But Disney owns the copyright to that tune, from *The Three Little Pigs* and they won't grant permission. We have to sing it like this."

He then sang it in the out-of-copyright version.

"Don't ask me what the title means. It means nothing. It's absurd. Albee meant it that way, so don't waste your time."

Sylvia spoke up with a slight frown creasing her brow.

"I assumed that the title wants us to think of the Big Bad Wolf."

"Yes," said Michael. "That's what I think too. And the Big Bad Wolf is any, or all, of the destructive themes in the play."

"If that helps you get to grips with the play, be my guest," said Adrian. "I personally think it is a part of the entire absurdist or existentialist movements which expostulates that human existence has no meaning, so all communication breaks down. In this 'Theatre of the Absurd', irrational and illogical speech supplants logical construction and argument. The ultimate solution is, therefore, silence. Would any of you like to pursue that line of argument with me?"

There was a long silence.

"I thought not. Leave the analysis of the psychology of the work to the intellectuals, if there are any left in this country. We must concentrate on the sheer drama and the emotional honesty that Albee infuses the play with and deliver that to the best of our ability. OK?"

In Michael's mind, for an actor, there are three stages in exploring a play. The first is coming to grips with the dramatic potential of the work itself. This involves deep consultation with the director and other casts members and the hard slog of getting the dialogue off pat. The second stage is more exciting, with the characters solidifying and the acting – especially the reactions – becoming clearer and more satisfying. The third part is the most rewarding because it involves getting into the mind of the author, especially one like Albee, and mining all the subtleties woven into the script. Such was the destructive venom of the two major characters that Michael and Sylvia could hardly speak to each other after each rehearsal, and it took all their self-control to become colleagues again. Adrian's acidity didn't help. He fully expected total professionalism from all the cast and, as to any carryover into the psyche of each character, his usual response was to tell them to 'get over it'. Out of the raw and relentless rehearsals emerged a superb reading of the play and the audiences responded to it enthusiastically from opening night to the final performance. Michael basked in attention and the glory and all else faded into a dim remembrance of his 'real' life. It took just one meeting with Dominick to bring him back to reality with a thump.

Chapter Twelve

An actor who thinks him or herself lost in a play is indulging in self-deception which is the bleakest bird that ever hung between two wings, because, when you act in front of an audience, you are never alone. Actors who pride themselves that they can fool an audience are blind to the fact that they are, in fact, fooling themselves.

This meeting took place not in the lush State Theatre restaurant but in Dominick's austere office on the top floor and there was little of the usual bonhomie in his manner.

"Thandi Kubeka. You remember her?"

He waited while Michael guiltily but hesitatingly cast his mind back to her, as if she had merely been a character in a play with him.

"Of course," was all he said.

"Well, she's in trouble."

"What sort?"

"The usual. She's part of, or about to become part of, a bunch of troublemakers. That much we know. But she's elusive and keeps one step ahead of us. We need to get in touch with her before she gets in too deep."

"Too deep?"

"Don't waste my time. Too deep means prison, for a very long time or even worse if her behaviour becomes sedition, even treason. And you know the penalty for that."

"What can I do?"

"You can help us find her."

"I don't know where she is."

"I know that. But you can find out and make contact. We'll take it from there."

"Wouldn't know where to start."

"Start with Bernard."

"Bernard?" asked Michael, with a sinking feeling.

"Bernard. We know he stays in contact with her."

"I couldn't, he's—"

"He's a traitor to his race. We could put *him* away for a long time. Here's what we want you to do."

"I'll not do anything to harm her. Or Bernard."

"I told you we just want to keep her from getting in too deep. As for Bernard, he's a useful idiot and there are many of them. We know where they are and what they're up to. We keep them on a long leash and watch what they do."

There was a long pause while Michael struggled with the idea. Betrayal. That's what it would be. Of both of them. Dominick watched him patiently for a long while before leaning forward and looking him straight in the eye.

"Consider where you are right now. Two great performances behind you. Two more to come. You have been granted those by us. You don't want to jeopardise the project, surely? Consider also that you are a citizen and therefore, within our power. Hell, you can't even leave the country without our consent. Now, get in touch with Bernard and get her contact details from him or get him to send a message to her to contact you. When she does, you let us know. When do you start the next rehearsals?"

"Em… in about three weeks."

"Good. That's all."

Dominick picked up a file off the desk and started to peruse it. The meeting was at an end.

"You want to contact her again!"

"Yes. I want to see her and warn her."

"She doesn't need a warning from you."

Michael looked at an expressionless Bernard.

"Please. I'll meet her anywhere. Anywhere in the country. I'll travel anywhere."

"If I contact her – and I'm not sure I will – and she agrees to meet you, you won't have to travel far."

"Oh, does that mean—"

"It means nothing. I'll contact her from a public telephone and if she wants to see you, I'll tell you where. You were good, by the way. In *Wolf*."

"Thanks. And… thanks."

Bernard nodded.

"I won't ring you. Your phone is tapped. I'll get a message to you, if she gives one."

The rest of the day was endless, and Michael's sombre mood wasn't helped by dipping into the script of *Long Day's Journey into Night*. The play is all about the Tyrone family, which is stuck in an endless cycle of broken dreams, conflicts, alcohol and morphine. It is set in one August day from breakfast to supper, followed by the nightly drunkenness, and it is clear that this stressful day has happened before and will happen again and again, the same wounds torn open, the same resentments expressed, the same cruel and painful conflicts, the same hurts and the same maudlin apologies. Even as he read it, he knew he shouldn't read it alone because not only was the sheer amount of dialogue daunting, but the repetitive nature of the arguments was confusing and depressing. On top of that, he didn't like any of the characters – least of all the father, James Tyrone, which was his role. James was a shabbily dressed actor who had, a long time previously, purchased the rights for a play in which he had toured for years and was so identified with his role in it that it curtailed whatever chance he had of being a 'classical' actor. His thespian angst dominates the play and prevents any possibility of a harmonious atmosphere in the home. Having struggled with the dialogue for several hours, Michael threw the script across the room and went to bed, where he tossed and turned for hours. Thandi intruded into his anguished thoughts of the play until she too seemed to be a character in the work and just as swept up in recriminations and disappointments as the rest of the characters. In those moments of confusion between consciousness and sleep, he and Thandi seemed embroiled in an impossible situation and unable to escape. His night's sleep was fitful and unsatisfying.

The first read-through was just like all read-throughs. Some of the actors were more fluid than others as they worked through the dense dialogue. The director, James Diggery, was a thin, intense, middle-aged man who intimidated them all by demonstrating that he knew the script intimately and word for word. He made it clear from the outset that he expected total fidelity to the playwright as he stopped them on the second page.

"Difficult as it may be to believe, O'Neill does not waste one single word of this dialogue, the stage directions or the character descriptions. We must not gloss over any of them but treat them with the respect they merit. The impending conflicts are signalled by this seemingly trite exchange in the first scene; breakfast is just finishing and Mary reacts to the laughter from the dining room by asking what the joke is. Tyrone replies – 'grumpily' note – 'that it's on him'. That it's always on the old man. There's his tone – and that of the whole family. Suspicious, resentful and braced for conflict. We are amongst a claustrophobic family group, each bone dry and ready to burst into flame at the slightest provocation. We are, indeed, at the start of a long, long journey into night."

And a long, long rehearsal, Michael thought but nonetheless, he was reassured that, with James at the helm, they would mine the script for all its potential. No wonder the work was considered by some one of the twentieth century's greatest plays. Even allowing for the current hesitancy of the readers in rehearsal, he knew that the full force of the work would be expressed by a talented and well-directed cast. So, he relaxed and went with the flow. For the rest of the day, as they got through a full reading, the dramatic power of the playwright was beginning to be plain for them all to see. Each day's rehearsal was gruelling and the cast was left limp and exhausted. For the first few days, thoughts of Thandi kept creeping into Michael's mind and destroyed his concentration, and this did not escape James's notice. At the next break he cornered Michael.

"You're not concentrating, Michael. Something on your mind?"

"Yes. Yes, there is. A friend of mine is in trouble and I'm worried."

"Well, you had better get your mind off it because I can see that none of this is sinking in. You'll never get into Tyrone's character at this rate."

"Yes. I agree. I'll block all thoughts of my friend and concentrate."

And he did. It wasn't easy but he knew if he didn't compartmentalise, he'd never get through, so he spent a quiet half an hour before each rehearsal, to clear his mind and think only of the play. It wasn't easy, but it worked, and James relaxed as they moved forwards satisfactorily for several weeks. Michael was particularly impressed by the young woman, Ria Van Vuuren, who played his wife, Mary Tyrone. She was very tall, just under six feet, and thin but shapely, with bright blue eyes in a mobile face. Her voice was cultured but she could summon up a whiney American accent and modulate it as Mary moved in and out of her many moods. During breaks, she and Michael would naturally seek each other out and commiserate with each other at the frequent and abrupt changes in attitudes and emotions, she to act out and he to react to.

"She is so unstable…" Ria said at one such break, "…that I want to shake her. I find her sudden moves from confusion to guilt to defensive very perplexing. All very hard to manage, without clutching my forehead in pure pantomime tradition."

"You must never do that."

"Of course I wouldn't, but these fast mood swings must be clear to the audience."

"Use your eyes."

"My eyes?"

"Look, there are no close-ups in theatre, like there are in film, so you must bring the audience close to you at those moments of transition, and you can only do that through the eyes, which may not be windows to the soul, but they are to the emotions. Your eyes, bright as they are, are great theatre tools. As Mary swings, you must show the alteration through the eyes. If you do you can be sure that every eye in the audience will be close up with yours. Then they will understand the poor druggie's torment. Tyrone does his mood swings through his great physicality; you must do it with your eyes as Mary reacts to his goads, whether they stem from love, from annoyance or from despair. When Tyrone lashes out, or reaches out, they will be looking closely at you to see your reaction. Remember, acting is *reacting*."

"That's so helpful. Why did nobody ever tell me that?"

"Not many people know it. It's the secret of the universe."

Thandi crashed into his mind, and he fell silent.

"What?"

"Nothing. It's just that…"

"What?"

"I said that to someone before."

"Oh? Who?"

Michael flushed and stood up.

"Nobody special. Let's get back. Can't keep James waiting."

Ria followed him with her eyes, wondering.

The rehearsal got under way again and James had something special to say.

"Now here is another, beautifully placed reveal. In a self-pitying mood, Mary reminds him of his affair and of the fact that, since, he had never given her a real home, or even a decent home to live in, and Tyrone responds, note, 'with guilty resentment'. He begs Mary not to dig up what's long forgotten. If she goes back in the past now, what will she be like tonight?"

Ria chimed in as she discovers more of Mary's evasion and denial.

"And she says she has to go to the drug store."

"And Tyrone rubs it in," Michael said. "'Bitterly scornful' as the instructions say and reminds her of how she screamed for her drug and ran out of the house in her nightdress."

"See how they goad and torment each other," James butted in. "It is a vicious play."

He continued to push them all deeper into the text until their confidence grew and their characters coalesced, and they all began to feel better.

Then a message came for Michael, so he went to see Bernard at the lunch break.

Chapter Thirteen

Every soul has a circle of antelucan darkness in which betrayals take place. A circle is a natural shape for a loving heart because it has but one centre around which it circles, but an ellipse has two foci, each as strong as the other, doling out short but strong leashes.

"I got a message," Bernard told him. "You must go to the public phone box in the station, the first box next to the entrance, at exactly 6am. The phone will ring, and you'll be told what to do."

When he got to the phone box, a woman was in it speaking loudly into the phone and shovelling coins into the slot from a pile on the ledge. He paced up and down impatiently, trying not to stare at her. At 6.05am she finally finished her call and left the box. Michael slipped in and took the phone off the hook, while holding down the button. *Ring! Ring!* he thought. And it did.

"Hello?"

A man's voice answered.

"Michael?"

"Yes."

"She'll be at the aviary in the public gardens, in ten minutes."

The phone was hung up and Michael burst out of the box and started to walk quickly away. He was so focused on seeing Thandi again that he didn't notice a tall man in a raincoat following him discretely. Nor did he notice a second man join the man in the raincoat when he arrived at the aviary, stood behind a large tree and looked around the open space in front. On the far side of the open space, in among the dense bushes, Thandi was standing and looking at him intently. The two men walked slowly towards her. She glanced at them briefly before starting to walk in front of them towards Michael. Within seconds, the two men were at her side, each holding one of her arms and shoving her quickly towards the gate. Michael gasped and started to run towards her, but a third man stepped in front of him and took a hold of his coat.

"Don't. It's police business," he growled.

A fourth man joined them, and they both looked at Michael as if daring him to do something.

"Go on about *your* business, Mr. Driscoll," said one.

Michael looked at their impassive faces and then at Thandi as she disappeared around a dense hedge. Their eyes locked and short though the contact was, in hers he could see something that would haunt him for a long, long time: sorrowful disappointment. When the two men confronting him turned their backs and walked slowly away, he realised that the state run by such men was impregnable. A kidnapping of a woman in broad daylight had been totally ignored by many passers-by as if it was a regular occurrence. He wondered briefly if it had been him that was kidnapped, would there be any tangible resistance? Not a chance, he concluded as people passed him by without a second glance. He concluded that, in spite of the privileges accorded to him, he was beneath the contempt of such 'guardians of the peace'. He had made his bed, so he may as well lie in its comfortable embrace.

"You bastard!" Bernard was livid and stomping around the room with teeth and fists clenched.

"I didn't know—"

"You didn't know! You've been walking around with your head stuck up your ignorant arse, buried in shit but ignoring the smell."

"What will happen to her?"

"How the fuck should I know? I know what has happened to many of the activists who stuck their head above the parapets, but I don't know what's going to happen to Thandi. Her future in their hands ranges from tough, degrading punishment to goddam hell. And it is mostly your fault."

"I didn't know—"

"I don't give a flying fuck what you *didn't* know but, by the suppurating Christ, you know now."

"How can I help her?"

"You can't. I don't even know where she is."

"Can't you find out?"

"So you can snitch on her again?"

"That's not fair."

"Very little in this country is fair. Don't you get it?"

Bernard eventually stopped striding around and sat down opposite Michael.

"I'll find out what I can. But you better stay away from her. You'll only cause her more trouble. They're cutting you some slack but don't think for one moment that you are out of sight or out of mind for them. Listen. Stay away from here. Any news I get I'll pass it on to you. But no heroics. You'd be better off if you concentrated on the American project and stayed out of their way. OK? OK?"

That night he parked his car where he had been told, at the end of the car park farthest from the entrances. Switching off all the lights, he crouched down in his seat and waited, feeling very nervous and exposed. He was not used to being alone in such deserted places, but the caller had been very specific. He would have to be at that place at that time if he wanted to hear about Thandi. The man had had a thick African accent and sounded brusque and angry. *As well he might, if he was a friend of Thandi's* he thought. The engine had cooled down and stopped ticking and clouds had obscured the moon. Bernard had been adamant. "Do exactly what they tell you and you'll be alright," he had said. A faint light caught his eye. An old big, black American car was coming towards him, its lights switched off except for two faint lights low on the enormous front bumpers. It pulled up beside him and the near rear door swung open. A hand beckoned from the driving seat, so he got out, locked his car and crossed to the other vehicle. In the gloom he could just discern two white eyes in three black faces, all looking at him. Their eyes gleamed in the gloom. He got in and the door slammed as the car took off and left the car park.

The city they drove through was in some sort of hiatus. Its past was ignored, its future uncertain and its present a state of schizophrenia. The car did not attract any attention in that part of the city which housed the corporate, the commercial and the political world. The wide and empty streets they drove through did not command or deserve much attention. Lofty buildings on each side exemplified the difference between the concept of building and the concept of architecture. They served the need for accommodation and commercial functions and did not waste space on any subtle proportions or unnecessary ornamentation which are an essential ingredient of worthwhile architecture. The sense of continuity that exists in a city at peace with itself was absent. In a self-contained spurt of sudden growth in the mid-twentieth century, the builders of this downtown area had erected vast, featureless edifices that crowded the streets and cowed the citizens. The few nineteenth-century buildings that had stood there were long since demolished and with them the character of what the city had been. Once they left the downtown area, a more neglected and depressing expanse of urban sprawl took over. The buildings were lower, which conferred a modicum of benefits to the occupants insofar as it admitted more light into their lives, but a price was paid in mediocrity. The few open spaces grudgingly allocated showed a state of neglect that indicated contempt which, in turn, generated a total lack of civic mindedness in the denizens. As they drove further out, neglected, dilapidated and rusting, light industrial buildings predominated, and every other wall was covered in mindless graffiti. On they went, leaving the semblance of a tarmac road behind and moving onto sand and mud. The buildings were shacks now and there was very little street lighting. Michael began to feel very insecure and moved uneasily in his seat.

"Never been here before."

It was more a statement than a question.

"No. Where are we going?"

"We'll soon be there."

And sure enough, the car slowed down and one of the men got out, opened Michael's door and strode off into the darkness. He got out and peered around him. He could see very little, just the irregular shapes of the shacks and the occasional glimmer of light through the gaps in tattered curtains. He followed the man hurriedly in fear of being lost in the strange and threatening environment. Ahead of him, a door suddenly opened, spilling a path of light across the uneven ground. The man stopped in the doorway and beckoned Michael forward. He obeyed and was soon inside the hut which seemed not more than one room. There were a few items of furniture, including a table and four chairs. Sitting on one of them was a man who nodded Michael towards another chair. The man who had brought him moved to the wall and stood against it with arms folded. The man at the table watched as Michael took a seat. There was silence for a few heavy moments. The man offered Michael a cigarette from a silver case and when Michael refused, put one in his own mouth and lit it with a silver lighter. He was an adroit smoker. He pulled hard on the lit cigarette, inhaled deeply and let a thick stream of smoke slowly out of his mouth in a thick curl, straight up into his nostrils. Then he inhaled again and, moving his mouth as if he was chewing the smoke, he blew it out again, much diminished in texture, in a powerful plume up towards the light bulb that dangled from the ceiling. Cupping the cigarette in his hand, as if masking the lighted tip, he looked steadily at Michael.

"Thandi said you would be worried about her."

"You know Thandi? How is she? Where is she?"

"I know Thandi. Thandi is my cousin. She is well. She has been moved into the country. She must live alone. Not meet or mix with anyone."

"Why? Why?"

"Because she stood too high. Her people were admiring of her. They don't like that. She has had a taste of fame. Now it's time for a taste of neglect. It's a reminder to her that she is nobody special. Just another black girl."

"How long will she be—"

"Banished? In exile in her own land? We don't know. Until she has learned her lesson. Had her little experience of a living death. That's how they work."

"Is there anything—"

"We can do? No. Not now. Maybe when things settle down and they begin to forget."

"Forget what?"

"That we, too, are human and sometimes good at what we do, when they let us."

"I'd like to see her. If that's possible."

"Maybe. I know she would like to see you too, so maybe, when things have settled down, we might be able to arrange that. We mustn't be in a hurry. When the time comes, I'll tell you where she is and maybe you can visit. In the meantime, have you any message for her?"

"Tell her… tell her that I'm sorry I led them to her and that I send my love and best wishes."

"You send her your love? How is that to be done?"

"Just tell her. She'll understand."

"If she does, she'll have spent too much time among white people."

"Can I write to her?"

"If you write something now, I'll try to get it to her."

Michael was in the habit of writing down long pieces of difficult dialogue which he had to memorise. He felt in his pockets and took out a single page of the *Journey's* script which contained a drunken conversation that his character had with his son Edmond. Because of the drink, the logic of the words was askew, even though the emotional force at work was sequential. Knowing it totally made his playing of the scene easier. He turned it face down on the table and took the pen that the man offered him. While the man did his smoking routine, Michael concentrated on writing a meaningful epistle to Thandi. One that would be both an apology and a reaffirmation of his regard. This took some time, two cigarettes in fact, but he was satisfied with what he had written. He folded it and handed it to the man who put it into his pocket and nodded at the man who had taken Michael into the shack. They left the shack and drove back to Michael's car in total silence.

They were almost completely off the *Journey* script and Michael and Ria went for a stroll on the roof patio for a breath of fresh air and a rest from the rehearsal. After a companionable silence, Ria stopped and looked over the rail and down into the after-hours streets which were relatively quiet with just a few people strolling along and three or four cars. *Not a bit like the busy upper town area around the Arena*, Michael thought. That place was noisy and vibrant. Ria turned to him suddenly.

"Who did you talk about acting and reacting to?"

"A girl I acted with once in *Richard the Third*."

"Thandi Kubeka?"

"Yes."

"I saw her in *Richard*. She was magnificent. Especially in the horrible wooing scene. Whatever happened to her?"

Something clutched at his heart as he recalled that look in Thandi's eyes as she was dragged away.

"She… dropped out of sight. I don't know why or what happened to her."

He flushed and turned back towards the rehearsal room.

"Well, duty calls," he said. "Can't keep James waiting."

He walked away quickly, and Ria followed him closely, wondering what had just happened.

Michael had a penchant for falling for his leading ladies. Perhaps it was the shared adventure of seeking and sharing the deep-down essence of the characters that were playing together, or perhaps it was the experience of having a person of the opposite sex blossoming as their characters impinged into their real word and overflowed into their real life. The fact was that Mary's inadequate and drug-prone character did not impede that attraction. In fact, her vulnerability made Michael feel sorry for her and admiration that Ria could play Mary realistically deepened his admiration for Ria herself. Above all, in the hothouse of the rehearsals under the relentless direction of James, emotions were very near the skin and, therefore, more than ready to develop as they struggled with and helped each other reach for the depth needed to bring the characters to full and vibrant life for the supercharged atmosphere of a theatre crowded with knowledgeable and expectant theatregoers. Michael's and Ria's comforting hugs at the end of gruelling rehearsals evolved into friendly embraces that quickened both their bloods. So, as the opening night approached, Michael was, he was ready to admit, in love with Ria. And she with him. James left the cast alone before the opening performance, but his skilled assistant director pushed, bullied and cajoled them through the warm-up exercises so that each stepped out onto the stage with their minds and their bodies keyed up to the required degree of readiness. The play unfolded as O'Neill had intended and every scheduled emotion and mood change followed faithfully the pattern laid down by the playwright. As the curtain fell, the audience was on its feet, applauding, shouting and fully satiated, as the cast and James took nineteen curtains and retired into their respective dressing rooms to accept the plaudits and the praise of the throng.

James stayed with the show for the first five performances and handed out notes to all the cast on slight deviations he had seen from O'Neill's instructions until he was satisfied that they were all acting at their peaks. Then on the Saturday night, he gave final instructions to the assistant to keep them on their toes. He also left them with a final pep talk.

"You have all done well. I'm sure O'Neill would have been pleased. I have seen this play performed three times and I can honestly say that your readings are up there with the best of them. For that I thank you. It was a privilege working with you all. Towards the end of the run, I will come to see it but, relax. There will be no notes. I will come to see the play because it always moves me, and I would like to experience it as objectively as I can. So, good luck to all of you. I'm sure you will all move on to greater roles and deeper performances."

He then shook hands with them all and took his leave. When they had cleaned up, Michael and Ria met in her dressing room.

"Come home with me."

"To your flat? I'd like that."

"I mean come to my parents' home, where I grew up. It's about two hours' drive from here. You can stay over until Monday morning, if you'd like."

"I'd like."

Chapter Fourteen

A kingdom is to hand. Among the startling magenta flowers of the sprawling, exuberant bougainvillea against the green and gold of regimented vines. Everywhere, the heady embrace of hedonism. But this paradise has its Eve. Quod est eius Heva.

The drive down to the Van Vuuren home was soothing for them both. The road wound through rolling hillsides, with vineyards dotted here and there, and dense pine forests loomed along the skylines. As they drove onto a minor gravel road, the moon broke free of the scudding clouds and its soft light bathed the landscape. The sign over the gate, which was wide open, read *Paradyse*. He drove through it and Ria directed him towards a small clump of white-washed, thatched cottages to one side of the main house, which was also white and thatched, with delicately curved gables that rose gracefully into the sky. He pulled as directed into a parking area between two cottages and switched off the engine.

"Your room is in that cottage. My brother stays there when he comes home on leave. You'll find clean linen in the wardrobe. Help yourself. This is my room. Come to me in half an hour."

Then she was gone. He left the car and entered the cottage. It was compact and cosy, and there was indeed plenty of clean linen and casual wear. He showered hurriedly and changed, and it was precisely half an hour later that he let himself into Ria's cottage. It was in darkness except for the room furthest away from the front door, which was softly lit by moonlight shining through the uncurtained window and dim, flickering candlelight. Inside, Ria lay on the bed, her long, pale body totally and startlingly naked. She looked straight at him, with a faint smile hovering around her lips, and watched attentively as he undressed and climbed onto the bed beside her, surveying her long limbs which lay like swords of ivory along the sheets. The dim moonlight and the flickering candlelight sought out and found her soft swellings and rounded crevices. She candidly examined his body, including the rising hardness of that between his thighs. Then the two of them, she supine and him crouching, moved slowly towards each other until their breasts and their lips met. He kissed her, softly at first and then firmly, as their mouths opened and melded in a delicious, moist mingling.

The night was enchanting for Michael. They made love several times and drifted off into a comfortable sleep afterwards and, when the sun shone into the room the next morning, they turned towards each other in one mind, and this time Ria was more forceful and set the pace. Spent, they lay in the sunshine looking out over a rose bush and towards a distant, purple mountain and listened to a songbird welcome the new day. His reverie was broken by a smart slap on his buttocks.

"OK. Enough of this debauchery," she said as she clambered out of bed and headed towards the bathroom. "Breakfast will be served in a few minutes."

"Breakfast!" He snorted but suddenly he felt very, very hungry. "Actually, that's a good idea."

"Hurry up then," she called over the noise of the shower.

When he returned, in a plain white shirt, she was seated at the dressing table in a long, flounced white dress, pinning her hair back.

"Will this do?"

She looked at him and nodded approval.

"Perfect. Sunday breakfasts here are very casual."

She took a last look at herself and headed for the door.

"I hope you're hungry. There'll be plenty to eat and my parents take pride in feeding their guests well."

The entrance hall to the main house was framed by a blaze of purple bougainvillea and the double doors were wide open to reveal a pale wooden floor that ran right through to an open balcony at the rear, in front of which white lace curtains billowed gently in the soft breeze. The walls were panelled in a dark, glistening wood on which hung gloomy portraits of jowly men and haughty women who seemed to glare at him disapprovingly. Ria led the way down the hall, calling out, "Mother? Father? It's me."

She turned into the room on the left and crossed to the dark wooden table where she bent down to kiss a dignified lady at the table end. Then she walked to meet the tall, thin man who rose from his chair at the table head and moved to meet her. They embraced lovingly and looked into each other's eyes for a moment before she turned to present Michael.

"Mother. Father. This is Michael Driscoll, the absolute star of the show. Michael, my mother, Mrs. Van Vuuren and my father, Dr. Van Vuuren."

Michael hurried to the lady who held out her hand with a gracious nod and a smile.

"I'm so pleased to meet you, Mr. Driscoll."

"Michael, please, Mrs, Van Vuuren." He took her hand and bowed over it. "I can see where Ria got her loveliness."

She nodded as a faint blush crossed over her face, squeezed his hand slightly and turned towards her husband who held out his hand to Michael.

"Michael," he boomed as they shook hands. "Delighted to make your acquaintance. We went to see the play, and I loved it. Mrs. Van Vuuren thought it a trifle long."

"Doctor. Very pleased to meet you. Not as long as I felt it was as we rehearsed it."

"I'm surprised you remembered all the words," said Mrs. Van Vuuren. "There were so many of them. I said that to Ria after the show, didn't I, dear? We went to her dressing room, but we didn't have time to come and congratulate you. It was *so* late."

The Doctor took charge.

"You must both be starving. Come, help yourself."

"He gestured towards the enormous black sideboard on which stood several silver dishes, some crockery and several plates stacked on a warming dish. Ria smiled at the black lady who was standing ready to assist.

"Martha! How nice to see you again! This is Mr. Driscoll, and he is ravenous."

"Hello, Martha. I *am* ravenous."

"Hello, sir. I'm glad." Martha handed him a plate and lifted several lids to reveal the contents. "Would you like some fried eggs? I can do them for you."

"Thank you. Two, sunny side up if you don't mind."

"I'll do them right now."

She slipped out of the room and Ria filled a bowl with cornflakes.

"Have some cornflakes while you're waiting," she said. "And coffee."

They each took flakes and coffee back to the table.

"Well, Michael," said the Doctor. "You have another play coming up I believe."

"Yes. It's Arthur Miller's *The Crucible*."

"And there's talk of me being in it with him," said Ria.

"That's marvellous! Isn't it, dear?"

"I do hope it's not as gloomy as the one you're in now," said Mrs. Van Vuuren nervously.

Michael took over.

"No, thank goodness. The two main characters play dangerous emotional games with each other, but it rattles along at a great pace. I don't think you'll be bored at all."

"Good. I like to enjoy myself at the theatre. Don't I, dear?" she ventured.

"Yes. And you generally do."

"You're not a drug addict in it, are you?" she asked somewhat anxiously.

Ria laughed and reached out to touch her mother's hand.

"No. It's nowhere as dismal as this one."

"Good. Then I'll go to see it. Ah! Here's Martha with your eggs."

Michael rose and took the plate from Martha, filled it with sausages, fried tomatoes and bacon from the side dishes and brought it back to the table. Taking some toast, he buttered it and tucked in heartily. The others looked at him in amusement.

"You must have been starving," said the Doctor. "Acting does take it out of one, I suppose."

Michael blushed and, glancing at Ria who was smiling wickedly, blushed again and concentrated on his breakfast.

"When will you know if you have the part, Ria?" the Doctor asked.

"It will have to be soon. There's a lot of rehearsal needed."

Michael finished his breakfast and dabbed his mouth before sipping at his coffee.

"The theatre manager thinks it would be a good idea to position us both as an acting couple," he said, sipping at his coffee. "The theatre-going public likes that sort of thing and, after all, there aren't too many interesting actors on the scene right now."

"He might even manufacture a romance between us, to get us into the gossip columns." Ria was still grinning wickedly, and Michael averted his gaze.

"Oh, how vulgar!" Mrs. Van Vuuren blurted. "Dear, can't you prevent such a thing?"

The Doctor laughed dismissively.

"Wouldn't dream of trying. A bit of gossip will help both their careers. Have you had enough breakfast, Michael?"

"Plenty, sir."

"I really think you ought to try, dear."

"Don't worry about it, dear. Well, if we're all finished...?" they all indicated that they had, "Then, Michael, you might want to freshen up a bit and I'll show you the orchards and vineyards. They're in fine shape right now."

"It would be a pleasure, Doctor."

The early sun was burning off the remains of the night-time fog, part of which still clung to the vines with their precious burdens of golden grapes. The Doctor led the way in among the vines, plucked a bunch off one of the vines and passed it to Michael.

"Sauvignon Blanc. My specialty. There will be a good harvest this year, I'm glad to say. Take the large berry at the bottom of the bunch. It's perfect now."

Michael did so and enjoyed the burst of flavour into his mouth.

"Mmmm. Very—"

"Herby. Lime, apple, peach. The peach is particularly dominant this year, which will soften it somewhat. Oh, don't try to identify the flavours. Most of them are so subtle, even in the finished wine."

He took a berry from the bunch and tasted it.

"Coming along nicely. It's a pity that the Muslims now forbid the drinking of wine. Their ancient mystics perceived it as a highly beneficial drink and admired the transformations that it goes through, starting with the crushing which transforms the berry into a sweet-tasting juice, which is, in turn, transformed into a delicious wine, which transforms us humans into joyous, intoxicated creatures, or, sometimes into reeling drunks. Except for that last stage, it is a gentle process, beneficial to all humankind. Even Jesus himself said, 'I am the true vine, my father is the husbandman, and you are the branches.' This is in contrast with revelation, which says that all humankind will be tossed into the great wine press of the wrath of God, from which will flow an immense river of blood. Have another grape."

Michael laughed and took another.

"So, wine has had a bad press over the centuries."

"Not all the time. Another Persian extolled its virtues: 'here with a loaf of bread beneath the bough, a flask of wine, a book of verse and thou beside me singing in the wilderness—'"

"Wait. I know that…" He paused. "'And wilderness is paradise enow,'" Michael finished.

"Well done. You know your Khayyam."

"I've always loved him. Ever since I learned it at school. How does it start?"

Michael took up a regal pose and intoned, "'Awake! For morning in the bowl of night has flung the stone that put the stars to flight…'"

The Doctor joined in and they both, delighted with each other, continued: "'And lo! The hunter of the East has caught the Sultan's turret in a noose of light.'"

"Well, we better get back," the Doctor said when they had walked through the vineyard, listening to the birdsong from the surrounding trees. "Dominick is coming for lunch. He'll need freshening up before we eat."

Chapter Fifteen

A river runs through it. Singing, limpid, wayward. Silvered with trout, rippled with sunshine and very seductive. Soft sand on the banks, smooth pebbles on the bottom. Paradise enow. Except for the serpent at its heart.

Sure enough, when they returned to the main house, they found Dominick in deep conversation with Mrs. Van Vuuren and Ria, who was arranging some roses in a crystal bowl.

"Dominick brought some roses for Mother. Wasn't that kind?" she said.

"Pink too. He knows my favourite colours."

When the greetings were completed and the display of roses commented upon, Dominick stood and addressed the group.

"Would you mind if Michael and I had a private word. We have some theatre business to discuss."

They nodded to the rest of the company and Michael and Ria exchanged wry looks as he and Dominick went out. Dominick headed towards the wine cellars with Michael in pursuit.

"It's beautiful here," Dominick said, pausing at the open doors and sniffing the wine fumes that emanated from the whitewashed and thatched entry hall. "Many men of the Doctor's class do this sort of thing, grow wines, sample each other's vintages and generally have a life that is the envy of the world. They live in a cocoon of course but you have to admit, it's a very comfortable one and it is protected for their enjoyment. Did you know that Ria is the only living descendent and the sole heir to all this?"

They made their way down the wide wooden staircase to where the immense barrels with their precious contents were slumbering. They stopped and watched a man in a white coat, standing on a stepladder next to one of the barrels, holding a steel rod with a small cup attached to the end. This he lowered down into the barrel and drew it out slowly. Then he swirled it in a circle around his head, examined the cup and then took a tentative sup of the contents. They both watched as he sucked the wine in through his pursed lips and chewed it with a thoughtful expression on his face.

"Is it alright?" Dominick called out.

"It's coming along very nicely," the man said as he replaced the bung in the barrel and started to descend. When he reached the ground, he approached them and held out the cup.

"Want to try?"

Dominick indicated Michael forward and watched as he took a tentative sip. His face wrinkled and the man laughed.

"Doesn't taste like much, does it? It's only halfway through the process. In another two years, or, if we're lucky, one year, it'll be ready for bottling."

"How long has it been in the barrels?"

"Two years, but it's very robust so it needs more time. When it's ready, it will be one of our best vintages."

"Thank you for that information. And the wine."

"It's a pleasure."

They made their way back towards the house in a circuitous route, and Dominick became confidential.

"You and Ria are made for each other."

"Come on! We're just good friends."

"Very good friends. You spent last night together."

Michael drew up short.

"How the hell do you know that?"

"Someone followed you out here and saw that you stayed in the same cottage all night."

"You are spying on me! This is—"

"We are protecting our investment in you both. Two fine actors who have had all the resources of the State Theatre – even the state itself– lavished on you. Do you think for one moment that we would put you at risk?"

"This is an invasion—"

"Of what? You're privacy? Don't be naïve! You are part of the greatest single investment in theatre that the state has ever made. We keep a discreet but highly effective watch over you to ensure that you don't endanger our project."

Michael was stunned. He knew – as deep down as he could bury it – that the state was all-powerful and would fight against any challenge. Reality was pounding on the door and, resist though he might, it would not be denied access. He stopped and looked out over the vineyards; Ria's legacy, that was there for the… he tried to dismiss the thought, but it lingered.

"All of this, Michael. Reach out and *Paradyse* will be yours."

Michael thought of the verse from *The Rubaiyat* which spoke of wilderness and paradise and how a flask of wine could transmute them. Dominick stopped beside him and examined his face with clinical detachment. Then, with splendid bonhomie, he put his arm around Michael's shoulder and started to lead him back towards the house and the Van Vuuren family.

"Come. When two national treasures like you and Ria come together, it behoves us all to take the best possible care of them, so forgive me if I seem too proprietorial, even a little bossy. I have both your interests at heart, really, I do. Your level of acting takes enormous energy and focus, and I wish to make your lives as stress-free as possible so you can concentrate on it. Now lunch. I'm starving and the good Doctor keeps a good table.

Dominick was right. The lunch was superb: a succulent mixed salad, some perfectly ripe avocados, fresh, crumbly homemade bread with thick, yellow farm butter and, naturally, a four-year-old Sauvignon Blanc, at its prime and chilled to perfection. The Doctor and Dominick were in fine form and the talk was lively and amusing. Even Mrs. Van Vuuren was gay and mischievous and exchanged toasts with them all, especially Michael who was seated at her right. The only dark moment in the meal was when Martha and another maid were clearing the plates off the table. As Martha took up Michael's plate, their eyes met.

"Thank you, Martha," Michael said, and he was greeted with a bright smile which froze and faded as Mrs. Van Vuuren hissed in a vicious undertone, "Martha! Don't place one plate on top of another!"

Martha mumbled something and withdrew, and Mrs. Van Vuuren smiled a little tipsily at Michael.

"It's so difficult to train them. They never learn."

A falling piece of cutlery drew her glare, but she turned back and leaned towards Michael.

"I can't tell you how often I have to replace crockery in this house. If you're not careful, they'll rob you blind."

"Michael. Stop flirting with my wife. A glass of wine with you."

They toasted each other and Ria commandeered his attention.

"I haven't had a word with you since breakfast. I insist that you accompany me to the stream. It's my favourite place on the whole estate. How is the fishing, Father?"

"Not bad. I landed a nice trout last week higher up the river and I'm afraid I didn't release it again but took it home for

Martha to poach in a little of my wine. It tasted marvellous, but I mustn't do it again. Not for a long time."

When the lunch was over, Michael and Ria wandered lazily across the estate towards the foothills of the purple mountain that stood guard over the serried ranks of vines. Beyond the vineyards was an extensive swath of grass that sloped upwards to a bend in the river which flowed slowly through the estate and, as the ground levelled off, widened as it approached the gravel road that delineated the Doctor's grounds. A stately row of tall willows nodded over the bank and the pebbled bed of the river, their silvery leaves shivering in the sunshine and the few remaining yellow catkins drooping down towards the lush grass. They strolled along the bank hand in hand until a particularly welcoming carpet of grass and small flowers in the dappled shade of a massive, lopsided willow prompted them to stop and embrace. After a long, lingering kiss, Ria stepped away from him and started to unbutton her blouse. He took his cue from her and moments later they were both naked and admiring the play of the sunshine over each other's bodies. She stepped down the bank into the water and took a shallow dive into its embrace. Her white body was a shade lighter than the pebbles as she took slow, easy strokes out towards the river centre. He followed and, covering her body from behind, lifted his head up between her legs until it rested on the swell of her buttocks. His mouth slid up the soft rounded cleft until it reached the base of her spine and then moved out to one of the two dimples that framed it. She rolled onto her side, as did he and he penetrated her from behind. The natural buoyancy of their bodies kept them clear of the pebbles as they made slow and lazy love. It was different to the love they had made the night before. This was languid and gentle, and the orgasms seemed to go on forever.

Supper that night was interminable. The Van Vuurens had invited several neighbours who all looked the same; the men were burly, suntanned and casually dressed, the women were clones of Mrs. Van Vuuren, mild, diffident towards their husbands and sipping more wine than was good for them. Dominick was his usually ebullient self, flattering all the women, respectful towards the men and attentive to their rather limited conversations. This time, thankfully, Michael was not sitting next to Mrs. Van Vuuren but next to a small, nervous woman who concentrated on her husband across the table and did not respond to his half-hearted attempts at small talk. Between the two of them, the Doctor and Dominick managed to create the illusion of wide-ranging discussions, and Michael was cajoled by each in turn to take part, but his mind was on Ria who was opposite him. She tried to draw him into some of the small talk. His mind was also on Martha who had changed into a more formal housecoat and, assisted by a young black girl, served them all dexterously, not once placing one plate on top of another. What intrigued him was that she seemed to be invisible to them all. In spite of her physical closeness to them in turn, not one of the group looked at her. There was not the slightest indication of gratitude as they were served. They talked around her as if she weren't there, each of them knowing that a slight raising of an empty glass or a look around the table for a condiment or a sauce would bring her to them with the wine bottle or the desired container. Every so often, Michael would catch Martha's eye and they would exchange very faint smiles of amusement. Mrs. Van Vuuren, of course, watched Martha like a hawk and her hiss would be audible at any supposed clumsiness or lack of exactment. One of the guests raised the subject of labour in the area and how it was getting expensive and the workers getting more reluctant and truculent. All the men joined in on the subject and Michael became embarrassed at the rudeness of the comments made and the viciousness of the opinions held by them all on the subject. Even Ria seemed oblivious to the manifest racism. Martha seemed unaware of what was being said about her people, apart from a slight, ever so slight, stiffening of her mouth at some of the more outrageous remarks. Deciding to give her a healthy tip in the morning, Michael's mind slipped into neutral and his reaction to the various topics raised became meaninglessly automatic. Dominick remained imperturbable and relentlessly urbane.

Chapter Sixteen

Sometimes the actor is called upon to step outside the role, to view it through the prism of the audience's mind. And cope with the inherent tensions between personal prejudices, the playwright's intention and the audience's sensibilities.

The play ran for eight weeks, and the response from the audiences and the critics was ecstatic. The glossy women's magazine featuring Michael came out and he was gratified to see the cover featuring his face prominently displayed in several windows in the large shopping centre close to the theatre. He purchased one and accepted with becoming sangfroid the gushing compliments from the shop assistant who sold it to him. The article itself was accurate but very superficial. Still, he put it in his file, along with the other press clippings he was collecting. That afternoon he was interviewed by a young TV presenter who knew very little about theatre, and nothing at all about the play, and Michael found that very draining as he waffled along for the fifteen minutes, speaking far too much about O'Neill and the difficulty of delivering the play night after night while keeping the energy level high. A later radio interview by a knowledgeable theatre critic went much better as they discussed the issues raised by the piece and the playwright's intention in creating it. The hour-long interview flew by as they discussed what the play meant and its importance to theatre in general. Towards the latter part of the run, Dominick was seriously considering mounting it in three other cities but, to Michael's relief, nothing came of the thought. At the closing night's celebration, Ria told Michael that he had been invited to stay at the family estate again for a few days, but they decided that they both needed a more peaceful break so they booked a week's stay at a luxurious seaside hotel about two hours' drive along a particularly spectacular coastal route. The bookings were made, and they set off in her father's Mercedes which she had borrowed for the trip. The weather was glorious, the scenery dramatic and the service at the hotel was excellent. They both ate far too well, made love far too often and generally felt very smug at their situation.

"Well, you two look fit and well, I must say. Are you both ready for the next blockbuster?"

Dominick had called Ria and Michael to his office before rehearsals which were due to start later in the day, and he was at his smoothest.

"I thought I would speak to you about our decisions for *The Crucible* since it concerns the two of you especially. This is Miller at his most indignant. He hated that slimy bastard Eugene McCarthy for the damage he had done to some of the best actors in Hollywood by accusing them of being card-carrying communists or naming some of their friends who were, at the infamous hearings held by the House Committee on Un-American Activities. Miller's way of combating him was to write about the seventeenth-century witch-hunt in Salem, Massachusetts in which most of the town's population was hanged or even pressed to death on the flimsy evidence of a few hysterical young women they had consorted with and who were thought to be witches. The parallels were very clear to Miller's audiences and, although it took some time, the impact of the work had a major role to play in the reassurance of American society. We feel that this version of *The Crucible* will have a similar effect here."

"I'm not sure how," Michael intervened. "Communism is frowned on here and is, indeed, against the law, but there is not the same degree of fear of it."

"I'd argue that. But there is fear of blackness."

Dominick paused and studied Michael's and Ria's faces as they absorbed the thought.

"So, is the message of the play here that we shouldn't fear blackness?" Michael asked at last.

"Not to the same degree as the fear of witchcraft was in Salem. Blackness is a fact. In this country, as in a few others. We have lived with that fact for many generations but rather than fear it, we must live with it without hysteria and accept that it is not the work of the devil but the workings of the human condition. A firm control is required of course."

"Miller recommended no such thing," said Michael. "In fact, he offered no solutions. He concentrated on dramatising the hysteria that drove people to extreme solutions."

"And we are forcibly making a point about *our* society by having several black actors in the cast."

Dominick sat back and waited for that to sink in. Ria was silent and Michael took some time to collect his thoughts.

"What will the audiences think of that?" he finally asked. "It's a complete reversal of government policy."

"They will be surprised, even astounded, but when they stop to think about it, they will be reassured that we are so confident and in control."

"Does that mean that from now on black people will be allowed to—"

"Certainly not! It will be allowed for this play and no other."

"And will blacks be allowed to attend?"

"A select few will."

"Then—"

A flicker of anger crossed Dominick's face, but he continued, "Michael, you will perhaps be convinced of our sincerity by the fact that Thandi Kubeka will be in the cast as the orphan Abigail, the instigator of the hysteria and your character's – John Proctor's – once lover who was taken into your house as a servant by you and your wife, Elizabeth – your character, Ria. That little trio alone will add immeasurably to the power of the play. It concentrates on the effect of hysteria on the individual rather than on the group.

Dominick sat back and watched as they tried to absorb the information.

"I know it's a surprise for both of you, and I would like to reassure you of our best intentions in this matter of casting. On a superficial level, it will pleasantly surprise the international theatrical community and catch our overseas critics unaware, all of which is in line with our international goals and objectives, but I would like to concentrate on the effect it will have on our local audiences and media. The inclusion of blacks in the cast will alter attitudes in this country. Many will be relieved that we are relaxing what at times are perceived as rigid and unthinking prejudices, and that is to the good, but the roles we assign to the black actors carry their own messages. The girl from Barbados, Tituba, will be played by a black actor too."

"Indicating that our blacks are prone to hysteria."

"As were the children of Salem. But think hard about the fact that all the horror of the play stems from the violent punishments handed out by the leaders of the community on their own kind. They too succumbed to hysteria, as did McCarthyites in twentieth-century America. Our approach highlights that fact very, very forcibly, which I'm convinced Miller will appreciate. Miller has sanctioned our casting so… the discussion is over. Our dramatic intentions will be made clear. That will be all."

He picked up the telephone and began to dial so Ria and Michael left his office in silence. On the way to the rehearsal room, Ria was the first to speak.

"I'm going for coffee. Alone."

Ria left Michael and headed for the coffee bar. She was a product of her upbringing, and she was both repelled and intrigued by the thought of acting with blacks. It was somewhat shocking, but the actor within was excited by the challenge. She understood that Elizabeth – her character – had known of the affair between her husband and the black servant and that knowledge would require her, Ria, to subjugate her personal feels to the demands of the role. She strongly suspected that Michael and Thandi had been close and while she disparaged such a relationship, her feelings, those of a sensual woman, were titillated by the thought. *This* fact shocked her as she gulped down her coffee. And scalded herself.

When he could gather his thoughts again, Michael took a long time to make up his mind about how he felt. On a personal level, acting with two women with whom he had made love would require a remarkable level of detachment and his guilt about Thandi increased the emotional pressure exponentially. The images of the two women seemed to merge in his mind, both so different and yet so similar in the strength of his attraction for them. He wondered if Ria suspected anything and if she did, would they – could they – share the thought? It was an unsettling idea. He hurriedly shuttled in his mind to Dominick's rationale regarding the unexpected inclusion of blacks and how the audiences would react to it. He wasn't convinced about his logic or his intentions, and he left the building to walk about for some time in a state of confusion. When he arrived back in the rehearsal room, the rest of the cast was waiting.

Chapter Seventeen

Profound social needs throughout the ages have demanded from theatre story, conflict, mimicry and high speech and it has supplied them for seven centuries. It thrives because of this and because it continually shows what one person is capable of doing, without evasion and with a great deal of difficulty.

The first meeting of the entire cast was traumatic for Michael and Thandi and a little unsettling for Ria. She felt immediately the undertone and thought again about both their involvements in *Richard the Third* and *The Kingfisher Couple*, not to mention whatever else had transpired. She also noted their restraint when they were together and deduced that there was some sort of unfinished or, perhaps *not* unfinished, business between them. Thandi was tentative with Michael and unsure of their relationship. She was unsure of his part in her recent clashes with the law but assumed that Michael *had* played some sort of role in her rehabilitation. This unexpected casting in *The Crucible* she could only perceive as a slackening of the state's antagonism and was grateful at the opportunity to rebuild her theatrical career. She could see that there was a closeness between Michael and Ria and assumed that, if there had not been a liaison between them before, there would probably be one after the play's run. Used to the imperious behaviour of white people, she accepted, albeit sadly, that Michael's avowal of love had been genuine but could not be depended upon to last. It was clear to Michael that Ria suspected something, and he was uncertain how to handle the complications between the three of them. To mask his confusion, he decided that he would throw himself wholeheartedly into the role of John Proctor, the adulterer. The director was James Diggery, who was as thin, as intense, as intimidating as he had been for *Long Day's Journey into Night*. He also knew this script intimately and word for word. Having given his customary summation on the playwright's intentions and their importance to every member of the cast, James got down to specifics. The first read-through had been arranged around a large table in the rehearsal room and the actors had chosen their own seating before the director appeared. They had instinctively positioned themselves according to race and James indicated immediately that this was not acceptable.

"Right. Let us get organised according to relationships in the play. All the young girls together please and that of course will include Abigail and Tituba. The Proctors will sit next to them. Then the villagers will line up in any order you chose. The village elders, including you Simon, will sit next to them."

They took some time to sort out the revised seating and there was an uncomfortable silence when it was done. James let the silence hang before proceeding.

"We have the playwright's guidance on each character. Miller wrote them as introductions for each, to be read out by an extra character called 'The Reader' between major scenes. This idea was performed only once and – thankfully – dropped. But Miller included them in the printed editions of the script, and they are enormously helpful to actors. The protagonist is John Proctor who is enmeshed in an internal drama involving his wife, Elizabeth and his ex-servant, the orphan Abigail with whom he has sinned, an act of lechery for which he will never forgive himself. Miller says in his introduction about him that he's powerful of body, even tempered and not easily led. But he is not untroubled. He thinks himself a fraud, and a sinner, not only against the morals of Salem but against his own vision of decent conduct. This is his weakness, and it will seek him out and trip him up before the end. This trio of Proctor, his wife Elizabeth and the orphan he fornicated with is the true moral centre of the entire work. The trio's problems and conflicts are the pivot around which the whole sorry saga revolves. Sins will emerge that dwarf Proctor's in horror and vindictiveness.

"Michael, as Proctor, you will be emotionally shredded not only by your guilt but also by the Salemites and their rampant hysteria.

"Ria, you will suffer as you watch the husband, whom you know as a good man, harassed and bullied to his death, and you will suffer almost as much as him while you do so.

"Thandi, yours is a difficult character. The most useful thing that Miller has said about Abigail Williams in his introduction is that she has an endless capacity for dissembling. She also has a hard on for Proctor. Your job will be to stop her coming across as a two-dimensional mischief-maker and doer. To give her depth you will have to work hard on the affection or love or lust or perhaps all three she feels for Proctor. Bear in mind that she is young and ignorant and frustrated by the simplicity of the villagers. And you must make her suffer at the end when Proctor is hanged because of her vindictiveness.

"Winifred, as the black Barbados slave Tituba, who initiates all the shenanigans of the impressionable young girls, you will have a difficult curtain call. You will be the focus of all the prejudice that this country is unfortunately prone to, and don't be surprised if you are received in silence or even booed or hissed at by some members of the audience. If that happens, take it as a compliment on your acting skill.

"As a bookend, as it were, and to avoid heavy-handed acting in terms of race, the Deputy Governor, Danforth, the very epitome of authority in Salem, is being played by Simon Mbeki, the distinguished black actor from out of town. Welcome Simon. Our audience will, early on in the performance, perceive that the race of the actors is irrelevant and will experience the play as close to Miller's vision as possible. As regards the subject matter, *The Crucible* will be hard for all of you as you are confronted by the unthinking savagery of the Salemites, but you must remember that they were surrounded by a savage wilderness. Outside their village was the domain of evil. They lived in an atmosphere of perpetual terror as they struggled to build a godly society that would help them evade the flames of hell. Now let's have a careful and thoughtful read-through and start to get a grasp of the dramatic potential of the masterwork."

After three careful read-throughs under James's careful direction, the cast had fully accepted the structure of the drama and the burden it placed on all of them. Such is the adaptability of human nature that the majority of them acted in accordance with their characters' psychology and moved away from their own ingrained attitudes, especially about race. The rehearsals were grinding, remorseless and incredibly rewarding to all concerned. Miller's powerful psychology insights were inherent in every character, every scene and every confrontation. The hysteria of the villagers, the pressure of the trials for witchery, the sense of impending death was all-palpable and all-invasive, and each actor's character brought his or her own angst to the process. So much fear and anxiety were generated that James Diggery felt it incumbent upon him, as director, to call frequent breaks in the rehearsals and order the cast outside into the sunshine to relieve the pressure. During one such break, Michael was on the roof of the theatre, sitting on the low wall that ran along three sides of it when James approached and sat down next to him.

"You looked a little perturbed during my last address, Michael. Is there something bothering you?"

"I've been wondering. Why has this government allowed this play to be performed here? In this theatre? Don't they realise this play is about them?"

"A few of them do. But they realise that putting it on will make them look good overseas and most of the audience won't see the connections anyway. It's about a small village in America nearly three hundred years ago! And about witches! So who the fuck cares?"

"But it's not! It's about—"

"McCarthyism. I know. But the right-wingers, the *real* right-wingers, are so self-absorbed that they can't see beyond the end of their self-satisfied noses. The McCarthyites in America didn't think this play was about them either. They were born into an ongoing, decades-long red scare so fear of communism was ingested with their mother's milk. And to the righteous everywhere, including here, everybody is out of step except them. The un-fucking-American trials in the fifties that ruined so many people were so insane that one man was sacked because he was innocent of any connection with the left. His boss said that, since he had nothing to give the trial, he was a slur on his company, so he had to go. That's how fucked up the thinking was there."

"And here?"

"Here we're struggling with a deep-down terror of the blacks, so anything that sets up a subjective reality, like a genuine witch-hunt in an obscure American village, will let them sleep easier in their beds. 'That's genuine wickedness,' they'll say. 'We could never treat anybody as badly as that,' they'll whisper to themselves in the night. And they'll believe in the subjective reality of Miller's play about witches rather than the reality of black hordes that are crouched out there, thirsting for white blood."

"You're making me feel uncomfortable."

"Good. That was always Miller's intention. Shall we go in?"

The Crucible was a bombshell and ran to packed houses for its scheduled period. The fact that the cast was multiracial was the first factor that the theatre-going public had to come to terms with. Tituba, the Barbados slave, was easily absorbed. After all, they were used to seeing black people in such subsidiary roles. Abigail was another matter. To see a young black actor mingling with other young girls as their equal was difficult for them to accept and when it became clear that she had been intimate with John Proctor, many among them felt very, very uncomfortable and squirmed in their seats. When the highest official, the Deputy Governor, Danforth, strode on, manifesting as a large, black man, it became almost too much to bear. But such is the power of theatre and the readiness of an audience to go along with the playwright's – in this case a brilliant playwright's – intentions and storytelling, that the overwhelming majority of the watchers accepted the situation on stage and, in doing so, were reassured and coaxed into involving themselves in the play. When Proctor admitted under cross-examination that he indeed had sex with Abigail, the fact of interracial sex passed by almost unnoticed because it was subsumed by the drama of the confession to the Deputy Governor that he was a lecher, and that he had known her in the proper place – where his beasts are bedded.

Peter had been right – Abigail and Danforth received their fair share of applause at the curtain call, but when Tituba took her bow, there was a noticeable drop in the volume of the applause. But it continued so enthusiastically that those offended watchers were cowed into acceptance. With a few insignificant exceptions, the reviews were highly favourable and almost self-congratulatory at the sophistication of it all. The government gloated, as did the Minister for Culture who pitched up at the closing party in fine, bombastic style, nodding and winking at the favourable comments as if he had, almost single-handedly, made it all happen. The more conservative section of the population was nonplussed; races mixing in the theatre? Was this acceptable? Was this legal? Was this the slippery slope to full integration? A few official speeches and media blasts from the government soon pulled them into line, and they acquiesced since none among them intended to go to see the play anyway. *The Crucible* ran its full term, and Michael became a national celebrity and could hardly walk down a city street without being waved at, smiled at or asked for his autograph. Ria was also feted and invited onto radio programmes and interviewed for the various women's magazines. Thandi was allowed to bask in relative fame and kept up irregular contact with Michael. Sometimes he and Ria met at the Arena coffee shop, and were each served a slice of cake by a proud Bernard.

Thandi was another matter altogether.

Chapter Eighteen

Of what moral value is theatre if we do not examine and analyse our own lives the way we do a play? And then act upon it? Lest we be left adrift holding Ahab's smashed quadrant.

Dominick was so ebullient it made Michael slightly queasy.

"Look at you! Basking in the sunshine. Admired by hundreds of thousands, envied by millions. You blush! Not quite lost the common touch, hey? Well, I've seen plenty of people whose heads were turned by a fraction of the exposure and admiration that you have earned."

"Well, thank you, Dominick. It's very kind of you to say so," said Michael.

"Actors get so few rewards beyond the acclaim that follows a good show," Dominick continued. "Ria too, remains very much in the public eye. I hear on the grapevine that she's been asked to write a series of articles on acting for a magazine, and that's very good for her. The public's memory is fickle, and it pays to stay in sight after the glow of a great performance dies down. But I'm sure she'll get the roles she deserves."

"Oh, she will. She has a great future ahead of her in theatre. I've been thinking about Thandi too. She deserves some recognition. First *Richard* then *Kingfisher* and now *Crucible*.

Yet she seems to have disappeared. Is there anything that can be done about her?"

Dominick's face went cold.

"Thandi Kubeka? She's had her time in the sun. Much more than she deserves. Forget about her. There's nothing more that can be done. There were… repercussions about her role in *Crucible*. Simon Mbeki's role too. Rumblings came from some very important people who could not see or understand how necessary they were or how they helped improve our image among theatregoers here and in the world at large. It was an experiment, a brave one, but we cannot afford to make those important people insecure, so it has been decided that there will be no more black actors on our stages. Not now or for the foreseeable future. Perhaps someday, when the situation changes or the more conservative element in the upper echelons of government are, shall we say, no longer around, we can try the experiment again. But not now. Not any time now."

He paused and watched Michael closely as he absorbed this. It took some time.

"You, however, don't have to worry about slipping out of sight. Every theatre in the country wants you. Every established playwright and theatrical promoter is eager for you to grace their endeavours. I hope it doesn't give you a swollen head."

Michael was nonplussed.

"I… I've heard nothing. Nobody's approached me."

"No. They wouldn't. They know better than to do that. Since your astounding successes, they all know they shouldn't approach you directly. They approach me. That's how it should be now."

Michael felt a sinking feeling in his stomach. He had heard that expression many times but never knew what it meant until now. In fact, there was an emptiness, a coldness in his bowels, as if part of his innards had imploded. He was silent for a long time.

"What's the matter? You look surprised."

"I... I am. Surprised is not the fucking word. I'm astounded. Shocked. The... the decision as to what I do next is—"

"Ours. The decision is ours."

The ebullience was gone. Dominick's face was suddenly stony. His eyes lost their sparkle. His voice was cold and a full tone lower.

"We have invested in you. Heavily. Consistently. We have made all your successes not only probable but inevitable. With future successes in mind, we have decided that your... experimental days in theatre are over. You will no longer act in such unorthodox – and risky – ventures as *The Kingfisher Couple* and put your career in danger. You will participate in mainstream, acceptable productions which reflect on the glory of our theatrical endeavours. World-class theatre is our aim. We are investigating the existing major roles and commissioning similar roles to be created for you. We have received several submissions and are examining them closely. The nation's leading academics are being recruited to ascertain the works most suitable and most appropriate. Both the international works which have already proved themselves on the world's stages and the ambitious works drafted by our leading playwrights. When we have made our choice, your acceptance will, of course, be obtained. So why not take advantage of this gap in your performances and build up your strength for the exciting and very demanding roles that await you."

The pause in Dominick's dialogue was so prolonged that it was clear that he had nothing to add, and Michael had no option but to get to his feet and shuffle towards the door. Holding some papers in his hand and without moving from his seat, Dominick stopped him at the threshold.

"Michael, how about you going on an all-expenses-paid tour of the international theatre festivals and a visit to the major theatre productions to see what the world is watching? That should stir your dramatic soul. I'll have my team draw up an itinerary and prepare the way. Rub shoulders with the theatrical greats, writers, producers and managers. Broaden your mind. See what makes international theatre tick. You'll have some well-informed personnel to smooth the way for you."

There was a silence and Dominick broke it.

"I regard your silence as acquiescence."

He went back to his papers and Michael went through the door, closing it after him. He could hardly breath. The thought of official minions and faceless civil servants choosing his future roles was horrific. He could imagine the anodyne subjects that would be sought, the bland and totally forgettable dialogue that would be written. It would be the death of him. His creative soul cringed at the embarrassment that would result. Fuck them! He would go back to the Arena and seek out Rupert's searing criticisms, his acid comments. Playing the required roles would reduce his income, that was definite, and his lavish lifestyle, that was inevitable, but what price would he be paying if he submitted? Subservience? Conformity? Surrender to what he knew, with certainty, was unjust and unthinkable. But there was always international theatre. No impediments there. Only opportunities. They would remember his greatness with O'Neill, Miller and Albee. His reputation was good, and he would be welcomed in the world's theatres. But hold on! He remembered with a sinking feeling the conditions of his change of citizenship process. The one condition that he had not given the amount of thought to that it merited. The one stipulation, the small print of which he had glossed over in his readiness to accept what he had considered a worthwhile privilege: no dual citizenship. For an actor feted and supported by his own government, the doors would open, but as a lone foreigner from a pariah country, with no clout, access would, most probably, be denied.

A stiff drink was mandatory, and Michael soon sat slumped at a nearby bar trying to get his head around the situation. To have the dead hand of official correctness guiding the choice of his performances was appalling, in spite of the fact that such hands had chosen his last four roles which had catapulted him into the international scene. He could well imagine the anodyne plays that the 'leading playwrights' would produce. Such work that no serious, self-respecting theatregoer could witness without throwing up. After the third drink he dragged his self-pitying self out of the self-centred mood and thought of Thandi. Again. Perhaps Bernard would know something.

"What do you *think* happened to her!" said Bernard, glaring at him. "She's been put away again, having served her purpose. Yes *purpose!* The powers that be earned some international brownie points and gloated appropriately before tucking her away out of sight. She's a non-person now. Nobody's *ever* heard of her and, I suppose, never will again."

"Jesus! They can't be that hard-hearted!"

"Want to bet? They're adaman-fucking-tine, those bastards! Thandi Kubeka is, officially, no more. She's most probably been put under house arrest again, in some distant town where nobody has ever even *heard* of the theatre. She's a non-person. Jesus! It must be hell for her. After all that recognition. That acknowledgement. Back on the ash heap."

"Isn't there anything—"

"We can do? No. There isn't. If you try, you'll only make it worse for her. They're vindictive, that lot."

Bernard looked at Michael in silence.

"Michael. Best forget her. You'll never see her again, believe me. I know of a few people who have been… disappeared because they rocked the boat. It's death. A legal death."

Chapter Nineteen

What is it in the make-up of a character that makes him do what the world tells him he shouldn't do? In the event, the strong character walks towards trouble but, if the danger is to someone else, should the real hero walk away?

It was cold in the car, despite the rays of the setting sun that shone through the fly-spattered windscreen. The indigo hills and slopes stretched across the dull, inhospitable landscape, as if attempting to take its desolation further. A wide, dusty road lay from left to right at the end of the equally dusty road on which he had stopped the car under the branches of a sprawling thorn tree. Wooden telegraph poles lined the wider road ahead, the wires sagging as if half melted after the heat of the day. Dotted along it at irregular intervals were several woebegone cottages with crumbling walls and rusty corrugated iron roofs, but he was focused on the one that faced the road he was on. It had a narrow wooden door and one half-hearted window on the wall facing him. Next to it was a wooden outhouse, an outside toilet with a sagging half-open door facing the side door of the cottage, as if the privacy of its users was of no concern. Apart from a few spiky weeds, nothing grew in, around or alongside the cottage. As he surveyed the bleak edifice, a dangling piece of tattered cloth was pulled aside in the front window and a black face looked out. Even at a distance, he recognised Thandi. The coloured shop owner he had spoken to in the small village had been correct. This cottage at the end of the road was where the African woman, who had moved in three months previously, lived. The face looked towards the car for long moments before the tattered cloth was dropped back over the window. He waited as the sun departed and darkness crept across the desolate scene, and when the gloom provided some cover, he left the car and walked towards the cottage. The closer he got, the more decrepit it looked. The window frames sagged away from the wall, and the cast iron roof, torn loose from the supporting wall on the side facing away from the outhouse, was buckled. A dim light came on inside the window. It was low down, as if placed on a table, and shadow passed before it. He approached the cottage and, passing through the gap where a gate had once hung, he went to the door and rapped on it. After a pause, the door opened jerkily as if caught on the floor, and there stood Thandi, barefoot and wrapped in a cotton blanket. Her face was in shadow but what light there was shone on his.

"Michael! What are you doing here?" she said after a long pause.

"I came to see you of course."

"How did you find me?"

"Never mind. I just did."

She stepped back and opened the door further. He entered into a room with a mud floor on which stood some assorted bits of unsteady-looking furniture. She closed the door and turned to face him. They surveyed each other in silence.

"You're looking well," she said.

"And you're not."

"No. I'm not. In this dump, in this township – ha! – in this climate. How can anybody look well?"

"How long will you have to—"

"Stay here? How do I know? Until I die probably."

"It's so unfair."

"Unfair? Unfair? What sort of word is that? There's *nothing* fair in this country if you're black. Fairness is for *you* people. *We* have to do as we're told. Do this. Do that. Don't live there. Live here. Here? I wouldn't send my worst enemy here. No. I would. I'd send that fucking policeman who escorted me here *here*. I'd send him here and make him stay here. With a monthly allowance taken from his earnings, as they do from mine. And I'd throw away the key. Except you don't need a key here. Everybody around here knows that I'm under house arrest. Anybody who helps me will end up like me. Like. Like…"

Her rage made her incoherent. All Michael could do was to stand there silent until she either calmed down or burst a blood vessel. She finally ran out of breath and stood there sobbing and half screaming – whimpering – until it was all out, all the anger, all the rage against the system, all her pent-up fury at the unfairness of it all. Then she flopped down on one of the chairs, which wobbled dangerously under her weight, and stared at the floor. The blanket slipped slightly off her shoulders as she slumped, and he could see that her neck had shrunk, and the muscles stood out further than he remembered. Her scalp was dry and flaky, and she appeared to have lost the nubile bloom that he had so loved. The rage he felt well up in him clashed with the guilt about the part he had played, however inadvertently, in her downfall. He moved to her side and tenderly moved a side of the blanket back onto her shoulder. She seemed unconscious of his presence and his movement and continued staring at the dirt floor. An age passed and Michael felt that his coming here was a great mistake. What could he do to alleviate her plight? What could he say to offer any hope? Was there, indeed, any hope? Was this government so pitiless and so vindictive as to rule out any possibility of Thandi returning to a normal life? He gently laid a hand upon her shoulder, but there was no reaction, so they stood there in silence as a nightjar whistled and churred in the distance, making the land seem empty and desolate. Finally, Thandi spoke.

"Why did you come here?"

"To see you – as I said."

"And what will you do now that you have seen me?"

"I… I don't know. What *can* I do?"

"Get me out of here."

"But how?"

"How would I know. You're free, white and privileged. Think of something."

There was another long silence as he struggled with the situation. What could he do? Nothing. Why *had* he come? To see her. But to what end? To comfort her? He took a deep breath to say… God knew what. Anything to end the silence which seemed to be so bitter, but what?

Thandi suddenly stood, walked to the window and pushed the sagging curtain aside to peer out into the darkness. The nightjar called again.

"What's that bird?" she asked. "It calls every night."

"A nightjar, I think."

"How do you know what a nightjar sounds like?"

"Somebody told me. On a night drive."

"In a game park?"

"Yes. It was—"

"I don't want to know. *We're* not allowed to go into any game park."

"That's—"

"Don't say 'unfair'. I'd hate you to say 'unfair' again."

"I won't."

"Good. I supposed they followed you here."

"I don't think so."

"How would you know?"

"I wouldn't, I suppose."

"Just as you didn't know that they followed you into the park that day, near the aviary. That was the start of my journey into exile."

"I didn't think—"

"No. You didn't think."

"I wish we had stayed in Edinburgh."

"Why?"

"Well... we were safe there. Except for those thugs."

"*You* were."

"So were you. Those two policemen—"

"Those two policemen were just as bad as the thugs."

"Come on—"

"Just as bad. They stopped *you* from being harmed."

"And you!"

"Me? They looked at me as if I deserved to be attacked."

"I didn't see that."

"No. You didn't. They weren't looking at you. They were looking at a black woman who had been treated as she deserved."

"That's..." He stopped, realising that he had intended to say 'unfair' again and he knew that Thandi knew.

"You came back, you know," he finally said.

Thandi looked up at him, her face blank.

"That was really cruel of them. Opening the door slightly and then slamming it in my face again. How grateful I was. How hopeful. And then being in *The Crucible*! That raised my hopes again."

Her gaze drifted away from him.

"And that was the unkindest of all. I knew they were cruel, but they were so *vindictive*. There's a special place in hell for them. All of them. All white people."

His sharp intake of breath made her look up at him.

"All white people. You're all so smug. So blind and so... so..."

She moved back to the chair and slumped on it with her hands on her knees. He noticed that she automatically compensated for the short leg at the front of the chair. He moved to the other chair at the table end and sat on it. It too, wobbled. They sat in a silence that was heavy and loaded. Then the nightjar called again. Twice. He tried to envision it lying still on a dusty road in its mottled plumage gazing out over the emptiness it called to, endless and empty except for the insects which would come, inexorably within reach. They both sat in silence. In a tiny all-purpose room, in a dilapidated hut in a vast emptiness. No fences for miles in every direction. No fences of any kind except for those of the mind. Or of the legal strictures of a vindictive ruling class, afraid of its people but accustomed to the limitless freedom that existed in that darkness and through which all the people whom it suspected would eventually stumble into reach. To be incarcerated or, crueller still, released again into that vastness on an invisible but unbreakable leash by which they could be hauled in again at any time. *Jesus*, he thought, *Thandi is one of those insects. Dropped down into vastness, to be pulled in again at any time.* Whenever the state felt anger or revenge or sheer bloody-mindedness. He looked at her in silence and pity. Was there anything he could do? Anything to ease her situation?

"I'm going to see what I can do," he finally said.

"About what?"

"About getting you out of this place."

Thandi looked at him for a long time before snorting and looking down at her hands, which he could see were chapped and some of her nails were broken.

"I'm serious."

"Don't, Michael."

"Listen." He reached out and took hold of her wrist. "I could get a boat. Hire a boat. A big one. Take you off the coast somewhere around here and sail up north. Beyond the border. Beyond their reach. Up there they don't care about the laws down here. They would never send you back." He shook her arm gently. "Listen. Once up there we can get you back to Europe somehow or other. Edinburgh maybe. Anywhere. I've got some standing. In the theatre world at least. I could get in touch with that Lord... what's his name? At the Edinburgh Festival. And the British Arts Council. I've got some clout over there. A track record. Internationally. I've been in touch with some very influential theatre people in England. And the States. I could easily get some work there. So could you."

In his excitement, he let go of her hand and started to walk up and down. Thoughts flew through his mind so rapidly that they became incoherent: his career, his savings, Ria, *Paradyse*, Dominick, the apartment he had looked at in a great part of town, the plays in his future, the great roles that awaited him, Ria again, Ria naked and loving. The glamorous car he had recently ordered... he stopped suddenly and looked at Thandi wrapped in a blanket, hunched, unkempt and dusty. She was looking at him, stony-faced. He sat down and they regarded each other in silence. Which she broke.

"Michael. You're dreaming. It can never happen. You can do nothing. It is what it is. And I'm what I am. A once-upon-a-time-successful actress, stuck here until they no longer worry about me, or feel threatened by me. Soon I will have been forgotten by the people who saw me on stage and... admired me. Maybe they have forgotten me already. Theatre is so... unforgiving, and I'm looking older by the day."

This last thought hurt, and it showed in her eyes. Any optimism seemed futile. Any notion of a restarted career for her seemed a cruel mockery. The room was darker now. He moved the chair he had been sitting upon closer to her, sat on it and took one of her hands which were clasping the blanket around her. She let her hand lie inertly in his and gazed across the room. So, they sat for a long time until the darkness enveloped them. Then she let his hand slip out of hers. She stood up and, crossing to the bed, she let the blanket drop. He could barely see her body, bulkier than he remembered but still curvaceous enough. He rose up and crossed over to put his arms around her. She leaned against him, and they stood there as she moaned as if in despair. He took her in his arms and gently lay her on the bed, freed her of the thin shift and undressed rapidly. Within minutes of their embracing, he felt his ardour ebb and his body flag. It was the first time it had happened to him, and Michael was distraught. Not only at the inadequacy of his maleness but at the thought that Thandi would think that he didn't want her. He frantically searched his mind for a thought that would quicken his flesh. An image came into his mind of Ria naked in the river and his body responded almost instantly. Aware that this constituted a disrespect for Thandi, he tried to let his mind go blank and allow the friction of their private parts to cause an orgasm. It did. Too quickly for her and too detached for him. He lay there unresponsive as his body relaxed and hers quieted. *Why had she let him do it?* he wondered. Perhaps she was trying to thwart the powers which decreed sexual congress between races illegal. Perhaps she wanted to feel momentarily a human body and not just an entity defined by legalities. They both lay naked in each other's arms, drained but dissatisfied. The saddest part for both of them was that there was nothing to say to each other. The state had done its work. Fulfilled its mandate. Obeyed its own laws and proved that sex between races was, indeed, against nature. He dressed himself and she slipped beneath the coarse blanket on the bed. He stood there for a while as she turned her face to the wall. The silence was a palpable force in the dark room and there was nothing left to say.

"I'll…" he said in a constricted tone of voice. "I'll do what I can."

As she was silent, he had no option but to leave, pulling the door closed behind him. The moon was shining. Its light pallid. And the night was as cold as his heart. He walked along the dust towards his car, his mind strangely vacant. The nightjar's call seemed to have a mocking tone and the trills at the end faded sharply, as if fallen down into the dust.

Chapter Twenty

Out of the sweat of a playwright's brow comes a tocsin that alarms an expectant audience which is an abyss into which the playwright hurls his words. In the minds of such an audience, genuine resolution of conflict comes not at the end of a play but afterwards.

Michael was thinking about the script they were about to read as he sat looking at the rest of the cast sitting around the central table. It was the first of the new plays that had been commissioned for the New Drama series that would stretch over the next three years at the State Theatre and other theatres around the country, and he was committed to play in whichever plays were chosen. He had scanned through it the previous night and, in spite of his reservations, was impressed with the concept, the overall structure and the writing. In an about-turn by the authorities – according to Dominick – the play would be multiracial, as would the audience, with a separated entrance and the balcony for the black people. It would be directed by James Diggery, who had directed the *Long Day's Journey into Night* and *The Crucible*. Most of the large cast was gathered on this occasion, among whom were Ria, Simon Mbeki who had played the Deputy Governor in *The Crucible*, a white, bushy-bearded elderly man whose name Michael had forgotten and Dominick, who opened his manuscript, prompting the rest to follow suit. On the cover of each was the title *The Colonist and the King*.

"This is the first of several plays which have been commissioned recently. It's set over a hundred years ago and is quite Shakespearean in tone. It could be a new voice on the stages of world theatre," said Dominick. "There will be enough budget for the enormous cast, although some of them are not integral to the drama and will be trimmed, I'm afraid, Professor."

The bushy beard winced, opened his mouth to speak and finally shrugged, a movement that Dominick seemed to interpret as acquiescence as he proceeded.

"Professor Blake is, as you know, the author of the play and the writer of the lyrics. We are in the process of appointing a composer and a musical director; all the singers and dancers are black and, as it turns out, many of them were born in the area where the play is set."

He flipped through the hefty script and then turned to the opening spread.

"You've all had a chance to read it so you will know that the story is based on happenings that took place there during the last century. The roles of the colonists' leader, the larger-than-life wife of the colony's governor and the black king are superb and the three of you, Michael, Ria and Simon will, I'm sure, rise to the challenge and deliver mesmerising performances."

He looked in turn at the three actors sitting across the desk.

"After the nationwide tour, we envisage taking it to the international stages, where it will be appreciated as a new theatrical direction for this country of ours. The cast will be racially mixed as was the highly successful *Crucible*. This… yes, Ria?"

"I understand that I will be expected to sing in this play. Well, I can't sing."

"Nor can I," said Michael. "Not professionally anyway."

"Doesn't matter. You both have trained voices and you, Simon, have a magnificent baritone. Anyway, we are going to use an age-old technique called sprechgesang, which means speech song. This allows you to shape the patterns of the dialogue without sustaining the pitch. James will tell you more."

James leaned forward and addressed his remarks especially at Ria and Michael.

"A perfect example of the technique is the style of delivery that Rex Harrison used in *My Fair Lady*. I have copies of the film and we will watch it together. On top of that, we have contracted with a voice coach to guide you in the technique. He calls it expressive gradation, and you will both be able to handle it with some training. Simon, I'm sure that your splendid singing voice is more than adequate for the role, but you will be required to resort to this technique to meld with the white singers."

The bushy beard spoke up. "I have recently been introduced to the technique and I'm very excited. It will bridge the gap between the way in which black and white singers perform. All the time, the white singers, especially you, Ria and Michael, will be supported by Simon of course, as well as a capable black choir and some beautiful black music. It will be magnificent and totally new. Even revolutionary."

"Now," said Dominick, "we will have a read-through."

They all settled down into the process. Michael liked such full read-throughs, in which the spirit of the work and the balance of the characters first emerged. His previous reading of the script had been superficial and distorted by the fact that he was, as usual, concentrating on his dialogue rather than that of the other players. This time the work would register with him in all its aspects. James started the read-through, taking the parts of the few actors who were missing. The bushy beard indicated where the music would intervene and recited the lyrics in a strident voice. The shape of the piece was good, and the ebb and flow of the action was dramatic and fully engaging. Shakespearean it was, with some intriguing monologues and stirring clashes of personalities. The structure was sound, and the emotional baggage of each character clearly delineated. The plot was dense but reasonably easy to follow and there were several soliloquies which related the thoughts and feelings of key characters at emotional high points. These were well written and flowed off the tongue, even at first reading. However, as they read through it this time, he began to be a little uneasy about the overall thrust of the work. The key characters who generated all the conflict were the Colonist, played by Michael, the Governor's Wife played by Ria and the black King played by Simon. Each has equal stage time and opportunity to express emotion but subtly, an overall power structure emerged. The King's journey was clear, noble and tragic but he inevitably succumbed to the pressure – and the superior… (morality, was the most appropriate word) – of the Colonist and Governor's Wife. This bias was never clearly stated but it was there. Stripped of the drama and emotional power of the piece, the King, sympathetic though he was, ended up where he belonged, a subdued drunkard and no longer a threat. In spite of the undoubted brilliance of the work and the power of the overall production, the hegemony was as it should be. The audiences need not worry. It was all an exercise in theatrical legerdemain. Nothing, basically, was at risk. They could all go home, feeling sophisticated, smug and sleep easily in their beds.

They'll love it here, but overseas, they'll puke, thought Michael as they finished and all of them murmured approval and congratulations, which the Professor lapped up.

"Does the King have to end up a drunkard?" Michael suddenly asked the meeting at large.

"But it's true. He was," the Professor said, sounding offended.

"Perhaps," said Michael. "But the audiences won't know that. They'll think it is a matter of common prejudice."

"No need to worry about that," said Dominick firmly. "The fact that it is historically correct will be widely advertised and the facts will be printed in each programme. We are not distorting history here."

Dominick's tone of voice prevented any further discussion of the point and James went into some detail regarding the approach he would take to the work. Then he closed the script and addressed them all.

"Take the script home, become familiar with it but don't try to memorise it yet. We have a lot of preparatory work to do with each of you before full rehearsals begin."

Dominick took over in a brusque tone of voice and when he had finished his harangue, the gathering obediently dispersed. As Ria and Michael walked down the outside steps, she spoke. "About the King being drunk—"

"Yes. I know. It's history."

"Yes. It is," she said with some asperity. "We should be accurate."

"Yeah, I know. It's just that it reinforces the general prejudice that—"

"That all blacks are drunkards? Well, the colonist is brutal, and the governor is arrogant and uncaring. As they were back then. All of them. We, my people, are comfortable in our places in society and we understand our histories. It doesn't mean that we have to live out the mistakes of those people. We were carving out a country and we behaved appropriately for the period. We *have* moved on, you know."

The conversation was veering dangerously towards forbidden areas into which he knew he should not stray, so he steered into generalities. Ria was excited and proud about the play and, in fact, so was he, in spite of his reservations. It was very well written, had enormous potential and would be very popular and profitable overseas if stereotypical portrayal of the black King didn't create a furore, which he didn't really think it would. It wasn't too blatant and had a ring of truth to it. *Besides*, he thought wryly, *it was true*. They collected their car and drove out to *Paradyse* where his welcome had grown, and he was fully accepted as Ria's inamorato. In fact, some heavy hints about possible nuptials had been dropped, which he and Ria had steadfastly ignored. Neither of them was in any hurry. They were too busy enjoying their lifestyles among theatre folk, Ria's wealthy friends and her parents' equally loaded acquaintances. One of the latter was a financier and keen yachtsman and had invited them both on a weekend afternoon cruise, during which Michael had taken the tiller and acquitted himself well enough for the owner and he to have an in-depth conversation about the possibility of Michael purchasing his own boat. He had messed around on boats as a teenager and loved it, so he found the possibility of having his own very attractive. One balmy and sunny Saturday afternoon he and Ria set out to visit a friend of the financier who owned a firm of boatbuilders, and they were both interested, he more than she. When they arrived at the boatyard, the owner was busy on an enormous sleek, three-deck motor yacht, and he looked up and smiled as Ria called out.

"Mr. Barrington? Hi. I'm Ria Van Vuuren."

Barrington flashed his sparkling teeth and stopped his chore to advance to the rail and reached out his hand towards them. He exuded a bristling bonhomie in his blue slacks and short-sleeved white shirt which was open to his chest to display a broad, tanned, sinewy neck while the sleeves stopped just sort of equally tanned and impressive biceps.

"Rafe. Call me Rafe."

"Rafe. This is Michael Driscoll."

Rafe shook Michael's hand. Not as caressingly as he had shaken Ria's, Michael noted, and indicated the gangway as he walked towards it. The yacht was a three-decker beauty, with a massive centre mast smartly raked.

"Welcome to *The Ocean Sprite*. I believe you're interested in buying a boat. How do you like this one?"

"It's great. But it looks a little too rich for my blood and my bank balance," said Michael.

"Well, have a quick look around anyway. See what you think. I have a couple of pre-owned, older boats here, so we can work something out."

They toured the boat and gushed over the appointments, at least Ria did. Michael was intimidated by it and said so.

"Rafe, I just need it for weekends, maybe even day cruises up and down the coast. But this is far too glamourous."

"Tell you what, Michael. I have another one a bit smaller but very similar. It's had one previous owner, but he hardly ever used it. I bought it from him, well, from his widow actually, and she was glad to see it go. It could handle the deep ocean if you were keen on it, or indeed, capable of crossing an ocean."

"No thanks. Up and down this coast is all I would ever want to sail."

"Then *The Gretchen* is one you should be looking at. I'm refurbishing it right now, but to tell you the truth, he kept it in such great condition that there's not much to do. Let's go and see that."

So off they went to another part of the boatyard where a smaller boat very similar to *The Ocean Sprite* was moored. Slightly used as it was, it actually looked much cooler, with none of the out-of-the-box gloss left. He had a warm feeling about it as he looked at the sleek lines, the folded-down mast, the swoop of the hull with two windows on the side of the lower deck, wind scoops at deck level and two powerful-looking motors tilted out of the water at the stern.

"She's got two Volvo engines with just over two hundred hours on them. We've serviced them fully. There's a drop-down sail, in case you want to cruise gently without the noise of the engines. It's very easy to call into play. Just takes a little more care with the tiller. There's a retractable keel too, for cruising in shallow water. Let's look inside."

An entire forest was echoed inside the boat. It gleamed with polished teak and mirror-finished mahogany fastened with copper bands to oak frames, and light brown wooden panelling covered the walls. There were three steps leading down into a very comfortable and well-ventilated cabin. The various rich woods throughout reflected the light, and all the working surfaces were at hip-height and no more than four feet away from each other.

"Always a firm fixture within arm's length," said Rafe. "To avoid being thrown around in a rough sea."

There was a gas-operated stove with oven, plates and a grill and an adequate fridge/freezer next to a tiny sink. Along one side was a comfortable sofa and a drop-down table to eat from. There was a pump-action toilet, wash basin and shower behind a bulkhead at the stern and a single fold-out berth under the very smart cockpit which was up a short flight of stairs. Along the sides were bookcases, small cupboards and two slanted parallelogram windows on both sides. A double berth folded out behind the stateroom. It was all compact, comfortable and very capable looking. While they were inspecting the cockpit, Rafe told him the price and Michael was pleasantly surprised as he ran his hands over the controls and looked with sudden slit-eyed, professional skill out through the wrap-around windscreen like the salty old dog he had always known he was.

"There's another couple of toys for you to see."

Rafe led him up to the stern deck to a raised and waterproof locker which he opened to reveal two collapsible bicycles neatly tucked away.

"If on your trips up and down the coast you feel like doing a bit of exploring these will come in handy. They're rugged and very practical and each, as you see, has a collapsible basket to hold provisions or souvenirs or whatever takes your fancy as you move from seaside town to seaside town. Now, if you buy *The Gretchen*, I'll have one of my captains take you out in it and cruise around until you get the hang of it," said Rafe. "You should do that a couple of weekends under our guidance until you're competent and we will get you a proper proficiency certificate.

OK? Now let's take it out into the bay and show you how she handles."

Out in the bay, what little boat lore Michael had acquired in his teens came back. When he took the wheel, he enjoyed again the tension between the boat and the sea, the rhythmic thumping as he sailed across the waves, the surge as he went with them and gunned the motors to outreach the movement of the water. Very quickly the knack came back, helped by the enormous power of the highly responsive engines. Each thump against a wave as he made a sharp turn sent a shower of spray across the boat, and Ria stifled a shriek at the sensation of being soaked. Rafe swayed in a very relaxed manner as he saw that Michael was in control. By the time they made a tight swing around the bay and moved slowly and carefully back to the dockside to cast a line ashore, Michael was sold on the boat and the deal was sorted out very quickly back in Rafe's office. The payment would wipe a fair proportion of the money that Michael had accumulated. The thought flitted through his mind that, rather than let his earnings through his fingers like this, he had better start investing it.

Chapter Twenty One

Prophetic plays are built by words and action and the real hero of a story is he who pays most and stands to lose most. In the course of a play, the joy of recognition of the truth by some is balanced by the pain of reality for others.

The boat outing was the last break Michael and Ria had before they plunged back into the long and rigorous rehearsal schedule for *The Colonist and the King*. James and his associates had pushed them all hard, and they had all become familiar with the script. Familiar enough for James to meld them into a tight team that could handle the work demanded by the complex drama. In the meantime, James had recruited a musical director to write the score. This was Dick Black, an emaciated bewhiskered musical maverick who hovered on the edge of respectability, working as a producer, composer and guitarist in a recording studio located in a converted factory in a suitably semi-industrial neighbourhood containing a spectacularly dangerous elevator. He wrote and produced jingles for radio commercials, soundtracks for TV spots and commercial presentations and he was a member of a rock 'n' roll band which played regularly in hotels and pubs. He moonlighted with black musicians and was familiar with their music, even playing with them in makeshift performance areas in their badly lighted and dangerous slums. He took on the job of composer and musical director, worked with the sprechgesang instructor with enthusiasm and was not in the least fazed by the short schedule.

"If that Italian bastard Rossini could compose *The Barber of Seville* in three weeks…" he declaimed, "…I can write this fucker in a month."

He identified and recruited the members of the small and mixed-race orchestra and choir, and the result was a pounding sensory assault on the senses, interspersed with crossover melodies of surpassing and haunting beauty. The black members of the choir took to sprechgesang as if they were born to it, which, in fact, they were. They would instinctively slip into harmony with the white actors and singers while supporting and amplifying their vocal efforts. Michael's role as the Colonist in a nineteenth-century land was very physical, so he hired a talented trainer who had worked betimes on the national rugby team and who knew how to coax extra effort from Michael's muscles and sinews. This soon added to his chest, thigh and bicep measurements which Ria enjoyed the few times the schedule allowed them some intimacy together. Simon's black King was a noble figure and tragic in his descent from an independent and revered ruler to a co-opted, ruined and totally demoralised drunk, kept in thrall by the Governor. Ria's Governor's Wife was bitchiness personified, a fact that prompted Michael to hazard out loud the view that Ria didn't have to act much and receive a hefty thump for his pains. There was a complex relationship between the Colonist and the Wife which came perilously close to consummation but hovered instead in a frustrated and tortured state which added to the Colonist's vindictiveness and the Wife's frustrated and vengeful lashings out. The black King took the brunt of the tensions and frustrations of both and when the inevitable disempowerment manifested, retreated increasingly into despair and alcoholism. There were some powerful scenes, several psychologically sound soliloquies as well as some explosive confrontations and violent clashes between the colonists, the Governor's forces and the tribesmen. The writing never quite achieved a Shakespearean level, but it came close. The sprechgesang worked beautifully, both in terms of the storytelling and the musicality, and the superb choir and orchestra gave it a rich and satisfying dimension. After several sessions with the voice coach and innumerable playing of the *My Fair Lady* soundtrack, they all became surprisingly good at the technique. For the bulk of the rehearsals, the cast worked to a guide musical track recorded by Dick Black. The Professor was in perpetual attendance and, apart from some valuable tweaks to his script which cleared up some anomalies, he also made some minor alterations to the sprechgesang lyrics, to make the cadence better. Simon's effortless and expert segue in and out of the technique delighted them all and gave his role an additional weight and importance because he could guide them through the difficult parts. But Michael still felt uncomfortable about the King's drunkenness, although he seemed to be alone in this. Simon himself was unperturbed and seemed surprised when Michael raised the issue with him when, during a break in rehearsals, they were standing alone.

"Drunkenness?" said Simon. "It's still all too common in that area, I'm afraid."

"But don't you think it plays into the stereotype of the drunken black man?"

"Perhaps. But I personally sympathise with the King's predicament. As will all my people. If they are allowed see it."

"But don't you think that your people will feel demeaned by the portrayal?"

"No. They know it was true, and they will feel for the King. They will understand."

Michael sensed that Simon was being careful, but he was not close enough to him to probe into what could be a delicate area. He let the subject drop and went with the flow. The fact that he seemed alone in his reservations suggested that he keep them to himself. The play, after all, was magnificent, and his role was a once-in-a-lifetime opportunity. Word had spread in the industry and he and the other leads, including Simon, were approached by the media to talk about the work. On this subject Dominick and Peter were clear. They should all give the play a positive spin and duck any questions that probed too deeply into any aspect that detracted from the positioning of the work as anything other than a giant leap forward for theatre. The press releases had all stressed the historical accuracy of the piece and that seemed enough. But deep down, Michael felt uncomfortable, especially when, towards the end of rehearsals, with a temporary music track in support, Simon gave a powerful physical and emotional performance as the Governor forces him to relinquish all his land to the white government. The King knows he has lost the support of his people and is banished into exile among the mountains. The sequence ends as the King leaves in an inebriated state, bemoaning his loss in sprechgesang, supported by drums and ululating women. It was tragedy at its finest, and the entire cast was moved by it. Simon himself looked as if he needed time to recover, so James decreed a long break. The actors dispersed in different directions, and several went out onto the enormous balconies that stretched across the side of the theatre, overlooking one of the streets that led to the bus terminus and the train station. They all strolled around, deep in thought and avoiding each other. Michael too wanted to be alone with his thoughts but his gaze – and his footsteps – were inevitably drawn to where Simon was seated on the wall, looking down onto the streets. Michael moved to his side, nodded at him and sat down beside him. Simon returned the nod and carried on looking down onto the streets. Business hours were coming to a close, and the black and white pedestrians were all hurrying towards their individual departure points from the city. The black pedestrians, he noticed, were walking faster than the whites; some were half running; and neither of the races collided with the other, as if segregation had demarcated the very pavements under their feet. In spite of his hesitancy to approach a thorny subject and his respect for this actor who had acted from his very soul in his exit scene, Michael had to speak.

"Simon, I want to tell you that I respect you very much and I admire what you are doing in that last scene. No. 'Admire' is the wrong word. I am humbled by it. I know I could never plumb the depths like that. It was so powerful and truthful that it hurt, physically. It was… beyond… acting."

Simon carried on looking expressionlessly at the hordes below for such a long time before he spoke that Michael thought he was offended, but Simon's gaze when he turned to look at him was gentle, almost tender, as was the tone of his voice.

"Acting such matters is difficult. The situation is deep and important and there is such a burden on the actor to be truthful. So, every word hurts. The script is good. My job is to act the words. I am acting for all those people out there on the streets. They're all running away from… some sort of slavery, intending to stop at the bars and shebeens to drown their shame and prepare them for another return to an inadequate home, to hungry children and to a wife's eyes. What those men feel is difficult enough to show, but what a king feels as he is discarded forever is…"

He paused for such a long time that Michael felt he was intruding far too much. But, as he was framing a suitable reply, Simon started speaking again.

"I am sorry to say these things to you, but they are so near the surface, and I have been controlling them for the entire scene and singing at the same time! Is that not hard, Michael?"

He started sprechgesang, sotto voce:

"I go now. To hide from the faces of men. To hide my failure. My loss of kingship. And my spirit."

He looked again at the streets.

"They will understand. They are all hiding."

"But they won't all see this play, will they?"

"No. And that is the hardest part of all. You are not from here, Michael. You cannot know the pain. The separation."

"I can, Simon. I have lived with separation. Close up."

"Ah! Thandi."

"You know about Thandi!" Michael was shocked.

"We know more than some people would believe."

"You know where she is then?"

"Yes. Some of us know about it."

"And you can do nothing?"

"Nothing. The chains are heavy." He rubbed his wrists together. "And they are tight."

They both looked again at the streets which were getting less crowded as they watched.

"Michael! Simon!"

It was James calling. They both looked in his direction and started to get to their feet.

"Thank you for sharing that with me, Simon. Why did you, by the way?"

"There are some people we can trust."

"But how do you know?"

"We know. Believe me. We know the people who are not threatened by us."

Michael laughed.

"Except as an actor," he said.

"That is professional jealousy. We can handle that."

They headed back to the rehearsals, the schedule for which was the most rigorous that Michael, and indeed any of them, had ever experienced. This was one advantage of working for the system – there was budget enough to do things properly, providing it had the blessings of the governing party. The acting, singing, dancing all coalesced into a complete and satisfying whole, and all the participants were soon ready for the performances.

It was the most exciting opening night that Michael had ever experienced. The audience was of mixed race with the many black people constrained to the balcony and one designated toilet. The stage designer had exceled himself. The set was immersive and was an integral part of the in-your-face theatre from the start. As the lights dimmed, a faint drumbeat issued from the lobby, and through the door and down the aisles, in almost total darkness, came the singers and musicians, performing the theme song. They mounted the stage which comprised a curved concave cyclorama which enclosed the performing area. Onto this was projected a vista of wild country, into which the singers and musicians seemed to disappear under an overwhelming star-studded sky. This formed a background for the Colonist who introduced, in sprechgesang, the world of the story they were about to relate. The animals of the night were suggested by rolls on deep drums to simulate the roar of a lion, ululating women to suggest hyenas and screams to suggest kills. The Colonist outlined the basic tenet of the tale, the pushing back of the wilderness to create a living place for invaders. As he outlined the life of the small town on the edge of the untamed land, he slowly disappeared; the outlines of buildings emerged from the wings; and the light went from dark to a golden day. The principal actors came on stage and the play began. The audience was mesmerised; the bulk of it had no concept of the musicality of the population from whom they had carefully and deliberately divorced themselves. The sounds they heard were new to them. The music was new. The story was new, and the sight of accomplished black actors in full, supportive interaction with white actors was a revelation. For the duration of the performance, there was one nation in the theatre; the cast gave their all, sensing the momentous of the occasion, and they were amply rewarded by the reaction; in the silences, one could hear a pin drop; in the explosive applause one could not hear oneself think. It was a roller coaster for all concerned.

The key moment at which the overarching theme of the work was laid out was between the Colonist and the Governor's Wife. She was lauding him about his brave and glamorous life on the frontier, but he was having none of it. He perceived himself as a necessary tool in subduing the wilderness in preparation for such as she who would bring civilisation and order. His part in the process was far from glamourous. His job was to minimise danger so that society could be established and prosper. Then he, or people like him, would move on to other parts of the country. This passage was in sprechgesang:

He: *These people must know*
That they and the animals must go.
She: *Where? Where must they go?*
He: *That is not my problem.*
But my duty to make it so.
She: *No matter what?*
He: *No matter what.*
She: *And what is my duty?*
He: *To banish ugliness.*
She: *And then?*
He: *To bring beauty.*

At interval, the lobby was abuzz with excitement and even exhilaration, and when the bell went, signalling the resumption of the play, the refreshment area emptied quicker than the staff had ever experienced. The work thundered on. Individual conflicts played out against the clash of races. Treacherous deals were made – and almost immediately broken – and the King betrayed and fooled with empty promises until, tricked by unscrupulous machinations, his people lost faith in him, and he lost his status and retired to the hills in drunken despair. In the midst of such excited involvement, the King's exit was no way to finish a play, so there were two more dramatic scenes between it and the final lavish ending which had the Governor and his Wife bidding goodbye to the Colonist as they headed off, the Governor to be honoured and decorated for clearing the land so successfully, his Wife to continue an affair with her sorely missed noble General and the redundant Colonist for more 'empty' land further north. So, the King's downfall was consigned, as it were, to history, and the focus returned to the white characters. The final scene featured a sprechgesang trio, supported by the choir and orchestra, with the percussion section to the fore. The curtain calls were many and enthusiastic, the audience on its feet and the black people on the balcony nosily ecstatic. From them issued extended cheers and ululations when the King came back onstage and gravely took several bows. The entire theatre was electric, and the enthused audience piled into the front of house, talking excitedly and extremely reluctant to go home and end the spell.

Ria's dressing room was inundated by noisy admirers, led by her proud parents and their friends. Rupert and Bernard were there, and they both offered her their congratulations at which she nodded graciously. The Doctor had sent an enormous bouquet of yellow roses which had been given pride of place on her dressing table. She accepted the embraces and compliments in a glow of pride and self-satisfaction and almost squealed with delighted surprise when Dominick fought his way through the crowd, kissed her on the cheek, whispered in her ear and held his finger to his lips before departing again, bestowing smiles all round. Ria ignored the questioning looks from her parents and moved behind a screen to change, still laughingly accepting the accolades that were showered on her.

In his room Michael was heartily congratulated by friends and eminent theatricals and after they left, Rupert and Bernard pitched up.

"That was splendid," said Rupert. "It's a great play, remarkably honest. We've just been to congratulate Ria. I must say, though, it was a pity about the King's drunkenness."

"Yes. I was worried about that, but nobody else seemed to be, so I let it go."

"Not much you could have done about it anyway, was there?" remarked Bernard.

"The King was a great, tragic figure, and Simon played it superbly," said Rupert.

"He did, didn't he? I hope he feels good about it," said Bernard.

"He does," Michael agreed. "He felt it was the best part he's ever played, even though it hurt."

"We're off to have a drink with him, among his friends," said Bernard.

"Were there many black people in the audience? I couldn't see them."

"You must have heard them though. The balcony was full of them. Special concession," Rupert added. "They gave very necessary support for the King at the end. Dominick was wise to let them attend."

Dominick took that moment to bustle in.

"Well done, Michael. They loved you tonight. Absolutely loved you. Hello, Rupert. Bernard. What did you think?"

"Marvellous. It should travel. It deserves to."

"It will. It will. We've signed the contract with the Americans."

"For the whole show?"

"No. The concept, mainly."

"The concept?" Michael asked.

"They are going to adapt it to *their* history, and I can't say I blame them. Their production will involve their aborigines. The red Indians. The Apaches to be precise. The script will have to be adapted."

"How does the Professor feel about that?"

"Great. He's going over there next week to do the research, as will the musical director. They're both very excited about it. The American production company has already submitted some historical facts on which to base the revisions. But the Professor will tell you about that. The good news about you, Michael, is that they want you to play the main character. The producers remember your magnificent performances on PBS. In this version he's a ferocious Indian trader, and Ria will play the wife of the army officer who's in charge of the area. The rest of the cast will be Americans. I've just told Ria and she's… here she is herself."

At that moment Ria burst in. She smiled at Dominick and moved past him towards Michael to embrace him.

"Michael!" Ria almost shouted. "Have you heard? America! We're both going to America! Isn't it so, Dominick? And isn't it wonderful? Hello, Rupert. And Bernard. Isn't it exciting?"

"Very," said Rupert, and Bernard was nodding by his side. "Congratulations to you both. You have earned your parts and congratulations to you, Dominick. Well played."

"Thank you." Dominick nodded at Bernard and left. Bernard shook Michael's hand.

"Big time, old buddy!"

"Yes. It looks like that."

Rupert also shook hands with Michael and spoke softly to him.

"America. Big money, Michael. Have you contacted my advisor friend yet?"

"No. Not yet."

"Do so. Soon. Goodbye all."

He and Bernard headed towards the door but stepped back as Mrs. Van Vuuren entered, followed by the Doctor.

"You must both be proud of your daughter," Rupert said.

"We are… em… thank you, thank you," said the Doctor as he moved on.

"Yes. Indeed we are," Mrs. Van Vuuren chimed in.

Bernard and Rupert left; the latter caught Michael's eyes and nodded significantly.

"Michael. Well done, my lad," said Dr. Van Vuuren.

"You were absolutely marvellous, Michael," said Mrs. Van Vuuren, hugging him. "So, of course, was Ria, don't you think?"

"She was the star of the show," said Michael.

"The star of the show was Simon, don't you think?" said Ria.

"Yes. Yes. I do."

"Well, those in the balcony certainly thought so," said the Doctor.

"Can't think why they let all those blacks in," Mrs. Van Vuuren sniffed.

"For moral support, I expect," said Michael.

"Well," said the Doctor hurriedly. "Congratulations to you both again."

"That's not all the good news," Ria exclaimed and stopped. "I don't know what's happening. There's so much to absorb."

"What?" Mrs. Van Vuuren asked somewhat anxiously.

"We're both going to America, Michael and I. To play in the American version of the show."

"What? Oh. When? When?"

"Not for ages yet. We have to finish this run first."

"America? There's so much to… oh dear!"

"Don't worry about that right now, my dear," said the Doctor. "Ria, my dear! And you, Michael, sincere congratulations to you both. I feel very proud of both of you. You, especially, Ria. Now we must go. When will we see you again?"

"Next Sunday. OK?" asked Ria.

"Of course," said Mrs. Van Vuuren. "You too, Michael. Unless you're going to be swanning around on that boat of yours."

"I'll be taking it for a trip round the bay in the morning, but I can be with you after lunch, if that's OK?"

"That's fine," said the Doctor. "Congratulations again, my dear, and goodnight."

He kissed Ria, shook hands with Michael and forcefully escorted Mrs. Van Vuuren out.

"That trip? How early in the morning?" Ria asked.

"Not too early."

"Good."

"Let's get out of here. We need a bit of fun right now. OK?"

"OK."

Later that night, when Ria had left to go to her own apartment, Michael took down his script of *Kingfisher* and flipped through it until he found the name of the advisor that Rupert had suggested. Next to it was Thandi's number. The significance of both was clear, and it seemed as if it was time that he made plans for his own benefit.

Chapter Twenty Two

The perfect moment in which we all want to stay, the world's applause in which we all want to bask and the heady whiff of gratification which we want to inhale is all the devil needs to bind us to him with hoops of steel.

It was a long and exhausting run, and it travelled to two other cities. After seeing the show bedded down, James Diggery passed the direction over to a colleague who had attended many of the rehearsals as well as many meetings with James and had watched all the performances. His brief was to keep the show on track and the cast and musicians up to scratch, and this he did very well and sympathetically. It took the cast some time to accept him, having invested an enormous amount of trust in James. But they all soon adjusted to the new regime and took his occasional notes seriously. There were many interviews to handle, on TV, radio and the print media. Most of them were very elementary, and Michael and Ria sailed through them placidly, but a couple were with serious journalists who probed beneath the surface and wanted to discuss the injustices meted out to the local populations at the period in question. These probes could be handled easily for the most part, but when they moved on to present-day attitudes and practices, they were circumspect in their answers, Michael especially, knowing that the reviews would be closely scrutinised by Dominick and his associates. At a joint interview with him and Ria, only one journalist referred to the subject that had worried Michael at the start of the rehearsals: the King's drunkenness. He was hesitant in his reply until he thought of Simon's performance, and he gave a spirited and emotional answer:

"Simon Mbeki should be answering this question, he—"

"He played the King."

"Yes. Every night he gave a beautiful and powerful reading of that drunken scene, and when I asked him about how he felt about it, he had a very interesting answer. He said every man who stopped off at a bar on the way home would understand his performance, because each man had to face – he said – an 'inadequate' home, hungry children and his wife's accusing eyes. He said they would understand how a king would feel when he is thrown away."

Ria was icily silent during his reply, but the interviewer was intrigued.

"But Simon knew that those men would never see the play," he said.

"Some of them will. That's been taken care of, but that's not the point at hand. The point is that he knew they would understand, and that knowledge empowered him when he was acting that scene. I know I could never reach the heights Simon did. I suppose because I've never really suffered."

Ria rose to her feet and started to make 'that's enough' movements. But the interviewer was intrigued and ignored her.

"So, is it a comment on the present situation in this country?"

Michael ignored Ria's sharp intake of breath.

"I'm saying that it is a shrewd insight into the situation over a century ago. It has a universal truth to it, and universal truths don't tend to go out of fashion. No matter how uncomfortable they are."

The interviewer and he held each other's eyes for a long moment, and both decided that enough had been said on the subject.

"Well," said the interviewer. "The work is for all time, and it will not go out of fashion. That's for sure."

They both knew that enough had been said, and the interview came to a close. But in the car, Ria just had to get it off her chest.

"Michael! How can you do it? How can you say things like that?"

"What things? It is like it is. In this society, today, the King would be treated exactly the same way."

"And this country has been so good to you!"

"Yes. It has. And I'm glad to be here. But there are some truths you just can't ignore."

"So, my parents and their friends—"

"Ria! Don't take it personally, for fuck's sake."

The obscenity shut her up and she spent the rest of the trip in icy silence. Without commenting, he dropped her off at her flat and they parted with barely murmured goodbyes.

The Professor, Michael and Ria attended a seminar mounted by the university's history department and were subjected to an intense dialogue with the students and their lecturer, all of whom had attended a performance. It was gruelling but interesting, and it gave the actors some additional information and insights which they could use in their interpretations. The Professor was another matter. He took any perceived criticism very personally and tempers flared, which the lecturer had some difficulty in controlling. On the way back to town, the three of them assessed the evening; the bruised Professor had not budged at all in his total mastery and understanding of the period and the historic characters, but Michael and Ria felt that they were empowered to nuance their performances and they said so. The rest of the journey was travelled in silence.

At the end of the play's run, Michael had decided they should both take a long cruise up the east coast, stopping at towns and small harbours along the way. He broached the idea with Ria, and she was enthusiastic and entered into the planning and the shopping. With Rafe to guide them, they bought a stock of pastas, vegetables, rice and eggs, several sealed camping trail mixes, supplemented by cheese and nutritious snacks. They also bought tea, coffee and creamer, tinfoil, plastic wrap and assorted bags of snacks. A selection of meats was sourced and frozen for the trip, enough to last them for several days, they would replenish stocks at the towns along the way. Michael had been boating almost every weekend and was sufficiently confident of his ocean skills for the trip. He had mastered the sail too and could handle the boat in light to medium winds, switching to engine power when the going got rougher.

And so began one of the most enjoyable periods of time the two of them had ever spent together. The spring weather was glorious; the choppy sea was a sparkling carpet over which the *The Gretchen* wended her way with gay abandon. Michael hoisted the sail as often as he dared and, with the passing of the sea miles, he dared more and more. Storming into his mind came the youthful delight he had experienced when he first delved into sea stories. When he had soaked up thrilling tales of the sea in a heady brew of history and fiction. He had circumnavigated the globe with Magellan and Anson, cauterised the Spanish Main with Drake, served before the mast with Dana, delighted in derring-do with Hornblower, ached for death with Matthew Lawe, thrilled with the bravado of Lord Cochrane, raced through the adventures of Richard Bolitho and Jack Aubrey. Sighed with satisfaction as the upper yards of the *Pequod* sank below the vast billows with the foot of a sea hawk nailed in place by Tashtego the Indian. He had secretly vowed to go away to sea until his mother intercepted a letter from Cunard Line refusing him employment as a ship steward! Occasionally the wind became wayward as if to remind him of who was in charge around here. At such times, he gave the wheel to Ria, furled the sail, switched on the two Volvo engines and let them rip. The disconcerting yawing gave way to a purposeful and throbbing plunge through the brine. Ria, with sparkling eyes and legs akimbo, grasped the wheel and took control.

He found the smaller towns they stopped at to replenish locked in some weird time warp. It was a late Saturday morning and the few white inhabitants strolled along pavements, through the seething black people as if they were invisible. He had to go to the crowded post office to send some postcards to Ria's family and stood obediently in a queue as it inched towards a dumpy and frowning girl behind the counter. She scowled at each person as if they were asking her to do some unmentionable thing. When Michael moved forward to be served, the girl's frown changed to a delighted smile. Michael immediately changed his expression to a ferocious frown as he brusquely demanded some stamps. Her astounded double take sent him out of the place in high good humour.

They cruised several kilometres up the coast before gliding into the harbour of a small town and mooring in a berth that was pointed out to them by a uniformed and officious harbour employee. They showed their documentation, filled in the requisite forms and paid a mooring fee to the official who never uttered a word during the procedure. Michael locked up the *The Gretchen* and they made their way towards the small but well-rated hotel overlooking the harbour, laughing as they staggered along on shaky land legs. While Ria soaked in a steaming bath with half a dozen fluffy towels waiting, Michael had a welcome shower, sought the bar and ordered a gin and tonic. A deeply tanned, bearded man in a vaguely naval jacket was seated at the bar and he caught Michael's eye, raised his glass in salute and took a deep sip. Michael tasted his gin and tonic and waited for the inevitable. Sure enough, the bearded man was at his side in moments with hand outstretched.

"Captain Jack Armstrong. Ex-naval officer. Saw you come into the harbour. Nice boat."

He resembled Rafe with the same self-satisfied and impregnable air.

"Michael Driscoll. You sail?"

"Yes. The yawl in the harbour with the brown sails is mine. *The Marlin*, I call her. What are you doing in this out-of-the-way place?"

"Needed to get away from city life for a while."

"Don't blame you. Too many people. The sea's the place. Where are you heading?"

"This is as far as I'm taking her this trip. Heading back tomorrow. Where do you stay?"

"On *The Marlin* of course. Room abord for six."

"Do you ever have six abord?"

"Frequently. I take small groups out fishing. It's good around here."

"What sort of fish do you catch?"

"Tuna. Plenty of bluefin around here. And Marlin. Some smaller stuff too, for the not-so-skilled fishermen."

"I suppose if I went out on a boat—"

"Yawl."

"Sorry. Yawl. Called *The Marlin*, I'd want to find a marlin."

"Finding them is easy. Catching them is not. Hemingway knew that. I've seen him drunk with tiredness after he'd pulled one on board. But he cut it up himself afterwards. Punching the slabs of flesh like a prize fighter."

Knowing he was in for a well-practised yarn, Michael couldn't resist.

"You fished with Hemingway?"

The mariner's eyes locked off into the distance, and the navigator's shoulders drew back ever so slightly.

"Yes. On *The Pilar*. The boat he loved. Big black seventy-five-horse Wheeler, thirty-eight-footer with a vertical bow and low stern for fishing. Could turn on its tail, thanks to two enormous Chrysler engines. Do sixteen knots through the waves as if she had a foaming white bone between her teeth, as EH used to say. Sailed with him from Key West to the Caribbean. Fished and drank there for a week. He'd go for everything: sailfish, swordfish, kingfish, barracuda, even sharks, as well as the marlin and bluefin of course. Learned what I know about fishing from him."

The captain gazed into this drink like a true naval officer before finishing it and placing it on the bar with a nautical flourish.

"Care for another?"

Michael caught sight of Ria at the door of the bar and finished his drink with panache but, unfortunately, some of it went down the wrong way and he hurriedly excused himself.

"Ooops! Sorry. There's the girlfriend." He nodded in Ria's direction. "Must go, I'm afraid."

The captain followed his gaze and straightened every so slightly.

"Ah! Let her join us for a drink."

"She... she doesn't drink I'm afraid. Refuses to enter a bar."

"Pity." And the look he gave Michael was certainly pitying.

"Well, it was very nice meeting you. Goodbye." Michael made his escape on this hypocritical note.

"Who was that?"

"Some salty old dog who fished with Hemingway," he replied as he grasped her elbow and steered her towards the dining room.

"Oh, I'd like to meet him."

"No, you wouldn't. Hungry?"

"Starving."

"Good. I believe there's lobster on the menu."

"Excellent. I hope they have a good wine to go with it."

After long days of rather basic food on board the *The Gretchen*, the meal was magnificent. The locally sourced rock lobster was delicious and paired with a light and slightly smoky wine which perfectly complemented the slight sweetness of the lobster flesh. There was a crisp and inventive green salad to accompany it. A local cheese which looked poisonous but tasted divine when spread on a fresh, crispy-crusted white bread. Finally, a robust arabica coffee and a plate of local fruits brought the eating to a close, but the gustation reverberated throughout their systems. The one false note was when Michael spotted the captain entering the restaurant and being escorted to a seat against the back wall by an obsequious waiter; he quickly swapped Ria's empty wine glass for one of the glasses of water that had been placed next to each of their plates. However, the captain seemed oblivious to them both, so Michael forgot him in the delight of the meal, the mellowness created by the food and wine, as well as Ria's increasing attractiveness, which increased when they both enjoyed the sweet sweat of freshly showered bodies as they caused the bed to rock almost as much as *The Gretchen* until the early hours of the morning.

Chapter Twenty Three

Sometimes it's wise to look beyond the footlights and the seductive adulation. Protection from slings and arrows needs the type of shield you won't find in the props department.

The next Monday morning after their trip, Michael awoke with one thing on his mind: to make sure that whatever money he earned over the next few years would be safe, that is, out of reach of the authorities, whatever happened. He felt trapped by the citizenship deal which had unnerved him, as did Dominick's machinations, and he didn't trust those in charge to leave his money alone. Thandi's treatment had added to his fears. He was sure that a file existed somewhere in the dark depths of whatever department was in charge of such as he, a man who had been involved – let's face it, had had an affair – with a black woman and had been caught at it. Governmental displeasure would be harsh on the perceived miscegenation. It was up there with treason, anarchy, killing one's mother and other nefarious crimes, and the punishment would be silent, deadly and absolute. He rang the number that Rupert had given him, and the phone was answered almost immediately. *Was that suspiciously quick?* he thought, but decided that he was getting paranoid and answered.

"Hello, I was advised to ring this number by Rupert Blenkinsop."

"The name please?" asked a smooth voice.

"Michael Driscoll."

"Mr. Driscoll. Could you be here to meet the senior partner at three this afternoon?"

Not many clients, Michael thought at he waited for several seconds before replying.

"Y… yes. It appears that that would be fine."

The smooth voice gave a name and address and hung up. The address turned out to be in an older and run-down part of town he seldom went to. In fact, he couldn't remember if he ever *had* gone there. At a quarter to three he entered a dark-stoned, four-story building on a dark and narrow street that had obviously seen much busier days, judging by the imposing doorways to almost all the buildings. Above the recessed porch of the building he had been directed to was the chiselled name 'International Building'. Under the image of a bee, a well-polished brass plaque announced in a hushed typeface, 'Menton Advisors. A member of the International Discretionary Fund'. *Nothing like giving the game away*, thought Michael as he entered the dark hallway and consulted the list of firms and floors on the wall. There were very few names on it, and all were in the small pushed-in white plastic lettering that older buildings were wont to wear for the guidance of visitors. Menton Advisors were on the third floor. Michael went towards the back of the lobby to where a cage lift lurked. Inside that was an old, bent man, perched on a small stool to one side. His head had a somnambulant slump, but it came erect as Michael pressed the buzzer. The door was pulled open so slow that he reached out to assist, but a glare from the operator stayed his hand. He stepped in as the door finally clicked opened and a palsied hand reached for the row of buttons.

"Menton Advisors please."

"They're the only occupants, they are."

Wondering what sort of decrepit business Rupert had led him to, Michael leaned against the cage side but hurriedly stepped away as a passing descending girder came perilously close to his jacket elbow. The lift shuddered to a stop, and the operator reached out and pulled the gate open.

"Fourth floor. Menton Advisors to the right at the end."

Michael nodded and headed in the direction indicated and was confronted again with the bee logo and the name of the firm. He pressed a buzzer (another refence to a bee?) on the wall next to the door and it clicked open. He stepped into a spacious, dimly lit room with the occasional gleam from the highly polished wooden wall panels. A large desk faced the door and he moved towards it, waited and looked around. One wall was covered from floor to ceiling with shelves full of dim volumes with gold lettering glinting on the spine. On the wall behind the desk was a framed photograph of an elderly, distinguished man in evening dress around whose neck, on a red and black ribbon, was a golden bee. He was studying the austere but dignified face when a door in one of the walls opened and the stately figure of the person in the photograph stood there regarding him silently.

"Good morning, Mr. Driscoll. I have been expecting you for some time."

"Good morning, Mr...?"

"Menton. Stanley Menton. Please come in."

He stepped aside and gestured for Michael to pass him. Inside was a room of the same dimensions as the first and another desk, a replica of the one in the entrance room, facing across two leather chairs and the door. Michael stepped past Menton and approached the chairs.

"Please be seated," said Menton as he passed Michael and took his place behind the desk, where he stood waiting until Michael was seated before sitting down.

"Rupert suggested I get in touch with you."

"Yes. He told me. He said you would be calling. He told me about you and your rather spectacular career. How can I be of service?"

"I'm not too sure. I expect to earn some money, a lot of money, in the next few years, and I should be considering some intelligent investments, rather than just putting it into a bank and letting it earn a modest income."

"You are not a citizen, I assume?"

"I am actually. I was persuaded to change my citizenship a while back. To ensure some very worthwhile roles at the State Theatre."

"Ah yes. Four major roles in four important American plays. I've seen them. You were very impressive."

"Thank you."

"And a very spectacular local musical too. Which I have also seen. Also very impressive."

"Thank you again."

"And you want to find a secure home for the funds you will accrue, with all reasonable access and a degree of confidentially."

"Yes."

"You realise that we do not indulge in any form of evasion of the taxes and other charges those funds may be susceptible to under any of the laws of the countries in which we operate."

"Of course."

"Good. Then let me explain who we are and how we operate. We are part of The International Discretionary Fund, a worldwide network of investment firms with offices in most major cities in the Western world and several in the East. From which funds may be drawn, as required and at any time, by clients of the Fund. You will have noticed our symbol: a bee."

"Yes. I wondered—"

"The symbolism is apt, and I must admit I devised it myself. I am an erstwhile beekeeper, and I have always been fascinated by the role they play in pollination and the production of honey and beeswax."

Menton settled down in his chair and steepled his fingers in preparation for what was obviously an enjoyable and oft-repeated exposition.

"I and my international colleagues consider ourselves as bees and each branch office as a beehive. Each hive has a queen bee which, in our case, is the body of clients we service. Our sole function is to look to the welfare of the queen and to this end we labour incessantly, our busy wings fanning the papers of commerce: bonds, bills of exchange, scrip, letters of credit and other negotiables, activating them, stirring them up, mingling them to generate the heat of compound interest and an increasing yield for our clients. We fill the combs of the hive to keep it warm and comfortable and the queen bee – our customer – replete. In each area of operation, we worker bees toil incessantly to seek out the greatest source of yield, and when we find it, we share this information with other beekeepers. We perform what apiarists call the waggle dance to guide them to the best yield. That's the dance the bee does to show the other bees exactly where the pollen-laden flowers are in relation to the nest. Just as we guide each other to the most profitable investments. The bee uses the sun's position in the dance because the bee can see its UV – ultraviolet – light, through the clouds. The bee has been revered for ages. Napoleon replaced the fleur-de-lis of the French monarchy with the honeybee as his symbol of prestige and power. And it proved of immense value to him, that is until he reached the great hive Moscow and found it empty. By the way, we have a branch in Moscow which does remarkably well considering the paranoia of the government there."

Menton paused and looked at Michael to see how he was responding. Michael gathered his thoughts before replying.

"Fine. I'm impressed. How does it all work? I assume the investment procedures are universal and aimed at generating the highest profit for investors – the queen bees."

Menton seemed delighted at Michael's use of his, Menton's, imagery.

"I'm pleased that our philosophy makes sense to you. The registration is in line with all contracts of commercial operations. The depositing procedure is very straightforward. The withdrawal system is simplicity itself. You will have a unique code for withdrawal and, on provision with the normal identification documents, you will have a secret number based on your middle name. Upon production of those, your withdrawal will be sanctioned and the amount you require, which must always be five per cent less that the funds deposited, will be instantly forthcoming. Would you like to register?"

"Yes. Why not."

"Good."

Menton picked up a pen and pulled a notepad towards him.

"Now, what is your middle name?"

"Aloysius."

"Unusual. Good. Now if we spell it backwards, it is SUISYOLA. If we give each letter a numerical value according to its place in the alphabet, it is so."

He drew the name and made the calculation on the pad before handing it to Michael.

"Very easy. Very difficult to work out and impossible to forget. Presented with your ID number, a cash withdrawal or a transfer to any bank anywhere in the world will be honoured by our offices in any city in which you find yourself. And now, some ID and a few forms to fill out if that's alright with you."

"How… do I have to pay to join?"

"No. We remunerate ourselves with a one per cent commission on all funds that you choose to withdraw."

"That sounds simple."

"As are all the best systems. Let me get the forms."

Fifteen minutes later, Michael was back in the narrow street, feeling a lot happier.

Chapter Twenty Four

The universality of suffering and oppression is the warp and weft of theatre and grist to every playwright's fine-grinding mill.

The adaption of the play to American history was a wonder of synchronicity. It demonstrated that each succeeding people in each country on the globe followed eerily similar paths. New cultures dominated old cultures with the same clashes, conflicts and inevitable uneasy merging and absorption, with varying degrees of success. The changes to the basic story in the play were minimal, but the changes to history were immense. The location was Arizona; the tribe chosen was the Apache; and the chief was Cochise. The title of the work changed to *Cochise and the Trader*; the part of the Governor changed to General George Crook; and the same dynamics and pecking order applied. The Indian Trader, Tom Jeffords – Michaels' role – was a friend of Cochise's and became the on-the-ground emissary between the tribe and General Crook, who served as the bastion of the government. Cochise had actually died of cancer, but the script had him descent into drunkenness first, to bring the story in line with the original. Nobody took exception to that but, in another, less important bending of the truth, the physical, if unconsummated, attraction between Jeffords and Crook's wife,

Mary Dailey, caused some minor controversary when the work played, but it soon died down except among a few descendants of Mary. Ria played the wife of the General which mimicked the role she had played in the original, and all she had to do was change her accent, which caused her no bother at all.

The Professor had adapted his script to accommodate American history and sensibilities while an American musical director altered the music to the rhythmic, driving, drum-dominated pulse of Apache music and to the American Indian form of less-melodic singing, with occasional melodies and solos in a more European tradition. The same sprechgesang technique was adopted, and it worked beautifully. The director, Professor Newland Emerson, was a caricature of a Boston Brahmin of the upper-upper class which stemmed from traditionally wealthy families who distained the lower-upper class that mimicked the former's manners and dress styles: ferociously tailored tweeds with unimpeachable accessories and immaculate evening dress with a subtle but defiant slope about the shoulders and languidly swaying trousers. The Prof, as Emerson was always called, was over six feet in height and startlingly thin, with an unnervingly straight stare which he directed at erring cast members who were slow to follow his explicit directions. The actors, with the exception of Michael, were in awe of him. Michael, on the other hand, treated him with a casual camaraderie that Emerson resented at first but gradually accepted as Michael proved his theatrical worth and skilfully integrated the Prof's suggestions with consummate and obvious skill. Indeed, their relationship became a source of envy with the rest of the company. Under the Prof's expert guidance, the play developed into a powerful and moving piece.

American sensitivity ensured that all the Indian roles were played by white actors with copper make-up but, in an exception to this, Cochise was played by Paul Johnson, a light-skinned man with a magnificent bass singing voice who had gained local and international fame and, consequently, was acceptable, even lionised, in the best society. The relationships between the major characters were not as clear cut as in the original version, but nobody seemed to be bothered by this. Michael, however, felt that some of the really deep dramatic potential of the play was lost. He was particularly uneasy by the attitude of Paul and tried to probe this in a conversation he had with him during rehearsals. Paul seemed totally unaware of the ahistoric drunkenness of Cochise and, dismissing its relevance to modern audiences, he refused to engage with Michael on the subject. Later, Michael raised his concerns with the Prof.

"I just think, for the sake of integrity of the play, I think his obtuseness is unfortunate."

"Obtuseness? Don't talk to him about obtuseness. He's a negro who has a rare – and tentative – acceptance among the elite here, and he is revered abroad. He knows he's fashionable right now. A social lion. But he could go out of fashion, be dropped and forgotten in a season."

"In spite of his international standing?"

"Because of it. They don't like what they call 'uppity niggers' round here. They'd ditch him in an instant just to spite their perceived opponents abroad. Obtuseness? He's being very, very careful. He knows he's where he is under sufferance so he's careful. If they want Cochise drunk, Cochise will be drunk."

"I just wish he would bring the same integrity to the role as Simon did to the King."

"Now. Now. He doesn't carry the same burden as your Simon. You can't expect him to be as sensitive to historic injustices as Simon is."

"Why not? He is after all an 'uppity nigger' as you say."

"Michael! As a guest in this land, you have to be polite at least."

Michael surveyed the Prof and was silent. This was a scholar who could bring history into life and yet he seemed relatively oblivious to right and wrong. However, when he brought up his reservation about the drunkenness of Cochise to the Prof, he found him mild and urbane on the subject.

"You must understand the American view of our own worth and our God-given manifest destiny. We conquered the Indians by means more foul than fair but our occupation of the country from coast to coast is our foundational epic. It appeared as our manifest destiny, so when the frontier raced across the plains like a Kentucky thoroughbred, we poured in to build what we thought – and still think – is the finest society in the world. Such a magnificent achievement overshadows any impropriety, any injustice and fealty to our history, not the Indians'. Whether Cochise was a drunk or not is irrelevant to our supreme self-confidence and self-image. Our intolerance for other races is now less histrionic. Less brutal. At least on the East Coast where my family had the common sense to set down roots. A drunk Cochise imparts a degree of poignancy to the play. The audiences will love him because it affords them an opportunity to sympathise with him, the tragic, noble – but flawed – great Indian chief. Empathy without embarrassment. They'll enjoy that."

And that was as far as Michael got with his reservations about any historic inexactitude. The play was a resounding success and got eight curtain calls on the opening night. When Paul stepped forward, the audience responded with increased enthusiasm and vigour. He took several lone bows and the crowd whistled and cheered. Clearly, they were not concerned with the bending of the truth. The run of the play was interspersed with interviews with all leading actors, especially Michael, who was gratified to discover that he was remembered for his PBS broadcasts. Often, he and Ria were interviewed in tandem where they played off each other and dodged any questions about their personal relationship. They met practitioners from a cross section of American newspapers and magazines which still carried the birthmarks and the attitudes of a communications medium that, over a few decades, especially in the western cities and towns, had helped shape the pioneering communities in which they wanted to – and did – flourish. The sense of power this gave resulted in the print practitioners displaying an abrasive tone and a dogmatic opinion of the people interviewed, especially theatricals, on whom they occasionally imposed their own moralistic strictures. The interviews were brasher and more confrontational than Michael and Ria were used to. Having created the moral tone of their reviews, they questioned hard and probed deep. After several such interviews, Michael tried to explore the drunkenness of Cochise, with the same exasperating lack of response. Later Ria confronted him.

"Why do you keep flogging a dead horse?" she asked accusingly. "Nobody here cares about one drunken Indian, more or less."

"I just find it strange that such recent events seem to be either forgotten or irrelevant."

"You were exactly the same back home. Why can't you let go?"

He started to reply but held his peace. He was not going to win with Ria.

After one rather tepid performance, Michael and Ria decided to slip away alone and go to a nearby restaurant for something to nibble and to drink. The place was quiet and almost deserted. The lone waiter smiled and nodded at them.

"Mr. Driscoll and Miss. Van Vuuren!" he said. "So nice to have you." He grabbed a menu and escorted them to a table at the back. They passed a table of four other diners who had finished the meal and were lingering over their coffee and wine. One of them stood up and staggered forward to confront them.

"Mr. Driscoll and Miss. Van Vuuren! Michael. Ria. We saw the play on Saturday night. Didn't we, darling?"

A blonde, slightly tipsy woman took several seconds to focus on them.

"Oh," she said.

"*Cochise and The Trader*," hinted the man.

"Oh? Oh! Of course. Wonderful. You were both wonderful. Congratulations. To both of you."

"Would you care to join us?" said the man. "We have finished eating but we would… we would love to…"

He had distinct trouble deciding what, exactly, they would love to do."

"Thank you," said Michael. "But we have some points in the performance we just have to sort out. Some… problems."

"Of course. Of course. Thespian matters. Of course. Congratulations again to you both."

He stood watching them reach their table, nodding and half waving until the waiter seated them and handed each a menu. Then he raised his glass and toasted them extravagantly until the tipsy woman jerked his jacket so hard that he almost fell across the table.

Michael and Ria started to glance at the menus, each carefully avoiding looking at the table of four, where a general argument seemed to have broken out.

"Some problems?" Ria asked with a grin.

"None whatsoever. A drink?"

"Yes. Cognac and coffee."

"Me too. That's all we want so bring the bill at the same time," said Michael to the waiter as he handed back the menu. He looked at Ria. "Tonight…"

"Tonight what?"

"I just got a feeling that tonight I was being very, very stupid. Standing there in front of a large audience, speaking words written by somebody else. Pretending to be an Indian trader. Expressing emotions that I didn't feel. And singing into the bargain. In sprechgesang. Very stupid."

"It's your job."

"I know it is. But it's a stupid way to make a living, isn't it?"

"There are worse ways."

"I suppose there are. Doesn't help."

The waiter appeared with the drinks.

"With the compliments of the gentleman over there," he said as he placed them down.

"Christ!" Michael muttered.

"Michael! Be gracious." Ria raised her glass at the frantically nodding man who started to his feet, only to be dragged back down by the tipsy woman, placing more glasses in jeopardy. Michael gritted his teeth and raised his glass.

The waiter arrived with coffee cups and a silver coffee pot on a tray.

"Just made this," he said as he poured. "Nice to have you in here. The actors do usually drop in for a refresher. You were both great."

"Thank you," Ria said. "Do you go there often?"

"Every show. I'm studying drama at the Juilliard."

In spite of himself, Michael was interested.

"How long have you been there?"

"I'm in my second year."

"And?"

"It's tough. But great. I've seen your show twice."

"Is that part of the rigorous training? Boot camp?"

"Yes. We're encouraged to go. Get in cheap too. I have to write a review of it as part of my project."

Ria grinned wickedly. "He says he felt stupid tonight."

"Stupid?"

"Yes. For speaking somebody else's words. Pretending to be an Indian trader."

The waiter looked so astounded and upset that Michael felt guilty.

"Hey! I go into this tailspin every so often. But… it's my job."

"Job!" The waiter looked as if Michael had committed a sacrilege.

"He's like this every so often," said Ria. "Ignore him."

"You could put that in your review," Michael said. "It'll raise a few laughs."

"Not with my lecturer."

The waiter moved away to the table of four. They had finished their drinks and paid their bill, so they left noisily, the waiter rushing to open the door for them.

"We're all pretending, you know," Michael said as the waiter came back.

Ria jerked his arm, but the waiter was unfazed.

"I'll be going to see the show again next week."

"I hope it's going to be free again."

"It is. I wonder…"

"What?"

"I know I have a nerve asking but…"

"But what?"

"After the next performance, could I…"

"What?"

"Interview you. For my review. My lecturer would be—"

"What's your name?"

"Fred. Fred Saunders."

"Just send your name in to me the night you come, and I'll meet you afterwards."

"Gee, Mr—"

"Michael. And Fred?"

"Yes?"

Michael took up the bill. "Oh! It's been paid for hasn't it? Fred, think up some interesting questions. I'm sick of the same old shit."

"Interesting?"

"Yes."

"Yes. Yes. Sure."

"Bye."

They crossed the brightly lit street and headed up a darker

one. She went obligingly enough until the lighted shops became fewer and the darkness increased.

"Let's head back. It's getting late," she said. "We could get lost easily."

"Lost? This city is laid out cleverly. It's easy to get around. The streets run from east to west and the avenues run south to north. We'll explore a little along here and then make a couple of left turns and make our way back."

Against her better judgements, she acquiesced, and they walked on. However, after three crossroads, the avenue got darker and darker and suddenly, out of the gloom, four dark figures crossed over and headed directly for them. They were black men, in dark clothing, and were strangely silent. His stomach dropped. They stopped and he wondered how the hell he was going to get out of this. But Ria let go of his hand and took half a pace towards the dark strangers. Drawing up to her impressive height, she spoke in a subdued but authoritative tone of voice.

"Excuse me!" she exclaimed. "Where do you think you're going?"

Her quiet tone of confidence stopped them in their tracks. She took another step and they started to move to either side.

"Thank you!" she said and walked between them. They almost scampered out of her way and she and Michael strode off back towards the brighter lights. She didn't look back and neither did Michael. They turned into a much brighter street – or was it an avenue? He didn't know. All he knew was that years of ordering black people about had imbued her with an unassailable self-confidence. They made it back to their hotel safely but in silence. She unaffected by their moment of peril. He vastly impressed by her sangfroid.

Chapter Twenty Five

Praise and premonition are sometimes comfortable bedfellows, as the dead, who have been there, know only too well.

As the run was coming to an end, one of the stagehands brought Michael a note in his dressing room while he was preparing for the show. It was from Fred, requesting the interview.
"He's at the stage door," said the messenger.
"Tell him to come to my dressing room half an hour after the curtain."
"Will do."
"And make sure he's let in."
"Yes."
After the show, he was changing out of his costume and Ria stuck her head around the door.
"I'm off to the hotel with a friend. See you later."
"OK. I'm seeing Fred."
"Fred?"
"The waiter. From Juilliard."
"OK. Bye."
He had taken the costume and the make-up off when there was a knock on the door.
"Come in."

Fred was standing there, holding a canvas bag.

"Hello, Mr. Driscoll."

"Michael, please. Take a seat."

Fred did so, took a small recorder out of his bag and got it going.

"I've done my research on you and your work. I was hoping for some insights from you that would be of interest to the drama students. Some sort of insights into the art of acting."

"It's more work than art. Hard work too. The harder you work, the better the acting."

"I have studied your stage history," said Fred who was hanging on every word. "I would really like to probe your acting philosophy."

"Philosophy? That's a hard-edged word. I don't suppose I really have a philosophy. I think, after many years on the stage, I have a repertoire of moves and techniques. I apply them to the various roles I'm given."

"Could you describe one of those moves or techniques?"

"Let me see. Yes. There is one that has guided me through many impersonations."

"Impersonations?"

"Yes. We impersonate people. We put on make-up, costumes, and we pretend to be somebody else. Someone we've never met. Someone who comes to us through the mind of a playwright who invents a fictional character or interprets an historic one. Gives us words and actions to perform as truly as we can and imbue those words with the emotions that we *think* those people had at the precise time in their stories that the script decides they were felt."

"How do you decide on the tone of voice, or the action at those times when you're planning your impersonations?"

"Well, fear is a useful technique."

"Your fear?"

"No. No. The fear that the character experiences at that moment in his story."

"What sort of fear?"

"Well. When a character experiences fear, the audience experiences it too. If even on a subliminal level."

"Fear of what's going to happen to him?"

"That of course. But it's what is going to happen *next* that keeps audiences on the edge of their seats."

"But that's surely in the script's function."

"That's what riggers off a tense scene, but if the actor is afraid, or makes the character afraid, really afraid, that fear heightens the moment."

"I don't understand."

"I'll make you understand. Supposing I dried up during this interview. How would you feel?"

"Emmm. Embarrassed I suppose. And…yes… fear, I would suppose, that you had lost the thread of your thoughts."

"Exactly. Let me tell you about an experience I had in my early teens. I had joined an amateur dramatics group, and I had devised and was directing a passion play. A shadow play. All the participants were to be seen in silhouette on sheets hung along the front of the stage. These were slung along ropes across the front of the U-shaped stage, and we installed a series of a hundred-watt light globes behind them. We couldn't get the sheets to hang smoothly, and they had come from several homes, so they were all of different thickness and colours. So, I draped them along some ropes in such a way that they fell in curved crescents from top to bottom. This distorted the shadows in an interesting way and helped to cover up some of the obvious faults in body types and costumes. It's hard when you're a teenager; you don't have any budget to stage a play. Anyway, the cast and the audience – we only had one performance on Good Friday night – were all afraid. The participants that it wouldn't work and the audience that they would be embarrassed. We had a pianist pounding the slightly out-of-tune piano. Mostly dramatic chords. No discernible melody. It was a recipe for disaster and from the start, the fear was palpable. It was like another mental audience that was waiting for something horrible to go wrong and hoping it wouldn't. As the show started, I was nervous until I realised that the audience was mesmerised and totally involved in what was going on. There was no dialogue. Just the music, the actions and the grunting and shuffling of the performers. When the crucifixion happened, the cross was raised up, with Christ in position, by a pole attached to it directly behind, so it's shadow wouldn't fall on the screen. The two brawny boys at the back who were pushing the cross had to crouch down low behind the raised bit, to avoid throwing shadows."

Michael paused and Fred was open-mouthed by the suspense.

"While the piano – ever so slightly out of tune – thundered out the opening chords of Beethoven's Fifth, *Da Da Da Daa*, the cross started to wobble and the boy who was playing Christ started to curse. In an undertone, which was audible across the room. Christ! The sweating stagehands were pushing the cross up and the audience were all – *all* – scared shitless. The fear in that place was palpable. The cross rose up, stopped, wobbled one last time and thudded into the hole in the stage. The release of the fear and tension caused a silence sooo deep! The deepest of silences. Even the piano stopped playing. The emotion was transcendental. And reverential. And I knew that fear had done it."

There was a long silence until Fred cleared his throat.

"But how can you… create that fear?"

"You have to choose those moments in the script when the character is faced with a choice. Even a small choice. How to answer a question? Where to put down a prop? Where to go to next? Even what to *say* next? Brando is great at that. You never know what he's going to say or do. Not even if he's acting in a well-known play and you know the dialogue. Those pauses of his are well planned and have the audience hanging on his every word. In fear. That scene with Rod Steiger in the taxi. When

Charley, Brando's brother, warns him to get wise before they reach a street address. Brando pauses to digest this, and we see the poor, beaten-up ex-boxer pause before he asks, 'Before we get to where, Charley?' It's heartbreaking. We know he knows what's waiting for him at that address. And James Dean was the same. His searches for what to say were mesmeric. You feared that he would never get the words out. His fans miss his pain. I miss his pauses."

Michael spoke about many such concepts and Fred recorded them all and asked some astute questions that set Michael off. The interview lasted an hour and a half. Then Michael and Fred walked to the restaurant where they had first met. They had two drinks and finished the interview, after which Michael took a taxi to his hotel and Fred, refusing a lift, took the 'el' to his home. He subsequently presented his interview to his class, where it was listened to with great interest by his fellow students and his lecturer. This led eventually to a position as junior theatre critic for the *New York Times*, which tempted him away from life as an actor and left him, in later years, bemoaning the loss of a career on the stage.

The play finished its run in New York and travelled to Boston, the Prof's home town where his family had played a major role in the cultural development of the city. The play was moving to the Emerson Colonial Theatre which had been founded by the Prof's forebears and its ornate building overlooked Boston Common in the Theatre District. The auditorium was spectacular and threatened to upstage the actors, all of whom insisted on having their photograph taken on the vertiginous Grand Staircase as had many of the stage and screen legends of the USA. The Prof was lionised here, and he insisted that Michael and Ria stay at his family's home, a rambling Victorian brown stone house, as befitted the descendants of the revered Ralph Waldo Emerson. It was on a sprawl of densely grassed slopes dotted with old trees, and a limo was put totally at their service, day and night. They were invited regularly to lunches in the tidy city and lionised wherever they went. This attention soon paled, and they suggested gently to Emerson that they needed much more time to themselves. He relaxed the pressure on the social occasions and left them – with his limo – to their own devices. The Boston run went well: good houses, appreciative audiences and respectful interviewers. They were both asked to lecture at Emerson College, originally a 'school of oratory' founded by Emerson's family in the nineteenth century and of which the Prof was a trustee. Ria didn't take to these duties. For a brave and technically gifted actress, she was strangely inhibited in front of a group of knowledge-hungry students and soon persuaded Emerson to excuse her from the lectures and he, with old-fashioned gallantry, complied. Michael, however, enjoyed his sessions immensely and, since he wasn't motivated to make any preparations for his sessions, relied on his raconteurial talents to get him through. He made his sessions experiential and dropped his students into various sticky situations, as actors or writers, out of which they were required to extricate themselves. The consensus among the class was that these exercises were of immense value, but Michael couldn't handle the marking system, so the marks handed out at the end of a series of sessions were arbitrary. However, nobody seemed to take exception to his teaching method, and he got paid handsomely, in money from the management and compliments from the students. While strolling through the city, which Michael loved to do, he came across the Harvard Book Shop across the road from the university. It was a sprawling emporium with several floors of books. He was greeted by a thin, enthusiastic man with thick eyeglasses, behind the lenses of which his eyes floated like dull goldfishes. He recognised Michael and launched into a gushing welcome.

"Mr. Driscoll. Mr. Jeffords. How honoured we are to have you in our bookstore. I'm Hank, and it is my pleasure to assist you in any way I can. May I say that I *did* so admire your performance."

There was a slight pause as if Hank was waiting for permission.

"You may... Hank?"

"Hank. Yes. I *did* so admire your performance. How may I assist you?"

"I'm looking for Steinbeck's *Travels with Charley*."

"*With Charley: In Search of America*!" There was admonition in the correction.

"*In Search of America*. Right."

"A fan of John's?"

"Oh? Oh, John Steinbeck. Of course. Who isn't?"

"He's 'John' to us all here. We feel we're bosom friends with him here in The Harvard Book Shop. It's over there! I'll show you."

'There!' was a section of shelves at the side of the store towards which Michael was escorted. In the centre of one of the eye-level shelves were copies of *The Grapes of Wrath* and *Travels with Charley*. Hank indicated them with a flourish.

"If you enjoyed *Grapes*, you'll love *Travels*. We're on single name terms with our really great books here. You *did* enjoy *Grapes*?"

"Immensely," said Michael hurriedly, in case *not* enjoying *Grapes* was a punishable offense.

"Of *course* you did. And the movie?"

"I... I loved the movie."

"I *thought* you would."

"Except for the end."

"The *end*?"

Ooops! thought Michael. *The end of a beautiful friendship.*

"The ending. Giving the 'I'll be there' speech to Tom Joad instead of Jim Casy was a mistake."

"A mistake? But I *cried* at that speech."

"I'm sure you did. But that speech truly belongs to Casy. He was the preacher, and it was his philosophy. But Hollywood thought it would be better if Henry Fonda had the speech, because it would sound better if Fonda – the star of the movie – said it and because it would make you cry."

Hank's bonhomie dropped several points and he nodded uncertainly at the shelf and sidled away. Michael took down the book with its rather sparse slip cover and moved to a table in the centre of the room, around which there were several chairs. Nodding at the two other people who were seated there, he took out the notebook that he had kept by him through his time in America and opened the book. He was soon reminded that Steinbeck had called the van that he and his dog had travelled in *Rocinante*, the name of Don Quixote's horse.

He started to flip through it, looking for the places Steinbeck had travelled through, until he got to the West Coast where his last theatre appearance would take place. After several minutes, he placed the book and his notebook on the table and caught the eye of the man who was seated opposite him.

"Hi. Would you mind keeping an eye on these? I just want to get a map of America."

"Sure," the man replied. "Maps are back there."

"Thanks."

He made is way in the direction indicated and came across a shelf full of maps. Riffling through them, he came across a large, thick atlas of America with large-scale maps of each state on each spread and a fold-out map of the entire country inside the back cover. It was perfect for his purpose. He returned to the table, nodded his thanks to the man and started to flip through the book, a copy of which he had bought – and enjoyed – some years ago. Steinbeck had started his journey on Long Island, headed north-west, had turned around in Seattle, driven down to Salinas, his home town, then through the Mojave Desert to Texas before he headed back east. The play would move to the West Coast and when the run ended, Michael had planned on hiring a van, as Steinbeck had done, and following his route back to the East Coast. He had not mentioned this plan to Ria, thinking that she would not be keen on it and also thinking that he would need a long, long, break on his own before heading back home. Two hours of browsing through the book and marking the map accordingly and he had a firm grasp of the trip he would take. At one stage he sensed, rather than saw, Hank seething disapproval of him drawing on the atlas, but he ignored it. When he was satisfied, he took the book and the map back to the counter, behind which Hank was still seething.

"It's OK, Hank. I'm buying both books."

Hank took the books and flipped through the atlas, tut-tutting as he went.

"Listen, Hank. I'm going to follow Steinbeck's journey from the west to east. As a sort of homage to him – and Charley, of course."

Hank's reaction was well worth the teasing. He gaped, gasped and stuttered so much that he could hardly make out the invoice.

"Why?" he finally asked as he slipped the book into a paper bag.

"Why? The play finishes on the West Coast, so I'll buy a van, just like John's and—"

"John *Steinbeck!*"

Obviously only staff members of reputable bookstores had intimacy rights.

"John Steinbeck. And I'll go where he went. See what's changed and what has not. I might even buy a terrier to take with."

"*Poodle*. It was a poodle. A *standard* poodle."

"A poodle. Of course. Hank! You're a real bibliophile."

Hank blushed and simpered.

"I mean it. The days of scholarship are not over!"

"Well. We *are* in the purlieus of Harvard!"

"And the apples of knowledge do not fall outside the purlieu."

Michael left the bookshop and the still blushing Hank and

made his way back to the boarding house where he and several other leading members were staying.

The play had a week to run, and the houses and the actors' energy were both dwindling when Dominick appeared in Michael's dressing room as he and Ria were getting ready to depart.

"Going well?" he asked after he had greeted them.
"Slacking off a bit."
"To be expected. It's done well. Very well."
"Yes. It has."
"I've got a small chore for you both before the next run."
"Yes? Nothing strenuous, I hope."
"Just a little. I've organised a screen test for both of you."
"A screen test?"
"Yes."
"Is there any possibility of some screen work?" Ria asked excitedly.
"Let's not get ahead of ourselves. Since we will be in the land of The Movie, it makes sense to have a test. Just in case."
"You have some sneaky scheme up your sleeve."
"I just like to be prepared. The tests will be done in Los Angeles. I've located a reputable company there which has done tests for a few of the major studios. They know what's wanted in the industry. They have identified many stage actors in successful plays there and notified the movie studios. We'll head back there as soon as this run has finished."
"They asked me to do some final lectures at the college. The Prof—"
"Won't have time, I'm afraid. The tests are much more important for us all."

Dominick was gone in a flurry of goodbyes and hurried comments on the value of screen tests for actors such as they.

"He gets on my nerves sometimes. No. At all times," Michael hissed.

"Screen tests, though. Who knows what they will bring."

"I'm not interested in the movies."

"Ha! Just wait until some fat, cigar-smoking movie producer whispers in your ear."

"Ha!"

"Ha yourself."

"You started it."

"What?"

"The 'has'. Let's go. I need a drink."

"No. I'll go to the hotel. Bye."

She blew him a kiss and left. Michael finished packing away his make-up bits and pieces and went out. He exited at the stage door and walked along the lane towards Boylston Street which overlooked Boston Common, a place that had been the location of many events that had helped shape an emerging America. There were several drinking spots along the street, but a full moon hung overhead, wisped with flimsy clouds, and the common looked peaceful and inviting, so he decided he didn't need a drink, he needed some time to think, deeply. So, he crossed over the street and passed through one of the ornate gates. Inside there were stately trees, stretches of well-tended grass, bodies of water glinting in the moonlight and pathways that meandered among and around them. In the shadow of some of the trees, the silhouettes of courting couples were etched darkly against the stretches of lawn, and in the background, the lights of the many and varied buildings, including the ornate Colonial Theatre, twinkled obligingly. He crossed over one of the splendid bridges and stopped to look down into the calm lake water. The moon was reflected in it and a dark bird shape moved across it, leaving a dappled wake arrowing out on either side. He wondered at a bird being abroad so late and walked on in a peaceful mood. Dotted around were fountains, statues, gazebos, bandstands, some low buildings, and in the centre was the historic burying ground, its tombstones ever so slightly aslant, their moon shadows looking for all in the world like parallelogram pits. He stepped over the low-slung chain and strolled among the graves, feeling a deep sense of peace among Boston's revered dead. His life was very fast, very frantic and very exciting. He felt that the many roles he had played onstage were, for the most part – no – all the time, very satisfying and rewarding. The names on the tombstones, many obscured by time, put him in a pensive mood. Was this it? Was this as good as his life got? Would it be all downhill from now on? Would he carry on, beyond his energies and capabilities, until he ended up a worn-out barfly, boring everybody with hoary theatre jokes and meandering tales of the great roles he had played to thunderous applause? He thought of the many giants of theatre that he had admired so much and whom he had regularly come across, loud at parties, smug in restaurants, sentimental in pubs and lachrymose in their cups. He hoped to Christ that he wouldn't go that route. No, dammit, he would *not* go that route. Not he. Damned if he would. He would stay on top of the world.

He suddenly felt the blood pounding through his veins, the retinas of his eyes sparkling with clear visions, his heart pumping with excitement at the next challenge and success, his muscles taut in their pent-up strength, his male blood throbbing in his groin. He knew by Christ, that the sense of satisfaction and exhilaration he felt right now, among the tombstones, would never diminish. Never leave him. Never fade away. Never become a forlorn memory of past glories. This was *his* moment, among the long-mouldered corpses. This moment of profound self-satisfaction would – should – last forever. He looked round at the tombstones, some commemorating Boston's best and held sacred by the city. That's how he would go. That's how he would be buried. At the height of his powers. Buried with reverence and respect, to be fondly remembered by his peers and his fans.

A soft but persuasive gust of wind shook the trees and many leaves fell spiralling to the ground. A cloud flitted across the moon and its shadow dimmed the image of the tombstones. Then the wind was gone, and the leaves lay quietly, commencing their season of rotting and returning to the soil, unless the city authorities had them collected and carted away to some out-of-town civic dump. His introspective mood slowly faded. He left the burying ground and headed towards his hotel. As he crossed the street and passed by the theatre, the thought of Dominick came, unbidden, into his mind. So smug in his rightness. So condescending. So goddam in command.

And so in control of his – Michael's – life!

Chapter Twenty Six

The never-ending slope towards the setting sun is a well-beaten track to be wary of. Along and at the end of it, many dreams and hopes have stumbled and plummeted, to drown in the golden ocean.

The rest of the American trip was a hectic blur. The Boston run came to an end, and the company and the lead actors made their way towards the West Coast. They were to traverse the vast American hinterland by train and they, especially Michael, were keen to experience the American trains, huge, powerful vehicles that had supplanted the Conestoga and other, lighter, canvas-covered wagons that had transported pioneers across the vast plains up until little more than a century ago. They first had to catch a train at the fabled Grand Central Station in New York, familiar from many dramatic hellos and goodbyes in movies, to the vast Union Station in Chicago. That trip to Chicago was spectacular enough but to the west of that city, they boarded a Super Chief, a blunt-nosed giant diesel electric train sporting what was called War Bonnet paint, a starling red and yellow with two round snouts that stabbed, snorting, through the paint as if sniffing the steel of the two and a half thousand miles of track it had to gobble up. The stripes swooped along the carriages, like speed lines in a cartoon. The train was aggressive, intimidating, brutal and beautiful, operated by that historically redolent company The Atchison, Topeka and the Santa Fe. Michael found himself humming the catching melody and lyrics by Johnny Mercer as he, Ria and their co-actors boarded the fabled iron monster – called the train of the stars because of the number of film actors who used it as a vehicle on their to-and-fro trips to Hollywood – and sought their seats. They were soon walking through the Pullman-designed cars, sleepers, dining cars and the dome lounge to find their places. Once settled, they were greeted by the stewards and handed menus for the dining cars as the conductor yelled, "All Aboard!" This was followed by a loud snort from the engine, the slight but impatient slipping of the massive, flanged wheels as they sought for traction and the slow but increasing thrumming which would accompany them all through Illinois, Iowa, Missouri, Kansas, Colorado, New Mexico, Arizona and California.

Once outside of the yards and onto the westward-thrusting tracks, each crossing and small town was saluted by the deliciously hoarse train whistle which was to punctuate their journey to the far and fabled West. As he sat mesmerised in the dome lounge, with the Steinbeck book spread out face down on his lap, he conceded that America was indeed beautiful; the landscapes through which the Super Chief hurtled were spectacular. At one stage, the train closely hugged the shore of a lake, whilst, on the other side, a veritable wall of pines rose from beside the track towards the heavens; at another stage it snaked along a mighty trestle bridge around the bulge of a precipitous mountain and plunged through a sequence of peaks that towered higher and higher, reaching towards a startlingly blue sky. Then it thundered through a dry and desiccated gulch with ancient tortured and twisted trees clawing at the thin air and the totally unnecessary whistle added a note of anguish to the sandy gash among the barren hills. At another stage, it meandered through quintessentially Amish farms, with bronzed men walking behind ponderous horses, raising an arm at the train. Then the illimitable prairie unfolded on either side, grasses waving in the breeze as far as the eye could see. There was a suicidal plunge straight at a solid wall of striated rock, only to find, at the last second, the gaping mouth of a tunnel through which it rushed maniacally. Between this unfolding grandeur and the smaller world of small towns and cities described by Steinbeck in his Charley-accompanied sojourns, Michael was in love with this mind-boggling land.

They finally reached Los Angeles, Hollywood and the Beverley Hills Hotel where they thought they had died and gone to heaven. At least Ria did. Through the porticoed front lay an army of obsequious men in uniforms and beaming reception clerks who confirmed their bookings and sent them, graciously escorted, to their rooms on the fifth floor with spectacular views of the Pacific Ocean. They dumped their bags and sought the lobby to do some star-spotting and were rewarded with glimpses of several movie stars, some famous and others who acted as if they were. Then they caught a cab to the Hollywood Pantages Theatre where Howard Hughes had installed his personal offices after he had acquired it. Having been the venue of the Academy Awards and many blockbuster movies, it was, after substantial renovations, repositioning itself as a venue for lavish stage productions, the first of which had been the enormous, worldwide successful musical *Bubbling Brown Sugar* and *Cochise and the Trader* was the latest.

Two days after they arrived, as per instructions from Dominick, they made their way towards the Pacific Coast to the studios of Sage and Company which was positioned as 'A National Stage and Screen Resource'. The receptionist welcomed them and ushered them into an enormous office with a small studio taking up considerable space at the end. There was a central stool positioned in the studio section in front of a roll of white paper which hung from a roller on the back wall. Around the stool stood an assortment of lights of varying size, some with barn doors on them, some with metal snouts in front of them to focus the light and some with sheets of dark metal on adjustable arms secured to the stands. There were two stands supporting adjustable frames of tracing paper – scrims to subdue the light – with three rubber wheels in front of an enormous light. All of this Michael noted before he and Ria walked towards an enormous desk at the far end, behind which, wreathed in cigar smoke, sat a man with an enormous head who waved at them as they entered. As he slipped off his chair and padded towards them, his head dropped almost to the level of the desk.

"Ria and Michael. Welcome You have created quite a stir here in the States." (Puff.) "I'm Roscoe Sage – Mr. Stygfeldt suggested that you were both prime material for the goddam silver screen. And," (puff), "I agree so I'll do screen tests of you both." (Puff.)

Puffing away, he courteously ushered them to two remarkably low chairs that faced the desk. When they had taken their seats and Roscoe, returning to his side of the desk, had seated himself, their heads were on the same level. Except, that is, when he threw himself back on his swivels, his hands behind his head, his face sank perceptibly lower, occasioning them both to raise themselves to keep him in sight. Roscoe sucked wetly on his cigar and expelled the smoke straight at them. Silently he examined them both, puffing away. The silence was beginning to be embarrassing when he suddenly threw himself forward in his chair and stabbed the sodden end of his cigar at them.

"Now that I see you both close up, my instincts were right." (Puff.) "Correct. As they usually are."

His dialogue was constantly interspersed with puffs on the cigar which never seemed to get any shorter.

"Good bone structure. Nice planes and curves. Eyes not so deep. Lips well defined. And cheeks. Noses straight. Slightly flared. That's good." (Puff.) "Smile."

They did. A bit awkwardly, and he looked from one to the other.

"Wider. Good. That's good. *Stan!*"

The name was shouted so loud that they both started. The door opened and a tall, gangly man entered and slouched towards them.

"This is Stan. My cameraman. Hollywood trained." (Puff.) "Best in the goddam business. What do you think, Stan?"

Stan took a long, long look at them both, walking around them as he did so.

"Worth a test," he finally said.

"Stan's the man. He knows his job. OK, Stan. Let's do it."

He slid off his chair and led the way to the further end of his office.

"Ria first," he said.

He watched carefully as she took a seat and Stan had fiddled with the lights around her. Standing back a little, Michael saw that, quick as he was, Stan obviously knew his job. The scrim with the light behind it was turned towards the stool, high above and in front of her and the light switched on. A seamless wash of soft light fell on Ria, bathing her in its highly flattering benison.

"The key light," Roscoe whispered.

One of the lights on a low, low stand was pointed at the white backdrop and switched on. The light faded away behind the lower part of Ria's face, bringing her face forward as her upper torso sprang into prominence.

"For definition," Roscoe whispered.

Another light was position behind her on the opposite side and a soft halo materialised.

"Back light," came through the cigar smoke.

A small light with a diffuser in front was positioned in front of her illuminating face, bringing her well-defined cheekbones forward.

"Fill," came the explanation. "That's good. Perfect. Some stills please."

From nowhere, Stan produced a Roliflex stills camera and started shooting while Roscoe called out instructions.

"Smile. Broader. Laugh. Louder. Hold your hand in front of you mouth. Lower, show surprise. Astonishment. Anger. Rage. Good."

The instructions went on as Stan instructed her to turn her face in various directions, gave her focus points, including the lens, to look at and clicked away using up several rolls of film. Finally, Roscoe stopped it.

"Your turn, Michael."

Michael took Ria's place and went through the same gamut until Roscoe was satisfied.

"Enough stills. Get the Arri."

Stan pulled the loose sheet off an enormous movie camera, wheeled it forward, pointed it at Ria and started to pull focus.

"Arri. Thirty-five millimetre reflex. Best in the goddam business," Roscoe said, as Stan took a reading.

"OK, Ria," Roscoe said. "I want the full gamut. Starting with you crying."

"Crying?"

"Yes. When you're ready."

It took some time, but Ria went into herself and nodded at the Arri. Stan started the camera.

"Rolling," he said.

On cue with complete conviction, Ria started to cry, sobbing first and then building up to a proper cry, complete with tears.

"OK. Now laughter. Michael, stand over there and feed her."

Michael stood to one side and made faces at her, waggling his ears, picking his nose, sticking out his tongue and Ria responded convincingly until Roscoe was satisfied. He then grunted at Stan who produced a sheet of paper which was affixed to a stiff board. On it was some puerile dialogue. Comic strip words about loving somebody forever. Then about hating somebody's guts for killing her lover. Then some 'disaster' dialogue about a block of apartments – the whole block being on fire. Ria memorised the word instantly and delivered them with an impressive passion, rage and fear, respectively, as the dialogue suggested.

Then it was his turn.

When the photo session was finished, Stan left silently, and Roscoe escorted them back to his desk and pressed a button on his intercom. When the thin voice of the receptionist who had escorted them in answered, he ordered coffee for three and settled himself back in his chair. He tossed away his sodden cigar and lit another. Michael and Ria sat forward in their seats and stretched their necks until the smoke-enshrouded head came into view. Roscoe sucked on the cigar with energy until it was well and truly lit and the smoke enveloped him in its murky depths.

"The purpose of the screen test is to find out if the camera loves you. If it doesn't, you don't have a career in the goddam movies. The average mouth is two to three inches across. A pursing of the lips, or a sneer, or a snarl or a shout does funny things to the average mouth. Twists, bumps, and stretches we see, and we understand at the usual social distance. We read the lips and we know the mood of the person and what he or she is thinking. It helps understanding and meaning. We look, we read and we know the mood of the person when he's at arm's length. If he is further away, say the length of the average theatre, we are not sure of the mouth, so we look at the body for meaning. You stage actors are good at using your body and your movements to show your mood. And that's fine. It works. Has done for years. But..."

The receptionist came in and Roscoe paused as she dispensed the coffee and cream and sugar and departed.

"But," continued Roscoe, "on the movie screen that mouth can be six to ten feet across. Every twitch, ever pursing, ever opening and shutting is as big as a goddam streetcar. And your face? As big as a goddam baseball diamond. So, every expression has to be true. You understand? Goddam true. Else you won't make it in the business. Got it?"

They got it.

Chapter Twenty Seven

Sometimes your looks are tested and sometimes your mettle. One is an ineluctable arrangement of the epidermis; the other is a confusing whorl of the mind.

Later that day, Michael was handed a message at reception. It was from Roscoe explaining that the screen tests were available for viewing, so he and Ria arrived at Roscoe's premises the next morning. After being subjected to several lungfuls of his cigar smoke, Roscoe escorted them to a small, steeply raked screening room and suggested that they sit in the back row. Stan's head poked around the corner and surveyed them blankly.

"Ready?"

"Ready," Roscoe bellowed, and the lights dimmed, and a leader strip appeared on the screen, followed by Roscoe's company logo and the titles: 'Screen Test. Ria Van Vuuren and Michael Driscoll. Sage and Company'. Onto the screen came Ria's face in close-up and in the small theatre, it was overwhelming. She looked lovely and the expressions on her face were powerful – her crying, her smiling, her laughter and her rage were utterly convincing. She delivered the banal dialogue with sensitivity and panache. She shone on the screen and Michael was stunned. Her test was closely followed by Michael's, and he was slightly disturbed at how mercilessly the camera captured his face. He looked much older than he thought he looked. His face was drawn and the creases around his eyes, which he had always considered charming and sophisticated, looked deeper, sagged more and were those of a much older man. More than that, he felt he was unconvincing. When the film ran out and the lights went up, Roscoe, who was seated further down, turned around and asked them what they thought. The looked at each other for a moment and both were rather overwhelmed. Roscoe was silent, giving them time to absorb the tests.

"You look great," Michael finally said.

"So do you."

"No. I look old."

"Old? You don't!"

"I do. All that face-pulling is obviously bad for the face."

"It's always a shock," Roscoe said. "I've had people threatening to commit goddam suicide after a viewing."

"Shouldn't we have used some make-up for these tests?" Michael asked.

"Never! They're experts on make-up here in Hollywood. They'd spot it a mile away. They expect honesty and that's what we give them. If you want my opinion…"

They did.

"Ria, you're goddam gorgeous. They'll love you for roles from mid-twenties up. You, Michael, are suitable for roles older than you expected. Yours is a middle-aged face. Strong, expressive. Great for dozens of good roles. So, swallow you pride. You're what they're looking for. You both are. Now I'll send prints off to some studio heads as per Mr. Stygfeldt's instructions. Anything else?"

"Can we have some prints of the stills?" Ria asked.

"Sure you can. I'll order them and have them sent around in the next few days. Anything else?"

There was nothing else so they both left.

Outside Roscoe's premises, they stood and looked at each other in silence for a long time. Finally, Ria spoke.

"What did you think?"

"Interesting. I suppose."

"Is that all you've got to say?"

"Well… it's a bit… disillusioning."

"Yes. The movie was merciless. I look so…worn."

"You looked great. You looked your age. Lovely and interesting."

"So did you."

"Those wrinkles. Don't suppose they matter on the stage but in close-up!"

"As I said, merciless."

"It's more than that. It's as if I was… pretending."

"Well, you are. It's called acting."

"I felt that my face was a mask. I've never felt like that before."

"That's why they use masks as symbols."

"It's… look I don't want to go back yet. I need to walk on that beach. A long walk. Want to come?"

"No. I'll go back to the hotel. I need a long soak in that massive bath."

"OK. See you later."

"Yes."

They kissed perfunctorily and Michael headed for the Pacific while Ria went bathwards. The walk to the beach seemed endless, and Michael tried to cope with the black mood that seemed to envelope him. By the time the Pacific came into view, the mood seemed impenetrable. Into his mind came the sobering thoughts he had had in the burying ground on Boston Common. Was this slightly unreal American tour the zenith of his career, as far as he would ever, *could* ever get? Was this lifestyle at risk? A life for which he had been striving, ever since he had smeared coal dust and lipstick on his face and regaled his mother and siblings with an Al Jolson rendition of the song 'Mammy', grovelling on his knees, wiping his eyes, blowing his nose on the tablecloth as he writhed in deep, down south anguish. Ever since he had held 'concerts' in the family garage for kids in the street (admission one penny). Ever since he had joined every amateur dramatics society in his part of town. Sought and fought for minor parts in professional theatres up and down the country. Slept in grotty boarding houses in grimy towns while performing myriad roles in repertory theatre. Clawing his way up through anxious auditions, heart-stopping opening nights and deflating (or exhilarating) last nights. And finally, he had made it. Good roles had come, increasingly better roles, deeply satisfying roles until he was known, wanted and approached by producers whom he had fruitlessly courted on his way up. Was it all on the cusp? Was a vertiginous plunge awaiting? He arrived at the beachfront and stopped and looked at the mighty ocean at which stout Cortez had stared with his eagle eyes and looked on his men in wild surmise – silent upon a beach in Darien. Christ! He was quoting again! Had he a voice of his own? Had he left his real self, the deep core of himself, on too many stages? Was he only a playwright's make-believe cypher, a mouthpiece for the writer's concept of life? Was he a projection of the hundreds of characters he had studied, got to know and got to perform for the benefit of a shadowy and demanding audience out there in the dark? Was that fucking thirty-five millimetre Arri the merciless revealer, the stripper of illusions, the unmasker with eagle eyes that were not to be fooled? Was the Arri the ultimate arbiter, avenging all those years of pretence, saying, 'thus far and not further, buddy. No fooling my lens. No hiding behind character on my vast cinema screen. That screen is perfectly reflective. It doesn't absorb your image. It scatters it in all directions. But mostly throws it at the audience. So that they'll see the *real* you. Not some make-believe character. But you. Warts and all. What do you think of that, Buddy?'.

  He stopped and looked around. Sunset Boulevard. Christ! They were all boulevards around here. No honest-to-God streets. It would take him to his hotel eventually, so he had time to think this out properly. Flog himself maybe but he had to get it straight in his mind once and for all, as straight as this fucking boulevard.

Back in his mental burrowing he came to the inescapable fact that this latter part of his career, the part that could – would – finally reward all his efforts was initiated, created and organised by Dominick Stygfeldt, the arch manipulator. Funny how he had appeared at exactly the right time, while he was basking in the righteous glow of the Arena and dwelling in the penumbra of poverty on its remuneration. What temptations Dominick threw at him! Dazzling. Financially rewarding. Irresistible. The sumptuous supper. The cajoling. The roaring success of the play. The adulation of the audiences and the press. The money. Ria and the *Paradyse* estate, the boat, the lifestyle, the first American trip. The realisation that it was all – all – within his grasp. Some prices to pay of course, having to change his citizenship, being offered specially *approved* roles. OK. So the first of these had been great, *good* for his career, very well paid, but he knew, deep down where he seldom delved, that the roles were going to change to suit the government's agenda, not the agenda of Michael Driscoll. He would, when the time came, be called upon to present some obnoxious political and social scheme as a theatrical anodyne. And there would be very little he could do about it. The movie industry might offer a way out. An alternative lifestyle that Dominick couldn't dominate.

And speak of the devil…

Chapter Twenty Eight

Beware the low-swinging chariot that comes to carry you home because, like it or not, the piper must be paid.

A massive, eye-popping red behemoth pulled up silently next to the kerb and who was seated in the nearside back seat, puffing on a huge cigar but Dominick Stygfeldt, basking in opulent leather luxury and emitting self-satisfied contentment.

"Michael! Just the man. Hop in, I'll drive you back."

Hiding a grin at the unadulterated vulgarity of the motor car, Michael crossed behind it to the far door, ducking as he passed the swooping massive fins that reached up to his waist, and noticing the double grill at the back, with the beautifully scripted Cadillac logo above it. He bet that the grill at the front would be more spectacular. The immaculate, white-walled tyres, peeking out from under the embracing side panel, caught his eye as he reached for the handle of the rear door, but it anticipated him and whispered open to reveal the same glossy, red-coloured leather inside. The uniformed chauffer nodded regally at him as he entered the cavernous interior. The upholstery reached up to embrace his nether regions as he slid towards Dominick's graciously outstretched hand. The door closed silently behind him, and his ears popped as the door closed to seal in the cold air and the cigar smoke. The car slid away from the kerb, as silently as he expected.

"Well? What do you think?" asked Dominick.

"Of what?" Michael's mind was still dwelling on his career.

"Of the car? I was speaking of the car. It's a Cadillac Eldorado. A V8. I'm thinking of buying one, taking it back home. What do you think?"

Without waiting for a reply, Dominick stroked the back of the seat in front of him.

"The yanks know how to make a car," he said. "They're saying that this model may be phased out soon. They're mad."

As Dominick started to speak like an American car advert and pointing out all the luxurious details, Michael took a hard look at him. He was handsome, no doubt about that but there was a hardness in his gaze as he looked around the interior and the creases on either side of his eyes looked as hard and sharp as crumpled metal. His hair swooped back over his ears, just like the swooping hood of the car, and Michael realised that he had never, ever seen a hair out of place on Dominick's sculpted scalp. There was a boyish excitement in his voice as he extolled the details of the car, but the expression on his face didn't change. It was as controlled and expressionless as it always was. There seemed to be no person behind the physiognomy. Even this childish admiration of the car didn't affect the facial features. Was there, in fact, any real person inside? Dominick stopped speaking and his eyes sought Michael's. There was an awkward pause and Michael realised that he had been asked a question.

"What... er... sorry. I was still thinking about the car. I mean... what it would be like to swan around in it back home. And the streets.... I mean, they're not designed for a car this size. I... I'd get a nosebleed every time I climbed into it. Besides, I don't have a flying licence. But... but it suits you, Dominick. You're image... perfect. Perfect for your image."

Dominick didn't reply. He gazed out through the window as they approached the hotel and nodded as the hotel concierge ran down the steps and reached for the door handle of the Cadillac Eldorado but was slightly disconcerted as the door anticipated him and whispered open. Michael stepped out and turned to thank Dominick, but he was looking straight ahead as the door closed and the vehicle oozed its silent way back into the traffic. Michael entered the hotel in a pensive mood. Had he, for a moment, seen through Dominick's careful carapace? Had his carefully contrived persona slipped? Was he not what he appeared to be? Could he be trusted? He caught sight of Ria, talking to the receptionist, so he shrugged off his gloomy presentiments and fixed a smile on his face as he approached. The receptionists looked at him and smiled, and Ria turned.

"Good. I have just booked us into the very best Chinese restaurant in Hollywood, The Formosa Café."

"It's *the* place to eat Chinese," the receptionist butted in. "Bogart and Gable used to eat there."

"And," Ria enthused, "Sinatra mourned Ava Gardner there, night after night. Imagine."

"Sounds great," Michael replied and tried to shake off his uncomfortable thoughts.

Ria grabbed his arm and thanked the receptionist before pulling him through the back of the hotel to where the swimming pools cooled off the clientele.

"You OK?"

"Yeah. I'm fine."

"You look a bit sad."

"No. Not sad. A bit… overwhelmed, I guess. What with the glitz and the glamour."

"Yes. It's a bit over the top. How was your walk? How was the Pacific?"

Michael made a big effort to be cheerful.

"Big and wet. Dominick dropped me off outside. He picked

me up as I was walking back. You won't believe the car he was in. Big – enormous – glaringly red. Fins you wouldn't believe. A million feet in length. He's seriously considering buying one and taking it back home."

"Just like Dominick."

"Is it? I suddenly realised that I don't know him at all."

"But he's been a big part of your life for so long."

"Yes. He has. But I don't know him. Not really. I feel sometimes that he's… well… sort of luring me along. Offering me things. Opportunities. Fame. I'm beginning to feel sort of threatened. Strange feeling."

"Yes. It is strange. You'll feel better when the show opens, and we get back to normal."

"Normal. Yes. That's the point. It's not normal. It's living by proxy. I'm not Michael Driscoll. I'm whatever character I'm pretending to be."

"That's your job. Pretending. It's what you get paid for. Paid well too, I might add."

"Impersonations," Michael, who had not been listening, said. "We do impersonations. Like those stand-up comedians. I put on some face paint and do an impersonation of an early American Indian trader who, perhaps, did exist once but he sure as hell didn't look like me. The Professor invented his words, made them up. Made Cochise a drunkard when I know and he knew that he died of cancer and that only Jeffords, my character and the remaining Apaches, know where he's buried. So I lean on my fake musket and look profound and pretend that I'm telling the truth about American history."

"You did the same back home."

"But back home it was true that the king died a drunkard, poor bastard. But here they seem to play fast and loose with their own history."

"But why should it worry you? It all happened so long ago."

"As long ago as Achilles? As Alexandra the Great, as Saint

Joan, as Caesar, as Napoleon, as Lawrence of fucking Arabia?"

"Michael!" You're being ridiculous."

He sighed at the enormous burden on his spirit.

"Perhaps I am. Sorry. I got into a strange mood on that walk."

"You certainly did. Now this is the last evening we have to ourselves before the opening. Let's try to enjoy ourselves. OK?"

"OK. I'll take a nap. Sleep this mood off and go and see the movie stars at the…"

"Formosa Café."

"Maybe we'll see Clark Gable and Humphrey Bogart there."

"They're both dead."

"Are they? Nobody told me. Well, maybe we'll see Sinatra mourning Ava."

"Maybe."

A few run-throughs, a rather stilted rehearsal with the orchestra, copious notes from the acting director and the opening night, all this seemed to happen at once. On the day, professionalism kicked in; they were all in harness; and the show was a success, judging by the applause during the performance and the enthusiasm in the dressing rooms afterwards. Some familiar faces to which they could not place names, came in, dispensed manly hugs and female air kisses all round and swore that they had never seen anything as fine – ever. Dominick was in best grand seignour mode, faultlessly remembering names and roles in movies and introducing the right people to the right people with consummate ease. No doubt about it, he was a social master as he dispensed empty promises to all and sundry. When his dressing room finally emptied, Michael took a shower and dressed slowly, promising Ria that he would join her, Dominick and some appropriate celebrities in the bar. When he was fully dressed, he sat looking at his image in the mirror and dwelling on his performance. It had been strange. He had been detached, scrutinising his performance as if he had been standing stage front and looking at Michael Driscoll being an actor being Tom Jeffords the Indian Trader. It had been unsettling. It had been faultless – on the outside – but he, and only he, it seemed, had seen the shield, the cover, the veneer, the sheer make-believe with which he had enveloped himself. Each movement, each expression, each line of dialogue was delivered as decreed by the author, the historic – albeit invented – facts and the director but he, Michael Driscoll, knew that it was all a sham. All so easy. Summoned up by his training and his experience – as an actor and not as a real character. The eyes were dead, the facial expressions mechanical, impeccably timed but as far away from real emotion as to constitute some kind of caricature of human nature. All created by unadulterated technique. Stage technique. But the fucking Arri had seen through this make-believe and denied him the incipient rewards of Hollywood. Had discovered the fraud. The fact that each important line of dialogue and each movement that he had carefully devised and imbued with the 'magic' of his technique was in no way susceptible to the merciless scrutiny of the thirty-five-millimetre lens and would not survive the presentation of the powerful projector onto the monster, highly reflective screen in a giant movie house. He had always used mirrors while preparing for and working in his professional life, to give him a sense of distance from himself. To imbue his face-pulling skills with a degree of objectivity so that he could measure his skill at pretence, at being somebody else, but the degree of scrupulous and totally objective examination that the Arri subjected him to was terrifying. Stan was a competent cameraman and knew the rudiments of lighting a face, but he was no Josef von Sternberg. He revealed the human face in a professionally competent way but was not a master of the subtle lighting that helps capture the emotions behind the acting, so Michael's face would join all the other casting submissions and slide through the system without a ripple. So it appeared that this final and devoutly to be desired pinnacle of his career

– Hollywood success – would be denied him. His musings on Boston Common were being answered. That was as good as it would get for him. Ria, on the other hand, had that indefinable ability to bring her emotion – whatever she decided it to be at that moment – to the surface, and the Arri had recognised that and recorded it for posterity or at least for the Hollywood producers. He shook the mood off with difficulty and headed for the bar.

"Here he is! The finest actor of his generation." Dominick had acquired the West Coast hyperbole and dispensed it with West Coast conviction, as to the manner born. Michael was welcomed noisily and had a drink thrust into his hand as he was hugged, pounded, kissed and fondled by people he had never seen before in his life. He managed to keep most of the drink in his glass and managed to reflect the unutterable joy that he felt in meeting them all and how much they all meant to him. He managed to catch a glimpse of Ria's wry grin as he made his way through the throng to join her.

"The finest actor of his generation," she murmured as he joined her and turned to face the accolades. They were many and varied as each sought to outdo the others in exaggeration. He responded with as much sincerity as he could summon up and slipped back into the introspective mood that had come over him in the dressing room. He watched himself as he had on stage earlier and there it was again, the carapace that separated him from the supposedly real world that these fawning strangers inhabited. He saw his own conditioned responses to their exuberance and marvelled at it as he tossed back two martinis in as many minutes. Ria glared at him warningly and sipped hers. After several long, long minutes, the crowd tired of such unresponsive recipients of their precious adulation and turned on each other for acknowledgement and, for sustenance, to their strangely unbalanced cocktail glasses, wide-bowled to ensure that the chilled aroma of the drink reached their noses as quickly and potently as possible. With the fumes and potency doing their work with the crowd, Michael caught Ria's eye and nodded towards the door. She nodded back and followed him as he sidled out. In the corridor they were confronted by a stern-faced Dominick.

"Where do you think you're going?" he barked.

"We're both tired," Ria said. "Opening nights, you know."

"That crowd in there is a ticket to the attention of Hollywood. They're important people. Their attention is an indication that you have come to town. They're—"

"They're all pissed," Michael barked back, and Dominick stiffened.

"Inebriated or not, you need *their* attention to get the attention of the theatrical community out here."

"Well, I'm tired," Michael said in a mollifying tone as he turned away.

"So I noticed."

Michael stopped and faced Dominick.

"I noticed that your heart wasn't in it tonight," Dominick said.

"Dominick!" Ria said. "I thought that Michael was—"

"Michael wasn't there. Were you Michael?"

"I was! They loved it and me. Their curtain calls—"

"Oh, they loved your technique. You're timing. You're singing. But you weren't there. Not fully there. You fooled them but not me."

They were all silent as Michael absorbed this. *The bastard!* he thought. *He's like the Arri. I wonder if he saw the screen test.*

Dominick stared at him silently as if in doubt as to whether he would continue speaking or not. The silence hung heavily on them all until Dominick took a deep breath.

"Why?" he asked and paused as they focused their complete attention on him. "Why do you think I took you – Michael – from the Arena to the Hollywood Pantages Theatre?"

"Because it's your job. You're a promoter. You promote."

"And you are a product."

They were both silent. Michael because he was offended and Ria because Dominick was focused totally on Michael and she was feeling left out.

"*My* product. You were good. I could see that very early on. And I plotted the path of your advancement carefully. Through the shows that defined your future and cemented your career and fan base. Then the big one, *The King and the Colonist*. That got you onto the international stage with *Cochise and the Trader*, after I had prepared the ground and drummed up the finances. New York, Boston and Hollywood, a carefully thought-out progression leading up to the movies. That was where all my efforts and all the investment would pay off: Michael Driscoll, the movie star! But theatre has devoured you, like a sow that eats its farrow. You have become *pure* theatre. All bombast and acting. All surface. No depth. Depth, depth, depth, is what the movies demand. Tonight your performance was flawless, but there was no depth. The audience was unaware, but you can't fool a screen test. You are fearless on stage but not on camera. I really thought you would be. But I was wrong. I have embargoed the test. No Hollywood producer will see it. They'll wonder why, but I'll divert them. They will believe that you feel you are not ready to go on film because that is what I will tell them. They're used to big egos out here, so they will find nothing strange in that explanation. They will wait until you change your mind but, of course, you never will. Now go back in there and mix. You need those people for your theatrical career. You too, Ria."

"I was going to ask you how I fit into this Svengali scheme of yours," she said.

"Svengali. Yes. That's apt. You are beautiful my dear and good movie material but not great, I'm afraid, so we will not waste our energy on that. You both have great theatre careers awaiting back home and, occasionally, on the world's stages. But when this run ends it is back home for all of us. Now off you go. Mingle. I have a meeting with a publisher who will assure us of great reviews. Goodnight."

He was gone, and they looked at each other with varying degrees of ire and disappointment.

Chapter Twenty Nine

If the fullness of life is the stuff of cinema, then the emptiness of life is the stuff of theatre, but print encapsulates the accolades of the future.

The run at the Pantages Theatre was painful for them both, and Ria had to battle to get her performance up to scratch for each showing. Michael found it easier, due to his strange new detachment, but Ria struggled each evening, and backstage and at intervals, Michael devoted much of his energy to building her confidence. Unexpectedly, the Professor arrived during the second week of the run. He bustled into Ria's dressing room where Michael was giving her his nightly reassurance, hugged Ria and shook Michael's hand with vigour and insisted that they come for a drink in the bar. Ria wanted to opt out, but the Professor insisted. He had some news for them both. The news he brought, which he had to bottle up while several people in the bar who had attended the show proffered their congratulations and drinks, was that he had written both versions of the play for publication and that an international firm of publishers had undertaken to publish them in one volume. The Professor sipped at his glass of red wine, winced, and, settling down as if for a good old lecture, explained the motivation for the book.

"Those two plays of mine are a demonstration of the importance of story in mankind's development. Story is the foundational fabric of humankind's psychology. The human child is fed the epics, the lives of heroes and nursery or fairy tales in early life. The more perspicacious of them will absorb the knowledge and values that they illustrate; the less intelligent will merely be entertained. However..." he paused for professorial effect, "...the rest of humankind will only achieve the intended impact if they are in printed form. The play, laudable as it is, and important as it has been in entertaining and educating humans, is limited by its very spontaneity and ephemerality. The great works Homer, Herodotus, Aristophanes survive because of their ubiquity in each of their societies, but later storytellers such as Thomas Mallory and his knights, Shakespeare, Hans Christian Anderson, the Brothers Grimm, even Scheherazade, survived in much bigger societies than the ancients had to contend with. And they survived for all time because of the greatest invention in history, printing from moveable type. Yes. Gutenberg gave us writers immortality and printing became the mother of revolution and thought. Books are imperishable, despite many efforts to destroy them, because the censors cannot burn every book in the world. And any dispute about Shakespeare can only be resolved with the printed word, not with the stage performance. Theatre can popularise stories and help disseminate them, as did the griots, the poets and the theatre, but they are all transient, as indeed film will prove to be. So, I will submit my work, however humble, to print."

He tossed off his wine, grimaced again and turned to the slightly stunned actors in expectation. Michael was the first to recover.

"Erm... yes. Well. I'm delighted, of course," he said. "Your work deserves printing, but the plays, the actual performances, did they... well, launch them?"

"Of course they did. And very successfully too. And a big Hollywood movie would have worked its magic too, on the *Cochise* one of course."

"A movie?" said Michael, and Ria perked up too.

The Professor caught the attention of a hovering waiter and asked for a Bourbon.

"Look what they've done with history in Hollywood. They have John Wayne and Alan Ladd resurrecting the heroes of the West, their great national myth. And what about *Cleopatra* with Burton and Liz Taylor and *Camelot*, a musical like mine. Of course they all had big movie stars. Heady stuff."

"Has Dominick said anything about the movie plans?"

"Oh, there are no plans. Not yet. Just ideas. Concepts. To get the juices flowing as they say. They say – the indefinable 'they' – that every major male actor, and/or their agent, is expressing interest in your role, Michael. Your's too, Ria, but not to the same extent. That's how they go to market here in Hollywood. 'Run it up the flag, to see if anyone salutes it', as one scriptwriter had it."

He sipped his drink and surveyed the two of them.

"But why," he asked between sips, "do you think he brought the play to Hollywood?"

They all sipped, Ria wistfully, Michael wryly and the Professor rather smugly.

"I suppose you thought Dominick was in search of a somebody to help make the show into a blockbuster movie."

"Well, I wouldn't have been surprised if—"

"Well, he tried. He really tried. It would have been a huge feather in his cap. But…"

"Well?"

"Well, without one of them on board no project of this nature has a chance in hell of being made. They all agreed to meet him – and me – because he has not *yet* wrinkled my rights out of my hands. So he had no alternative but to include me in all the negotiations. I attended all the meetings."

He drained his drink and beckoned for another.

"Dominick had got possession of the music rights, of course. Bullied the composer and musical director, Dick Black, out of all rights. He offered such a sum that Dick Black couldn't resist because he thought it was fabulously generous and it was, for the local run, but not the American performances which was infinitely more. He was putty in Dominick's hands."

The bourbon arrived, and he gulped half of it.

"But he couldn't bully me out of *my* rights. Anyway, after having had meetings with some of the serious producers here, he approached the really heavy thugs in the business, the ones who run the studios. The heads. These are the moguls. They have egos the size of an average American state. One particular example of the breed, who shall be nameless, is five feet nothing, and his huge office is an exercise in one-upmanship. The floor slopes subtly from the entrance to the far end where his desk is. As if the trek to his desk were not enough, that desk, which is of aircraft carrier dimensions, is on a dais. The walk from the entrance to the four chairs that face him is a lesson in humility. By the time you are seated, peering at his head which barely emerges above the desk…"

"We've been in one place like that. It's weird," Michael interjected.

"…but strangely effective. When you are finally seated. The head tilts; the divine countenance shines upon you; the basilisk stare pins you to your seat; and his beatitude waits for you to speak first."

"You were there with Dominick?"

"Yes."

"How did he cope with it?"

"Exceptionally well. He stared back. Expressionless. And waited."

The Professor paused, smiling slightly.

"And?"

"He waited until *I* was beginning to fidget."

"And!!!"

"The head spoke first, and I could see it hurt."

The Professor sighed and finished his drink.

"But it did no good. The fact that the head spoke first was gratifying, but it only increased the venom with which it refused all involvement. I tell you Mr. Dominick fucking Stygfeldt has met his match, several times over. They're hard-hearted bastards, the heads, the lot of them. All – *all* – of them wanted total control. *Total*. The rights to the final shooting script, the casting, the director. Everything. They would pay him vast amounts of money and major slices of what they call 'the back end'. They would pay me too. Damn. It would have been vast. But…"

Another drink, another signal to the barman.

"So, no deal?"

"No deal. Dominick wants to control everything too. That's his style, and I don't think anybody out here really understood that. Or maybe they did. Damn! But he tried hard. Damn hard."

So, having given up his dream – perhaps that was too solemn a word – his hope of a Hollywood career, Michael buckled down to the run and did his job, if not to the best of his abilities, then to best of his inclinations. Ria too, was disappointed, and her performance was almost faultless, insofar as she carried out her duties as an actress, but the inner fire was not there. Her and Michael were aware of their shortcomings, but the audiences were obviously not. They kept coming and applauding and being as congratulatory as ever after the show, but it became more and more difficult for both of them to immerse themselves totally into character as they had earlier in the run. But nobody seemed to notice or, if they did, seemed not to care. The director who had taken over from the person who had steered them through New York and Boston, seemed too intimidated by them both to take remedial action. The other members of the cast caught their mood and the show started to flag and loosen, but it carried on, night after night, filling the house and getting good, if infrequent, notices all through the run. Michael and Ria featured frequently on radio and TV and in the magazines and that covered up the cracks as it were, but all in all, they eagerly anticipated the end of the run. The entire company soldiered on, but it was energy sapping, and most of them looked forward to the closing night. It was a strange experience for Michael to see how ennui could sap the soul of a show. He was professional enough to deliver a faultless performance each and every night. Every line of dialogue, every movement and every song were delivered as written and devised. But inwardly he was shocked how completely the joy had disappeared. He was drinking too much after each show, woke up every morning with a thick head and a furry tongue, and the relationship between him and Ria faded until they were polite to each other but that was all.

Throughout all this time, Dominick was nowhere to be seen.

Chapter Thirty

The end of a play is the end of a surrogate existence. All that's left is the memory of the pretence, and if that dish is eaten cold, it sits lead-like in the belly. The dessert comes when it's all over.

"Thanks be to Christ that's over!" Michael bellowed as he reached Ria's dressing room where she was changing her clothes. She had thrown the stage costumes into a corner where they lay in an untidy heap.

"And I don't have to wear those clothes ever, ever again," she cried. "Michael, will we ever get our joy of acting back again?"

She was distraught and very teary.

"Don't worry. We're just sick and tired of this show, not of theatre."

"Are you sure?"

He took her in his arms.

"Yes. Very sure. We're thoroughbreds. Not cut out for long-distance slogging. This show was exhausting and with Dominick to boot. We should have used those two stand-ins more. That would have relieved the pressure."

"But you refused to consider them."

"Yes, I did. Pride, I suppose."

"And now what?"

"A drink. With the gang."

So they went to the bar where all the cast and some of the crew were closing the show in fine theatrical manner. The place was humming, and the moods varied from sadness to relief that the American run was over. Dominick had opened a tab and it was being honoured in fine style. It was customary for somebody such as Dominick to make a closing speech of gratitude, but the Professor took the duty upon himself so, with assistance from some of the actors, he mounted a table and held his hands aloft until he was noticed by some present who shushed the rest to silence.

"It behoves me to make the closing address at the end of what has been a remarkable tour," the Professor began. "I am proud of you all, and you should be proud of yourselves. All of you. The show was complicated and multifaceted, and through it all, I was – and still am – delighted by the performances. For the most part, it went like clockwork and the screw-ups were as one would expect from such a demanding show. As creator of this and the home country version, it is my privilege to say that a milestone in theatrical development has been created. The shows will take well-deserved places in history. I know that some of you were hoping that one of the Hollywood producers or studio heads would take up a movie option. This has not happened. Yet. But hope springs eternal and the possibility still remains. Both versions will go into print, thanks to the keen interest of an international publisher, and the publication of the shows in print form may, perhaps, motivate a movie. But beware, in Hollywood one can actually die of encouragement. So sufficient unto the day the rewards thereof. Once again, thank you and travel safely to your homes, wherever they happen to be, overseas or in this many-tapestried land."

To loud applause, the Professor was helped to the ground and embraced, and his hands were shook by all and sundry until he finally extricated himself and sought Michael at a corner table.

A drink was waiting for the Professor which he raised in salute to Michael and downed. Michael sipped his drink.

"So, what are your plans?" he asked.

"I'm off on a long cruise in the Pacific Ocean," replied the Professor. "I need a break from large countries full of large egos, larger delusions of grandeur and absolutely enormous misconceptions of who, what and how they are. I hear that you are contemplating a drive back across the States."

"Yes. Contemplating is the word. I haven't quite made up my mind."

"And the motivation for this odyssey?"

"I read Steinbeck's *Travels with Charley* and thought it would be a fun way to wind up my American experience."

"You will be grossly disappointed. The Great American Experience is far from fun, according to Steinbeck. He found American society oblivious to its surroundings – which is remarkable – its life – which is surprising – and its culture – which is understandable because, except for a few pockets on either coast, there is none. He said that Sitting Bull was the last person to be infatuated with the land and prepared to fight for it to the bitter end."

"Well, I thought his trip would be a good guide."

"To what? To a coast-to-coast conformity and a belief that speaking out against the government was blasphemy? We both have experience of such civil obedience. It's stifling."

"Well, it *is* a beautiful country. The land, the enormity of the mountain ranges, the—"

"All to be observed from a comfortable seat in a luxurious train."

"Yes. I *was* impressed on the way here."

"And so you should be. You saw America at 'see' level, through the windows of a comfortable train. Steinbeck was inspired by the resilience of life but only in the Mojave Desert, for Christ's sake! He was disillusioned almost everywhere else. Wastefulness.

Alienation. Fear of communism. Discontent with where they were, always wanting to be somewhere else or obsessing about how wonderful it would be. He felt lost. In a lost society. The only place that made a deep impression on him was New Orleans, and that was because of the invective that came with the integration efforts there."

"Thanks. You make it sound *such* fun."

"Listen. You and I know all too much about the fear that exists where differences between races are manifest. Fear about differences in how people *look* is, in a morbid way, understandable. But to fear and actively oppose the differences in what people *do* or are anticipated to do is where the real hatred exists. That is the dark, festering underbelly of humanity."

"Professor! Such invective! I thought you were a philosophical sort of person."

"Philosophical? Yes. I am. I can take most of the foibles and foolishness of people in my stride. It's just that every so often, I have to break my stride, move across and void the contents of my stomach on the side of the beaten track."

Michael was taken aback with the Professor's vehemence. He had always considered him a studious man with his emotions firmly under control. He watched as the Professor downed his drink and called for another. He caught Michael's startled look and laughed.

"Good," said Michael. "It's good to hear you laugh."

"And if the laugh is bitter, I'll laugh at the laugh. Thank you."

The 'thanks' was for the drink that the attentive waiter placed in front of him.

"The one thing you can't fault the Americans for is service. Where were we? Oh, yes. Fear and hatred of the actions of the 'others', whoever they happen to be. It's been around ever since man started to think. Take the Christians for example. Leaving aside the convoluted scriptural and doctrinal differences, just consider the way they make the sign of the cross on their bodies.

The Western Christians do it with an open palm, moving the hand from the left shoulder to the right. Whereas the Christians from the East do it with three fingers held together, to represent the trinity, and move the hand from the right shoulder to the left."

In spite of himself, Michael crossed himself to probe the Professor's proposition.

"And take that other crucial point of difference, the direction of Mecca and Jerusalem. In the Middle East, when you prayed, you faced in the direction of one of the other, depending on your beliefs. You observed the religious proprieties and bowed according to the strict structures – oops! that's hard to say – of your priest, mufti or rabbi. In the mosques of the world, there is a niche in the wall that faces the Kaaba. That's all very well, but from Western Europe or the United States, from where the exact direction of one holy site is indistinguishable from the other, who the hell cares? Well, millions do. And look at the way men and women button their garments, left over right for men and right over left for the distaff. Woe betide that couturier who gets that wrong. This obsession with the 'correct' actions was best exemplified by Jonathon Swift in his *Gulliver's Travels*. He had – now this is serious, young man – the inhabitants of Lilliput and… what the hell was the other place… oh yes, Blefuscu, open their boiled eggs on the smaller end, as opposed to the larger, on pain of death. This was because the son of one of the emperors cut his finger opening an egg at the wider end, so an edict was promulgated that, on pain of death, his subjects should open their eggs on the smaller end. In Lilliput six rebellions were raised in this cause and an estimated eleven thousand people suffered death or went into exile in Blefuscu rather than break their eggs at the wrong end. Snigger not Michael. That edict is not as trivial as some extant. However, your journey in Steinbeck's tracks—"

"I'm not going to do it."

"Have my persuasive powers proved too much for you?"

"I have been considering it carefully over the past few weeks. Mainly because of this… place, Hollywood."

"It *is* a place. It's on a map."

"See? The fact that it's on a map does not earn it a real place in the real world."

"Well, the real estate people—"

"That's a misnomer if ever there was one. They are *unreal* estate people here in what they call tinsel town."

"So your disillusionment with Hollywood has persuaded you to cancel your trip."

"Yes… actually I have only been reconsidering my plan but this conversation has convinced me."

"My prolixity has rarely had such an immediate effect."

"I've had enough of America."

"So you're going home?"

"Yes."

"How?"

"I'm flying. To London first and then home. Boeing all the way."

"And Ria?"

"She wants to go by ship. She says she needs to unwind."

"Good idea. When will all this travel start?"

"Next week."

"Well, in case I don't see you before…"

He offered his hand and Michael took it and pulled him into an embrace.

"Professor. Thank you for two marvellous roles."

"Thank you for the performances. Dominick was sceptical but I was adamant. I knew you were right for the roles."

"Dominick? I thought he was—"

"The instigator? No. He had somebody else in mind, but I persuaded him that you were the one."

"Oh. Well, thank you for that. Dominick said he had always—"

"Trust our Dominick to command all the credit. Well, goodbye. Travel well. I'll go and say goodbye to Ria."

He was off, dodging his way through the noisy crowd. Michael finished his drink as he pondered on Dominick's devious ways.

Chapter Thirty One

In the first act you strive to impress audience. In the last act you try to impress the actors. When the show is over you hope you have impressed yourself.

Michael sipped the gin and tonic he had ordered from the hostess and looked out the window of the Boeing 747 as the tall towers of New York slid past. What a country he was leaving! Huge, diverse, multifaceted and intimidating. Very intimidating. New York, Boston and Los Angeles. Three focal points where the complexities of the modern United States came into such a sharp focus that you could cut your fingers, or at least your misconceptions down to size on them. The Big Apple had been cathartic. All that was modern, all that was challenging and all that was exciting had been displayed there with an abandonment that was truly American. Boston had been soothing and stimulating at the same time. All that was extant from the European parentage, presented with an assured complacency and inviolable sense of entitlement. And Hollywood, a city, a state of mind, an ephemeral sleight of hand, where everything that the mind of man and woman could dream of, could imagine and could possibly desire was there – almost for the taking. And he had experienced these places from the most treacherous standing place of all: inside a theatrical persona on a theatre stage. He, a virtual pretence, was viewing a pretend world in obverse. His Tom Jeffords/Michael Driscoll persona had been accepted as one whole, an amalgam of reality and fantasy, while his perspective had been clouded by a carapace of make-up, bright spotlights and torrents of praise verging on adulation, as through a misty glass and darkly.

The cityscape outside the 747's window made way for a dull, uneasy ocean that went on forever. He felt – literally – at sea. Something had happened to him in that tumultuous year, something that would alter his philosophy, if he had ever had one, forever. A lifetime of pretend and play-acting had left him sadly adrift. Where was the senior statesman certainty that he'd expected as an old, seasoned and respected actor with a career of great and well-presented parts to his name? Where was the peace of mind and contentment to be expected after such a career as his? Where was the pride that should be generated from having created such characters as he had with skill and conviction? He didn't experience any such worthy feelings. He felt empty inside. Like a shell. The whiff of hot meat reached his nostrils and the stewardess reached out to him with a tray. He lowered the table on the back of the seat in front of him for the food, ordered a bottle of wine and, within minutes, was eating his supper, his mind drifting away from his gloomy career thoughts and onto the food. And the wine, especially the wine. It was a remarkable Cabernet Sauvignon to be offered on an airplane, first class or not. It brought back fond memories of the articulate and fervent wine descriptions he had heard on a trip he had taken to the renowned Napa Valley and the hundred-year-old Inglenook winery. At a guided tasting of a selection of the estate's most sumptuous wines, he had distained the stricture of sipping, chewing and spitting out the samples offered for his delectation. He had swallowed each glassful if not with abandon, then with appreciation. Knowing that there was to be no performance at the theatre that evening, he had lost himself in the wines and the sonorous descriptions in the mellifluous tones of the wine guide. The phrases came back to him as the aircraft's wine made inroads into his brain: ...*deep, tawny colour with an amazing touch of tannin astringency... red brick bouquet for a long, lingering sweet finish... big and rich in spite of ullage... alluring, lingering aftertaste... sealing wax nose mellowed by oak and bottle.*

Balance! That was the thing. The holy grail of vintners, vignerons and what was the other? Oh yeah... négociants. Ooops! Where was *his* balance as he lurched to the toilet and back to his seat, replete and tipsy? And what the hell was ullage?

He arrived back home long before Ria was due, so he made his way to the Arena where he found Bernard still slumped over his desk. He stood silently in the doorway and looked at him. He looked pasty, as indeed had all the people he had passed in the street. He had become accustomed to the bronzed faces in Hollywood, so the more accustomed pigmentation in the country in winter seemed pasty and etiolated, while the breast-out posture of West Coast Yankees made these people seem hunched and shrivelled. He watched Bernard as he typed something on his battered typewriter, paused and let his gaze drift as he contemplated his next word, phrase or thought. The gaze drifted past the doorway, stopped and snapped back to Michael who was pleased at the delighted grin that lit up his face.

"Michael!" he shouted as he rose to his feet and strode towards him. "Welcome back. So glad to see you, man."

They embraced and leaned back to look at each other.

"Bernard. You haven't moved from that typewriter since I last saw you. How are you?"

"Not as well as you. You look like an American leading man. Tanned as hell. Your hair even looks like its American."

"Yes. I'm well. And you?"

"I'm as you see me. Overworked and underpaid. As usual. Coffee?"

"Yes."

Over the coffee, they reminisced on the theatre both locally and in the States and within several minutes, Michael felt as if he had never travelled abroad. He was surprised that he felt detached and alienated from Bernard's world with its seemingly petty problems.

"And Rupert?" he asked, surprised that Bernard had not mentioned him in his summing up.

"Rupert? Well, Rupert seems to have lost his voice."

"Oh no. This country needs Rupert's voice."

"Yes. It does. Now more than ever. It's stifling here. More pressure on the few theatres that stage important work. We've had three plays closed down before they could make any money. Thank God for the few benefactors who keep sending in the funds. There's a lot of pressure on them but they're all – or most of them – independent enough to resist the pressure. Rupert is working on a concept—"

"Well, that's good."

"The problem is he's been working on it for nearly a year. Can't seem to come to grips with it. I think he needs to travel to recharge his batteries but he's not keen on the idea. I've spoken to him, but he clams up. I think, he's getting tired of being the conscience of the nation. I also think he's… running out of steam. The Edinburgh Festival invited him to become a member of the board and resident writer and director, but the government blocked the idea."

"Shit! Can they do that?"

"What's to stop them? Rupert took it hard, and I suspect that it got to him."

"He was always so ready for a fight."

"That's probably the problem. The fight seems to have gone out of him. That great voice is stilled – for the time being anyway."

"And Thandi? Any word of her?"

"No. At least, none that I have heard. She's still in the same place I hear, but things are tightening up. More and more people are disappearing. I've sort of lost touch. The network is being smashed or has been smashed already. Thandi is not the only one to be packed away into the murk. There's a lot of unrest and reaction from the authorities. Why did you come back?"

"Well, there's Ria."

"Yes. Ria. She's secure enough. And her family. What else?"

"My source of money's here."

"All of it? Surely you made plans."

"I did. I have."

"But you don't have to worry. You're not a citizen. Wait! Don't tell me!"

"I'm telling you. I changed my citizenship."

"Why for God's sake?"

"Well, Dominick thought—"

"Dominick! That slimy fucker. How did you get into his grip?"

"It made sense then."

"Made sense! You had what most of us dream of: foreign nationality. And you threw it away!"

"Well, as I said. It made sense. At the time."

"Jesus! Michael, you haven't the sense you were born with. Your success in theatre would have opened up a career in any country in the world. And now you're stuck in this one."

There was a long silence while the both absorbed what had been said. Michael looked so woebegone that Bernard felt sorry for him.

"Look Michael, I think you're a fool for doing what you did. But I admire you. For your talent and, well, for being a decent fellow."

"Thanks, Bernard, I need some moral support right now."

"Why now?"

"Well, I'm thinking of giving up acting for a while."

"For a while?"

"Yes. Maybe a long while."

"Once you slip out of mind, it's hard to get back in. Look, why don't you speak to Rupert about it. He's a wise old bird. Maybe he could help to straighten out your thinking. Here."

He grabbed a piece of paper, wrote something on it and handed it to Michael.

"There's his address and phone number. He's up the coast now, in some small town. Maybe you could even go and see him."

Michael took the paper, glanced at it and put it into his pocket.

"Well, I guess I'll see you around someday. Soon I hope."

"Better hurry up. I don't think I'll be here much longer."

"What? *You* leave the Arena? I don't believe it."

"It'll be more the Arena leaving me. We might make it to the end of the month. After that, who knows."

"But the benefactors?"

"Oh, they'll hang in. The problem is material and actors."

"There's plenty of material out there, and acting at the Arena is almost obligatory for an actor."

"It used to be. Now, the young talent is scared. They feel if they work here, they won't get in anywhere else."

"Is it true?"

"Probably. I hear rumours. And Dominick—"

"Dominick?"

"Dominick. He's hinting that anybody who plays here will not get into the State or any other legit theatre."

"Can he do that?"

"I think he can. He already has the young talent very nervous."

"I always knew he had hidden agendas. Shit."

They looked at each other mournfully for a while until Michael broke the silence.

"Well, Bernard. Got to go now. It was good to see you. Really."

Chapter Thirty Two

At the time of reckoning, when the bill is due, it's time to let go because too much reality is bad for the soul.

He turned in through the gates of *Paradyse*, looking forward to a few days in its hedonistic embrace. Not to mention Ria's. There she was, cutting some magenta and yellow bougainvillea clusters for the front room. He stopped the car slowly to watch her as she moved gracefully along the plants, holding a basket, but she heard the car slide to a stop on the gravel and turned to look. He flashed the lights and waved through the windscreen, but there was no welcoming smile or wave. Her face hardened and she stood still, looking at him expressionlessly. *What now?* he thought as he drove slowly towards her, stopped and got out of the car. She didn't move, not even when he approached. He stopped, facing her, and they were both silent for a long moment.

"Hello," he said.

She didn't reply. Her face was as if in carved stone; her eyes were hard; and he saw her hands clench.

"What's the matter? Everybody, everything alright?"

"No. Everything is *not* alright."

"What? What's happened?"

"You tell me." She threw the basket on the ground. "*You tell me!*"

"Ria, darling—"

"Don't you 'darling' me. Don't you dare!"

Ria, I—"

"Thandi!" She spat the name out and it hung between them.

"Thandi? Thandi? I don't—"

"She's pregnant! With your child."

His stomach lurched.

"Pregnant?"

"Yes. Pregnant. From you!"

"I haven't seen Thandi since—"

"Since you fucked her. Over a year ago."

He decided to fight back even though he knew he was caught on the back foot.

"You seem to be very precise in your dates."

"There's a child! A brat! A half-breed. And it's yours! God! The shame!"

"Ria, I didn't know."

"It doesn't matter whether you knew or not. You fucked Thandi while you and I were… I never want to see you again. Neither do my parents. You're not welcome here anymore."

Over Ria's shoulder, he saw her father come to the front door, pause and turn away. No. He wasn't welcome here. God alone knew how her mother had taken the news. He sighed heavily and turned back to his car. As he drove back towards the gate, he looked around. All this. All this could have been… he looked in the rear-view mirror and saw Ria still stony-faced. Goodbye, *Paradyse*. It was nice knowing you. Feeling very empty, he headed back towards town. A child! Now of all times? And how was Thandi? Was she coping? Up there in that bloody dumping ground? And how did Ria find out? Dominick! Shit. Bet it was him. He knew everything sooner or later, the bastard. Well, he was going to know exactly how he, Michael Driscoll, was feeling. Driving far too fast, he headed towards the confrontation.

"Of course I knew!" Dominick was as stony-faced as Ria had been. "I tried to keep an eye on you all the time, but I must say that you were quite slippery. I missed the contact you made with her cousin and that made me angry. When Thandi had a baby that was of mixed race, it could only have been you. Then I knew that you had visited her. Slept with her. I was furious. But I bided my time. I realised that I had another hold on you and that it would prove useful when the time came. Well, it did. I knew that when Ria heard about the child, the gates of *Paradyse* would be closed to you. And they are. Forever. You have been destroyed as an actor in this country and you will not be allowed to travel from now on. It wasn't convenient for me to tell anybody until all of you came back from America. Now, it doesn't matter who knows. You're finished in the theatre. I'll make sure that no parts will be offered to you in the legitimate theatre. You can try the Arena if you like. They're on their last legs anyway. A bit of scandal will probably sink them a little faster."

"Why are you so vindictive, Dominick?"

"Why? Because you have made fast and loose with our laws. Our sensibilities. Our customs. And after all we – I – have done for you. How dare you!"

"Because I refuse to be a racist."

"A racist! How boring. We are not concerned with skin colour, which is a simplistic indicator when it comes to separating the grades of humans. We are concerned with the continuing dominance of one set of people, a higher grade of person, over another. It was ever thus, and it was how each civilisation was an improvement over the preceding one. Your petty reservations about this inevitable progress will seem very trivial in the years to come, and your concerns now are quite simply naïve and ridiculous. And now, if you'll forgive me, I have some serious matters to contend with."

And he was dismissed. As an unimportant detail in matters of national security. As an errant minion. As an indulged state-sponsored *actor*! A spoiled make-believe practitioner who had sold his nationality for a fucking mess of pottage. It served him right. His moments of introspection in the Boston burying ground came back to him. *That* was as good as it got. From then on it had all been downhill. Down to this nadir. Well, fuck them! He was… what *was* he going to do? He had some money but so what? He couldn't spend it out in the wide world because he couldn't travel in the wide world. He was as much a prisoner as Thandi in that godforsaken town. Thandi! And her baby! His baby! Well, he could go and see her at least. See the baby. Was it a boy or a girl? What did it matter? What the fuck was he going to do? He was going to get drunk. That was what he was going to do.

Bernard was a good person to get drunk with, and he had as much reason to do so as Michael, as he insisted in their soul-destroying, 'I'm worse off than you' litany that went on for hours until they actually began to feel comfortable in their misery. The Arena was facing closure so, after they had been thrown out of the neighbourhood bar, they returned to the theatre and did a lachrymose tour of the staircase and corridors where the poster of all the shows were pasted to the walls. Each one brought up memories, good and bad. The great scripts. The towering successes. The magnificent failures. The hilarious screw-ups and amazing performances. The careers launched. The ructions in the newspapers. The raids and closures. Panned performances. The memorable reviews in the papers. The backstage flirtations, the covert couplings and the scandals. Michael had been involved in some of the shows and Bernard knew them all and both enjoyed the descriptions. When they had exhausted the reminiscences, Bernard made some coffee and that slowly sobered them up.

"What are you going to do?" Michael asked.

"No idea. I'll look around. See if I can drum up some work somewhere. In theatre if possible. Up north. Designing maybe. I was a good designer, you know. Could probably get a job in advertising."

"God! How depressing."
"Yeah! Or film-making. That'd be better."
"Much better."
"Yeah. Not much better though. That'd be all advertising too."
They sat and were depressed for a while.
"I need to speak to Rupert," Michael suddenly said. "Do you know where he is?"
"Yeah. I remember I gave you his address."
"Yes. You did. I'll go and see him."
"Good idea."
"Yeah."

When the hangover cleared, Michael made a decision. He was not going to be a victim. He would take command of what was left of his life. He would do what he thought was right and would be damned if he would roll over and be Dominick's victim. He had money and, more important, could move it anywhere. He would leave this country. Sail up beyond its border, seek a way of slipping into the adjacent country and make his way from there. First stop the next morning was Menton who, without blinking, gave him a letter of credit which would be honoured by any bank, no matter how small, especially in any country bordering the one which Dominick and his ilk called home. He had decided to sail up the coast to see Rupert who lived in a city on the coast and take advantage of his wisdom and experience. After all, Rupert had spent most of his adult life sparring with the government and was too famous and too well connected to be treated with anything other than respect, so he had pushed the envelope as far as possible and had got away with it. So far. After Rupert he would sail on further up the coast to see Thandi and make some sort of provision for her and the child. Having decided on this course of action, he ended the lease on his flat and paid the required severance penalties and other amounts. The only possessions there comprised his extensive wardrobe and some few items, mainly awards and mementoes which he left for Bernard to keep or clear out, to take his pick of whatever he wanted and give the remainder to anybody he knew who could use it. He had a duplicate key to the flat made and dropped it off with Bernard at the now empty and dusty Arena. Bernard was not surprised at his decision to leave and wished him well in his endeavours. That afternoon and over the next few days he stocked up *The Gretchen* with Rafe's assistance and advice regarding imperishable foods and other necessities for a long voyage. 'A protracted fishing trip,' he called it when Rafe asked what he had in mind. On his advice he stocked up on meat, fresh, dried and canned, pasta, canned vegetables, fruit, bread, meat, cheese, long-life milk, rice and eggs as well as a selection of nutritious hiking snacks. Then he went to a reputable sporting shop and acquired a selection of maps and charts of the surrounding ocean, a sophisticated magnetic compass and echo sounder which he had Rafe fit to the ship, powerful binoculars and of course some professional fishing rods, reels, lures and other tackle. He was shown a variety of sophisticated navigational aids but, without the necessary skills, they were of little use to him. Besides, he had no intention of sailing far from land. Then he withdrew a sizeable amount of cash for any eventuality that might arise and packed that into a waterproof box. He followed Rafe's advice on stocking the boat with adequate sailing clothing: several T-shirts, a few shorts, swimsuits, windbreaker, all-weather hats and sunglasses. A pair each of street, boat, and water shoes with non-marking, well-gripping soles and such things as a backpack and duffle bags rather than hard luggage that would be difficult to fit in closets and cabinets. He also bought basic linen and towels as well as an under-the-shirt security pouch. Oil-free sunblock and insect repellent, shampoo, soap and toothpaste, seasickness pills were all acquired, and *The Gretchen* contained eating implements and utensils and a first aid kit so, three days later, he considered himself and the boat ready.

Having stocked and equipped *The Gretchen* and purchased a selection of books to read, he went down to the harbour, informed the harbour master of his plans for an extended fishing trip off the coast of the country and filled in all the required paperwork. The next morning, with the boat as ready as possible for a long, long time aboard he had a final drink with Rafe and Bernard and cast off. Out in the bay, with a stiff wind from the right direction, he headed out to sea and into whatever the future held for him. As the boat heeled in the right direction and he headed for the harbour mouth, he felt a deep-rooted excitement and satisfaction at being, for the foreseeable future, outside Dominick's baleful influence. The boat behaved admirably, and the weather was kind to him. It held for the rest of the day and, by evening, he had reached the first of his stopover places, a small harbour in a fishing village, where he moored the boat and settled down for the night. After a rather unsatisfying meal and half a bottle of wine, it was time to take stock, for the first time, of what the hell he was doing. He was on a one-way voyage into the unknown, an irrevocable journey into the future. It was strange that he could sever all connections with his career and lifestyle so easily and with so little regret. He supposed that his being an actor involved a degree of being a vagabond which had made his life simpler and easier to let go of. That and the disgust of the system that was manifestly unjust and which he had pretended to ignore and, in the process, compromised himself while benefiting from the unjustness. He had made very few friends, a fact that was covered up or compensated for by his many and varied acquaintances. He had bedded his fair share of women, but Ria had been the only one he had loved sufficiently to consider being married to and, to be honest, the thought of becoming part owner of *Paradyse* had made that arrangement seem very attractive. But Ria's vehemence and disgust at his intimate relationship with a black woman and his fathering a child with her had opened his eyes which, he admitted, he had kept conveniently closed for a long, long time. His time with Ria was over, and their parting had been so abrupt and final that it was difficult to accept but not to understand. Besides, to be honest, the thought of buying into the lifestyle at *Paradyse* which it epitomised, was untenable. In the excitement and success of a theatrical career, he had made a lot of money but had never invested in any form of property, and his extensive wardrobe represented his only possession. So, he was unattached and free to go. He had held onto his original passport when he had acquired local citizenship and was confident that, in spite of the 'cancelled' stamp on the third page, he could renew it or at least apply for a new one when and where it became necessary to do so. He intended sailing up the coast in short hops, from small harbours in insignificant villages such as this one, to bigger moorings in sizable towns or cities, where he would find moorings and report to the harbour authorities when and if he was required to by law.

For the next few days, the weather remained favourable, and he took time to move closer inshore and do some fishing at which, to his surprise and gratification, he was lucky at. He caught three sizeable fish on one occasion which he could not identify but which looked decidedly edible. He gutted and cleaned them and ate one that evening with mashed potatoes and green beans, washed down with some white wine, feeling very capable and outdoor-ish. The days passed smoothly, and the weather was kind, turning a bit blustery from time to time but, paying attention to his coastal charts, he was ready to head for the nearest shelter when it became too intimidating. So, he crept up the coast slowly and carefully until he came to the city where Rupert resided. He checked in with the harbour master and filled in all the requisite forms, then went to a phone booth and called the number that Bernard had given him. Rupert's gravelly voice answered and said that he would be glad to see him and would drive to the harbour and pick him up.

Chapter Thirty Three

There are no answers in theatre, only questions, and the right questions are asked, by the real playwrights, again and again because nobody's really paying attention.

Rupert was very welcoming and hospitable and insisted that he spent some time in his house, which Michael was glad to do. After a wholesome meal and some superlative wine, they settled down at the fireside where Michael told him about his quandary at home and his plans for the future. Rupert was sympathetic and very encouraging. He commended Michael on his plans regarding Thandi and the child and was optimistic about their chances of finding a free life beyond the borders.

"The people up there know what's going on here, and they pity us all and not only our black people. Us whites too. They know that we have lost our way and some of our humanity. The pity they have for us is something that Dominick and his ilk would not understand. He can never accept, never contemplate, how much richer we all could be together. I intend to teach him and his like a lesson. In theatre at least."

"How? What devilry have you in mind?"

"'Angelry' would be more accurate. I have identified some

astounding black acting talent in this place and have been helping it realise its astounding potential."

He poured Michael some more wine and gazed into the flames of the fire as he collected his thoughts.

"In an adjacent township I came across a theatrical group who are striving to tell their own stories to those who will listen. Their passion, their honesty and their acting talent is amazing. I haven't seen the like before. They are raw, passionate and capable of telling the truth about their situation. In a fresh way. In a way that will astound the theatrical world, here and internationally. We are working on a piece right now that holds the oppression that they are all subject to up for all to see – and experience – because they have the ability to involve the audience in their work and fire it with the recognition of the universality of what they present. I have never seen such raw and passionate talent. All they need is a light – a very light – touch of technique to bring it in line with international norms. We are presenting it this Saturday at a church hall that is free of the baleful glare of Dominick and his cohorts. My aim is to expose them to the world, through the Arena initially but then Europe, the world."

"The Arena is closed."

"The building is still there, and I can source enough funds to refurbish it."

"My God. That's ambitious."

"There is only one way to help this group avoid the forces of oppression. Expose them to the world so quickly that the authorities will be caught on the wrong foot. We will blind-swipe them. Make key people in the city aware of this work before they can object and make this group and this work so manifestly successful that even those blind fools will not be able to censor them."

"That's taking a chance?"

"Isn't theatre all about taking a chance?"

"They'll be furious."

"I expect them to be. I intend them to be."

Michael stood and paced about in excitement.

"Rupert! You're terrific. I wish I could be a part of it."

"Not a chance. You are far too vulnerable to be part of this. You will have to be satisfied with a viewing of the group in Edinburgh."

"Wheeling out His Lordship again?"

"Exactly. He upstaged them before, and he'll do it again. That last show of yours put theatre in this country on the international map. Any repression of actors or scripts would undo all the good PR generated. The fools think that they are in control. This show will prove them wrong. We'll go to see it on Saturday. Meantime, relax while I finish the rehearsals. You need a break from all that voyaging of yours."

The intervening days went very fast, mainly because of Rupert's very impressive library which Michael made the most of, wandering from book to book, scanning the contents, dipping into the more fascinating chapters and promising himself that he would construct his own library, as soon as he was settled. Settled? Would he ever be so? Where would he go when… he stopped himself from planning ahead. How could he do that when he couldn't see further than Thandi and his child? The sea trip so far had been more strenuous than he had imagined, and he was more tired than he had ever been, so the very comfortable room apportioned to him in Rupert's wandering and intriguing house was very welcome. Rupert himself was at rehearsals for most of the day and collapsed when he came home late at night. He had a dog, a large, clumsy and endearing Border Collie which accompanied Michael on the walks he took around the house which was on the edge of a straggly wood through which many meandering paths wound. The dog led the way and kept at bay the mysterious forces which, according to its ferocious growls, threatened them at every bend. Michael had the sense to let the dog take him wherever it wanted and invariably it got him back to Rupert's house again. He was rested and at peace when Saturday came, and Rupert drove him to the church hall for the performance.

The village hall in the township was simple, unadorned and crammed with people when he and Rupert entered. The benches were full to capacity with men, women and children, all of whom seethed in delighted anticipation. There were several young men perched on the decorative lintel over the door, whistling and calling out friendly insults to people in the audience. Rupert was welcomed at the door and escorted to the front row, but getting there was slow. Almost everybody in the hall knew him, or about him, and were anxious to greet him and, if possible, shake his hand. Michael's hands too were heartily shaken by anybody who could reach them. Obviously, if he was with Rupert then he was worth meeting. Rupert's initial introductions of him were soon abandoned in the tumult, and Michael resorted to pronouncing his name and saying that he was pleased to meet whoever it was that was shaking his hands. This seemed to suffice, and he was escorted to a seat next to Rupert's where more and more people welcomed him and said that they were very, very glad to see him. Then Rupert stood to embrace a small group of people who came from backstage to greet him. By the delight and excited greetings on both sides, these were special people. In fact, Rupert introduced them as the cast of the play they were about to see. He tried to explain who Michael was, but the noise and excitement prevented any real introductions. Except for one man who took both Michael's hands in his and looked him straight in the face as he shook them. People around them stepped back to give them both room.

"Michael Driscoll," he said in a warm baritone. "My name is Tony, and I am delighted to see you here. I saw you in *The Colonist and the King*, and I was impressed. Very impressed. Simon has spoken about you with a great deal of respect."

"Has he? Well, I'm very pleased to hear that. His performance was superb."

"Yes. I thought so too. It was a pity—"

"About the drunkenness. Simon and I spoke about that."

"So he said. I shared your uncomfortableness. But he portrayed the king with dignity."

"He did. Are you in this play?"

"Yes. I have the most to say."

"Well that probably makes you the lead."

"There is no lead in this work. It is all very democratic, as you will see."

And see he did. The play exposed the everyday life of black people with searing honesty, sincere emotion and a humour that was both uplifting and cathartic. The opening scene used the device of that morning's newspaper read by Tony from a black perspective, and it was hilarious. It portrayed the white people's celebrations, worries and concerns so wryly that it was totally subversive, damning and overwhelmingly funny. Tony was in complete command and played the audience with a skill and sensitivity that impressed Michael. Halfway through this virtuoso performance a delighted howl of laughter came from the back of the hall, followed by a shout and a thump as one of the young men fell off the lintel. Tony paused and played the moment as the audience turned and admonished and encouraged the unfortunate young man as he was assisted back up on the lintel, still laughing. Tony let this go on for as long as was necessary and then stepped forward and held both arms towards the audience until they settled down and the theatrical order was re-established. He then proceeded with the monologue until another actor appeared, looking suspiciously as if he had been pushed on, and the play continued. It was a revelation for Michael. It was fresh and seemingly improvised but he could see that the work had a tight and meticulous structure and an ascending degree of involvement and acknowledgement of the injustice of the world in which it took place. Remarkably free of bitterness, it placed the characters in impossibly tough situations and let them extract themselves with creative cunning and an acceptance of their unjust situations with a humour that was at once heart-warming and appalling. It was universal too. Ever since societies had been formed, there had been underdogs, and these oppressed characters showed ingenuity and cunning in the face of the oppressor. It was a truly new voice and a new style of theatre that he knew, instinctively, would work anywhere in the world.

They were both on a high when they arrived back at Rupert's home, so they had some wine and snacks and discussed it well into the early hours of the morning. Rupert had laid his plans carefully. He would mount it at the Arena on a Saturday afternoon, one performance only, without any publicity but with a co-ordinated telephone blitz to all the heavyweight journalists and opinion formers who thought as he did and a wide selection of respectable people who he knew would support a highly publicised performance later when it materialised. The resulting coverage and enthusiastic reception from the invited people would, he was sure, catch the authorities off guard and prevent them from reacting when it was staged again the following weekend for a two-week run. Rupert's rationale was irrefutable.

"They don't realise that they are looking for subversion in the wrong place," Rupert said. "While they search out and hound the active and pissed-off young people in the townships, the real subversion is being created, more and more in the theatres. When the system eventually falls it will be the result of extreme dissatisfaction in many places and many minds, and the much-maligned middle classes will be a source of that dissatisfaction because stones may penetrate police stations and other foci of power, but words, the ammunition that you and I use, can penetrate the mind and undermine prejudice. We can change perceptions and tackle wilful ignorance, under the unintimidating guise of entertainment. It will take time, perhaps more time than I have left, but it *will* take place, and this work of ours will have a major role to play. When the pillars of the state come toppling down, one of the major catalysts will be the middle-class mind. Stubborn, evasive and self-deluding though it be, it will prove an unstoppable force for change. If you want a place to stand when levering the world's consciousness onto a different level, the stage will be it."

They both went to bed in a state of excitement, and Michael was sorry that he would not be attending the show but, Rupert assured him, he would see the show at a later date in Edinburgh, London or New York where, with the help of his Lordship and the managers of the Market Theatre in London and the Big Apple's Edison Theatre, he had arranged later bookings. All of these arrangements would be highly publicised internationally and at the same time, and there was little that Dominick and Co. would be able to do about it without being highly embarrassed in the process. The next morning Michael and Rupert parted company at the quayside, each trying to persuade the other that they would meet again under more salubrious circumstances. Then Rupert drove away, after asking Michael to remember him to Thandi. Michael watched him go and turned towards *The Gretchen*, his mind full of Rupert and the play he was putting together in the interest of the nation's theatre, hoping – knowing – that it would succeed and start a landslide of what Dominick feared most, sympathy and understanding of each other before the country tore itself apart in hate and prejudice. With this hopefulness in his heart, he boarded *The Gretchen* and headed out to sea.

Chapter Thirty Four

On this unpredictable planet, when the curtain comes down on one story, it rises on another. But when one actor leaves the stage, the big, wide world hardly notices.

Two days later, having sailed through some rough and intimidating seas, Michael turned to a small landing place, not substantial enough to be a quay and far from being a harbour. His chart was large enough to show it, but in reality, it looked as if no boat had used it for generations. He broke out one of the bicycles and then tied *The Gretchen* to the two rotting but serviceable wooden posts securely. He cut down some bushes to drape on top of the boat and down the sides until it was all but invisible to passing crafts and well out of sight from the dirt track that led past it. He placed a torch into the basket in front of the handlebars of one of the bikes, mounted it and set off down the dust road that he knew would lead to the road on which Thandi's place of exile stood. He pedalled towards it as the sun began to set, hoping he would hear a nightjar again, but the night was silent except for the sound of insects and the far, far distant sound of a train. He came to the tree where he had parked his car on his first visit and carried the bicycle to a shallow declivity in the ground away from the road. He covered it with some brambles and dried grasses in the hope that nobody would notice it and set off towards Thandi and his child, his heart beating strongly at the prospect of seeing them.

The house came into view – more of the corrugated roof was missing and the door to the outhouse was gone. Christ! It wasn't a fit abode for an animal! The fence in front was still sagging. Through the net curtain he could see a faint light shining, so he quickened his pace. It was now quite dark, and he had no fear of being seen as he crossed the road and approached the house. As he came to the door, he could hear a female voice softly crooning, the sort of comforting sound a mother would make to her baby. He stopped to listen and then realised it was not Thandi's voice but the frail, quavering voice of an old woman. He took a deep breath, pushed the door open and stepped inside. A thin, shawled old woman was sitting on a chair next to the bed, holding and rocking what was obviously a wrapped-up baby in her arms. He stopped at the sight and the old woman ceased singing and turned to look. She nodded as if he was expected and sat still. Then he saw a shape on the bed. It was the body of a woman, and it was perfectly still. It was Thandi, and her eyes were closed. Her uncovered face was drawn and still, and there was little of the healthy beauty that had been hers. The woman remained motionless as he moved next to her and looked at Thandi for the longest time without speaking or moving. Then a sigh slipped out of his mouth. A long, soft but deep sigh. He moved next to the bed and, leaning down, kissed the stone-cold brow that had often wrinkled in wry puzzlement at his obtuseness as she had called it.

When he straightened up, the old woman looked long and hard at his face and then uncovered the baby's head. A wrinkled light brown face twisted in the increased light, and the tiny, clutched fists opened and closed. The woman nodded and held out the baby towards Michael, and he took it in his arms. Did it look like him? He couldn't tell but, somehow, he was totally sure it did. It weighed very little as it stretched its limbs, moved its fists close to its mouth and sighed itself back to sleep. There was a folded blanket at Thandi's feet and Michael laid the baby on it and clumsily tried to wrap it. The old woman pushed his hands aside and wrapped the child snugly, tucking the blanket securely around it but leaving a long, loose flap over the face. While she was doing this, Michael took a wad of banknotes out of his pocket and handed it to the woman, making vague burying gestures with his arms. She gave him the baby and gestured towards the door. Then she took the money and, pointing at the baby, "Michael," she said.

He nodded as the tears suddenly came and, taking the baby, he left the house, blinking and staggering. Outside, he stopped and pulled himself together and then, using the loose flap of the blanket to wipe his eyes, he gently laid it back down over the sleeping face and headed towards the bicycle with his son in his arms.

The nightjar took that precise moment to churr into the soft night.

Back on board *The Gretchen*, he took the child from the basket of the bike and placed it in a large cardboard box, as a makeshift cot, with a thick towel folded to fit as a mattress. He then used blankets to make a raised edge on the small seat at the front of the cabin into which the cot fitted snugly. With some wide bandages, he made several belts that anchored it in place, looping them around a rail on the bulkhead to secure it. He then used a soda water bottle to make a drinking bottle. He made a plug of rolled bandage and massaged it into a point to protrude from the top. Filled with milk, he hoped it would keep the child full. Some watered-down and boiled milk would have to suffice for feeding. He sacrificed a couple of T-shirts to make nappies and that was about all he thought he needed to do as he cast off and headed up north. The sea was rougher now but nothing that he couldn't handle. He headed directly into the oncoming sea, hoping that the child – Michael – wouldn't get seasick. The trip to the border took three days, during which time, at stopover in small harbours and derelict landing sites, he fed Michael and changed six of the nappies. The child seemed content with the improvised bottle and voided his bowels four times; the contents of the nappies seemed healthy enough. The baby slept most of the time and, when awake, appeared to be content and comfortable, gurgling away at times, sighing heavily at others. The eyes, when open, did not seem to register anything, not even him when he was looking down at him. When *The Gretchen* passed the border post while far out to sea, he viewed it carefully through the binoculars and it seemed to be deserted, so he slipped out of the country easily and peacefully and felt the better for it.

"OK, Michael. You're going to grow up in freedom," he called to the baby and headed for the next landfall which, like most of them this far north, was a small one, hardly worthy of notice. On the far side of the border, the landscape remained unchanged except for more frequent clusters of straw-roofed huts dotted over the terrain, better tended and on better looked-after pieces of ground then those on the other side. Some in close proximity to others and looking relatively large and some more isolated and smaller. He sailed along looking for one of the smaller clusters near a landing place and, having identified one, he sailed in and tied up. Taking a wad of banknotes and the cot, he headed towards the nearest hut which looked quite prosperous, with vegetable patches arrayed around it and two small, fenced-in areas nearby, one containing goats and the other cattle. This looked a likely place, so he walked there and stopped outside the open door. A man came out, followed by a nursing woman. They stood there smiling at him, and the man gestured for him to enter which he did as they both stepped aside. Inside, the hut was sparsely furnished but well kept, and the floor was smooth and immaculately swept. The well-maintained interior was a far cry from the hovel to which Thandi had been banished. Michael walked to the table and laid the cot on it. At that point the baby within started to cry softly. The woman moved quickly to it and pulled back the blanket. The baby – Michael – started to cry louder, and the woman handed her baby to the man and, picking Michael up, lodged him at her ample breast which Michael immediately started to suckle. The woman looked at the two men, grinned widely, and started to walk up and down, humming softly to the sucking baby. The man chuckled and turned to Michael.

"That's what was needed," he said.

"Yes indeed," Michael replied.

"You have come here on that boat? From over there?"

He nodded in the direction of the border.

"Yes. I am leaving. I can't live there anymore."

"I understand," said the man, exchanging looks of understanding with the woman.

"I can't take the baby with me. I would like to leave him here. Is that possible?"

The man and woman exchanged looks and some message that Michael didn't understand passed between them.

"There is no life for him back there and his mother…"

Michael paused and stifled a deep sigh.

"…his mother is dead. She died in exile, in banishment, back there. I had to take him away. But he can't go back, and neither can I. Can I leave him here? There is nowhere else for him. Anywhere."

Again, the exchanged looks and the unspoken message. This time they were smiling.

"I would like to pay… for his upkeep… his name is Michael."

He took out the wad of banknotes and placed it on the table.

"That will take care of him for a while. I will send more when I can if you will give me an address. The nearest post office. Whatever. Where they can contact you when it arrives."

He stopped talking and gave them time to answer. They looked at each other again and she smiled at him, and he smiled back. Then the man turned and faced Michael.

"I understand the situation over there. We see people sometimes who are running away and we, the people here, give them all the help they ask for. Most of the people are black, but you…"

"I am in trouble down there. I can't work, and I can't leave legally, and the child's mother was put into exile where she died after he was born. He is the child of a white father and a black woman, so there is no real future for him there. I can't take him with me where I am going, because I don't *know* where I am going."

He stopped talking and the man took up the money from the table and approached the woman. They conversed quietly and at length in their language, looking at the money and at Michael from time to time. He watched anxiously until they were silent, nodding at each other. Then the man stood and walked back to Michael.

"This has happened before. And will happen again until…" he sighed and looked away. "But we will do as you ask. We have waited a long time for a child, and one has finally come. Your child… Michael?…will make a good companion for our little girl."

He waved the money.

"This will pay – generously – for his upkeep. If you can send more, it will be fine. If not, it will still be fine. You would be wise to move on, up to the city; there are a few prying eyes her so close to the border. Up there you will not be noticed."

Michael sighed with relief and shook the man's hand fervently. The he crossed to the woman and looked down at the child as he suckled away with obvious contentment. He placed his hand on the woman's shoulder and murmured his thanks. She smiled at him and looked down at her new-found son. The man tore a page out of a tattered notebook that lay on a shelf and scribbled something on it.

"Here is my name and the address of the nearest shopkeeper," he said as he handed it to Michael. "Any funds would be helpful, but we will take care of little Michael anyway."

Michael shook the proffered hand, nodded to the smiling woman, took a final look at his son and then almost ran to the door, left the hut and headed towards his boat. To his surprise he was sobbing.

Two hours later, in *The Gretchen*, he was far away from the village heading for the town, which looked sizeable on the charts and would hopefully contain some commercial and official places of business where he could start to arrange the rest of his journey. Pushing away the thoughts of his child whom he had created and then left in the care of strangers, he vowed that he would come back sometime and see how he was faring. That stalwart thought was wiped from his mind at the deterioration of the weather to which he had not been paying attention. The clouds were black, and there were flickers in them which could only be lightning. The sea had risen dramatically, and the boat was struggling to mount and pass over the heightening waves. He donned a sweater and waterproof jacket and trousers and tightened his grip on the wheel, taking a bearing to work out the direction in which he had to sail to reach the town which was ten kilometres ahead. According to the chart, there was a wide indentation in the coastline at this point and Michael, with the storm approaching, decided to cut across it, rather than follow the coastline closely as he had been doing until now. He estimated that he would reach the town before the storm reached him.

The sea in which Michael was sailing is on a broad, shallow edge of an ocean, a continental shelf which extends up to two hundred kilometres off the coast before plunging steeply to an abyssal plain far below in the wide ocean basin. Every such ocean basin on the planet has an immensely strong current on its western side and since time immemorial, this particular current, one of the mightiest on the planet, has flowed south along this shelf, carrying millions of cubic metres of water per second, many hundreds of times more than the rate of the Amazon River. Its magnitude helps this current play a significant role in global ocean circulation, and it is in the opposite direction to the swells, giant at times, that sweep northwards, driven by an almost perpetual wind. These two inexorable forces, current and swells, meeting face to face can – and often do – magnify the resultant waves to gargantuan proportions. Such waves manifest as rogue waves and, in that vast, and cunning, sea, one such wave was heading towards *The Gretchen*.

Halfway across the open stretch of water in the indentation, the sea rose in cataclysmic fury. The sky disappeared in spray and sudden darkness. Michael could barely see beyond the prow of the plunging boat between the blasts of wind and, in a stillness that suddenly manifested itself, he wished devoutly that he could not see what was coming towards him. It was a wall of water, curving up, up into the sky, moving towards his stern and then curving over him in his puny boat until the ragged crest, far, far above, looked as if it would fall down on *The Gretchen*. The rudder refused to respond when he tried to turn the prow of the boat towards the glistening wall. It was a forlorn hope. He let go of the wheel, stepped back onto the open deck, spread out his arms and, as the whole ocean fell on top of him, thought of Thandi, his child and – dammit! – Dominick.

About the Author

*Photo courtesy of The Theatre on The Bay,
Camps Bay, Cape Town.*

Dermod Judge has been typographer, designer, copywriter, creative director, dramatist, actor, broadcaster, film and stage director, script writer and script editor, international lecturer on storytelling and filmmaking.

Other books by Dermod Judge and published by the Book Club:

CLASH

TWO JAM JARS FOR THE MANOR

BOPPING IN BALLYMALLOY

MacBRIDE'S WARS

A HEALING PLACE

LOST ON THE SEA OF GALILEE

A TANGLED TALE

Other books by Dermod Judge and published by the Book Club:

CLASH

TWO JAM JARS FOR THE MANOR

BOPPING IN BALLYMALLOY

MacBRIDE'S WARS

A HEALING PLACE

LOST ON THE SEA OF GALILEE

A TANGLED TALE

About the Author

*Photo courtesy of The Theatre on The Bay,
Camps Bay, Cape Town.*

Dermod Judge has been typographer, designer, copywriter, creative director, dramatist, actor, broadcaster, film and stage director, script writer and script editor, international lecturer on storytelling and filmmaking.